JESSICA JUDE

Ace of Betrayal

First edition

ISBN: 979-8-9906231-3-2

Cover art by Haya in Designs

This book was professionally typeset on Reedsy.
Find out more at reedsy.com

To those with regrets,
and those who forgive us

Contents

Author's Note

This book contains mature content and potential triggers, including sexual harassment, cheating (prior to story), verbal abuse, violence, language, and explicit sexual content. It is not intended for readers under 18.

If you prefer to keep the bedroom door closed, you may want to skip over chapters 22, 25, 29, 32, and 45.

To listen to the playlist, visit JessicaJude.com/Ace-Playlist to be taken directly to Spotify.

1

"Coming Home - Part II" - Skylar Grey

Walker

I cannot afford to be spotted. I'm wearing a baseball cap I picked up at Heathrow that says "I <3 Big Ben" in blocky red letters. There's an Uber waiting for me outside, which I paid extra to stand by in case my flight landed early.

I specifically chose the red-eye because I assumed the airport would be mostly deserted at two o'clock in the morning. There aren't many people here, but I still keep my head down as a precaution, lifting it occasionally to scan for anyone who might recognize me.

There's a tired-looking mum in front of me on the autowalk, three bags in one hand and a toddler barnacled to the opposite hip. As soon as we step off, the little girl loses the contents of her stomach all over the gleaming tile floor and the front of her mother's quilted jacket.

I force my hand to stay at my side rather than covering my nose. I can't walk around them and pretend not to see, even if that's what my exhausted muscles are screaming at me to do, so I offer to get some paper towels. I like to think I'm a nice person.

I have immediate regrets.

Because inside the restroom, like the Ghost of Christmas Past, is none other than Lux Colombia-Clarke.

I don't know what she's doing here, but the look on her face makes it evident I'm the last person she expected to run into at WNX.

Our gazes collide in the mirror over the sink, where she is swiping pink gloss onto her luscious, already-cotton-candy lips. Even with my eyes closed, I would recognize that scent of rose water and vanilla anywhere.

Her long blonde hair is as flawless as always, flowing down her back like a golden river. My own brown mane is pulled into a sloppy ponytail under my hat. It takes approximately one second for recognition to light up her eyes, those perfectly pouty lips forming an equally perfect O.

That's when I bolt.

Tossing the paper towels at the mum still covered in vomit, I run for the exit, my Carl Friedrik trunk clanging behind me as it hits every bump in the floor. I slide to a halt next to the dark blue sedan waiting outside. The wind picks up and whips pieces of rubbish across the car park, and a travel brochure advertising *Wesbourne, the Land of Fairy Tales* smacks into my bag. I flick it off and lean down toward the open window of the car.

After confirming it's the Uber I ordered before leaving Oxford, I lift and heave my fifty-pound trunk into the backseat like a maniac and climb in after it. If the driver questions the wisdom of chauffeuring someone who appears to be a fugitive, he wisely chooses not to say so.

The car has the kind of fake pine scent that comes from those little trees people like to hang from their mirrors, but it looks passably clean. After a quick hello and a pair of raised brows, the man drives off without another word toward the address I entered into the app two weeks ago.

I tried to avoid this trip. I really did. But when I told Dr. Riordan I was going to write my dissertation on the effect G.R. Huntington is still having on horror literature today, he grinned as if he expected no less. Then he said the words I wish I could scrub from my memory: "You'll need to do your research back in Wesbourne, won't you?"

I shook my head. "I'm pretty sure I can access everything I need right here at Oxford."

"Walker, this is your dissertation. It makes sense to go to Huntington's homeland for research." He took a step closer, close enough that the scent of bay rum tickled my nose. "We expect a thorough analysis and a bibliography full of references." Then that smile, all white teeth against brown skin. "Besides, it will be good to go home, won't it?"

Good to go home.

I'd rather chew glass.

If I could hole up in the Wesbourne Archives with enough caffeine to keep me running twenty-four-seven, then maybe. That was my original plan.

Until I ran into Lux fucking Colombia-Clarke.

I have no doubt the entire country will know of my return before I even make it across town, never mind the fact that it's two in the morning. Lux has the mouth of a broadcast speaker. And while most of Wesbourne couldn't care less about me being home, there are a handful of people who will.

I'm not above a little social media stalking, and although I haven't posted anything in the past two years, my accounts are still active. The last time I checked, they were all still friends, posing in those ridiculously choreographed photos Lux is forever taking, grinning at the camera like they're in a teen soap opera.

What story have they been sold? It was impossible to tell from Lux's face. The only emotion I could read was shock. Although in hindsight, I'm pretty sure her eyes were also red-rimmed and glassy, like she'd been crying.

My brain trips over that last thought. Lux never cries. Ever. I can count on one hand the number of times I've seen her tear up, and they both involve faking it.

I give myself a mental slap. I can't be worrying about Lux, for god's sake. She's about to become the reason I won't be able to slip into town and quietly do my research without drawing the attention of the exact people I'd rather keep in the dark.

The exact *person* I'd rather keep in the dark.

I didn't expect it to still hurt this much, being back here. I prepared myself for pain at seeing old things changed, new things appearing, but I wasn't ready for the tight knot I now feel in the pit of my stomach.

The city streets glow from the light spilling out of windows as we cruise down Twenty-Fifth Boulevard. The occasional neon sign throws splashes of color onto the pavement. Ahead of us, the Bay River Bridge looms large in the darkness, its steel arches one of the city's most photographed sights during daylight.

We cross it, driving noises echoing across the water below us. I release the pent-up breath in my lungs. I haven't spent much time on the southern side of the bridge. The further from the river we get, the smaller the houses become. Streetlamps spotlight postcard-sized lawns. Discarded toys cast eerily shaped shadows against the buildings.

It gives me a strange feeling, like I'm home, but I'm not. Were I to see these same houses during the day, I'm sure I'd find them cute and charming. I would look at them and think, *So this is how the other half lives.* Instead, all I can do is question whether I made the right decision or not. Coming back *and* staying in this part of town.

When I found an old Victorian manor on Airbnb that allowed a long-term rental, I pounced on it. Bonus points are: a) it looks like something directly out of a Poe story; b) it's secluded and private, even though it's within city limits; and c) it's as far from the Hills as possible without making the trek to the Archives a nightmare.

I'm not planning to stay long. I'll get the research materials I need from the Archives and be on the first flight back to London and the safety of Oxford. As long as I keep to myself and stay far from the Hills and downtown, it should only take me two weeks, three tops.

As the car turns onto a street lined with broccoli-top trees, my heart rate kicks up. These homes are larger and farther from the road. Their intricate architecture screams "I was here before your grandfather was born!"

Wesbourne sits between the United Kingdom and the United States, and we've borrowed heavily from both of their styles. Brick-lined streets, glowing lampposts, arched porticos with floral arrangements framing the doors, perfectly trimmed hedges lining the driveways.

As we pull up in front of my Airbnb, I recognize the pointy spires pricking the sky. Stephen King would have a field day with this place. A single light illuminates the front door, which is set in an arch in the stone facade.

The driver stops the car a short distance from the house. Three stories loom above us, complete with several turrets and a widow's walk. I swing my tote bag onto my shoulder, laptop whacking my back, and hoist my trunk out of the back seat. The heavy thing bumps along the gravel path as I walk to the door, getting stuck in the tiny pebbles the whole way. The driver peels out of the driveway like he has better things to do than watch me struggle and absorb the guilt of not helping me.

Out of habit, I attempt to avoid a small crack in the cement. I take a step that's too large, and it causes me to stumble against my bag. When it occurs to me what I've done, I stomp on the crack to show anyone watching that I am not the same girl who left this place.

The house beckons like the old witch from Hansel and Gretel, motioning with her bony fingers for me to *step inside, take a look around*. But I'm exhausted. I booked a first-class ticket assuming I'd be able to sleep on the plane, but between the nausea in my stomach and the apprehension in my brain, I wasn't able to do more than fret.

Inside, the air smells musty and stale, like it's been a long time since someone threw open the windows. It reminds me of the library back in Oxford. I picture the rows of books lining the walls, where you can get so lost in a project you forget to eat, forget to sleep, forget that there's a whole other life you left behind.

I'll get some candles. They'll dispel the mustiness and put me in the right mood to keep my mind where it should be—on my research. Not on the drama that is about to unfold when Lux opens her big mouth.

Who knows, maybe no one will even care that I'm back.

2

"Poker Face" - Lady Gaga

Heath

I need to get my own place. Pierce's flat is great, but we're twenty-two floors up. I would kill for some fresh air. The closest we can get to being outside is the tiny balcony they call a terrace on the Atlantis's website, but that thing is cramped enough with a small table and two chairs. It could never hold the five of us for an entire game.

Once I have a house—on ground level with a sick outdoor space—I will fight for the right to host poker nights myself. All this regurgitated air is enough to make anyone claustrophobic.

I glance around the table. Maeve tucks that sleek black hair behind her ear. She will shit a load if I dare break the tradition of poker at Pierce's flat every Tuesday night. Pierce doesn't believe in half-assed efforts, which is why he's still wearing his suit and tie, despite having left the office several hours ago. Between the two of them, I'll have a fight on my hands if I suggest we relocate our games to a place with more sunshine and less . . . chrome.

When Pierce commits to something, screw anything that gets in his way. Even his game room looks like something out of the fucking Bellagio in Las Vegas. A baize-covered poker table dominates the center of the space, a dimly lit chandelier dangling above it like a woman in diamonds.

One whole wall consists of rows of small cubicles from floor to ceiling, and inside each one is a miniature collectible slot machine. Red mood lights glow from each box, making this both the creepiest and coolest thing I've ever seen in someone's home.

The whirr of cards being shuffled draws my attention back to the table. It's Rhett's turn to deal. His eyes are bloodshot and his dark curls smooshed, as if he rolled out of bed right before coming here.

He shuffles again, then looks around the table. "Antes? And what in god's name are we drinking tonight?" He holds the purple cocktail to the light.

"Black-*Beer*-y Whiskey Smash," Pierce says. Tradition dictates that he create a new cocktail for us every week. Depending on the night and the drink, this has been both a blessing and a curse.

"Oh god." Lux takes a sip of hers. Her face screws up into a tight ball. She takes a bigger gulp. "Good news. It gets better," she rasps.

I taste it myself. It's a little like drinking blackberry-scented wiper fluid. Not intolerable, then. I take another swig.

Maeve tosses a chip into the center. "I'll start. My manicurist didn't get the right shade. I specified chartreuse." She holds up her hand, showcasing neon-green fingernails. "Does this look *anything* like chartreuse?"

"I thought chartreuse was a liqueur." Rhett echoes my own thoughts.

"It's also a color," she says. "Could you possibly be any more stoned?"

"The night is still young," I say.

Rhett grins and tosses his own chip in. "Some hag yelled at me for double-parking. Total bitch."

"One of my assistants got my coffee wrong yesterday." Pierce's chip clunks against the others.

I wince. Pity the poor girl who has to take orders from the

domineering perfectionist that is Pierce St. James. I add my own chip to the pile and turn to him. "Your doorman looked at me funny when I came in."

He furrows his brow. "Leonard?"

"Oh, come on, Heath," Maeve says. "You can't submit Leonard!"

"Why not?" I say. "He stared at me the whole time I was waiting for the lift, *without* smiling."

"He was probably questioning your choice of footwear," Lux says, with a pointed look under the table at my flip-flops. She's been quiet tonight.

"Hey," I say.

"Is that the best you can come up with?" Pierce challenges.

"I'm saving my best." I cross my arms over my chest.

It's a lie. I've got nothing else up my sleeve tonight.

Maeve pipes up again. "You showed up with nothing for your ante? Do you even care about this anymore?"

I let the corner of my mouth lift in a half smile. "Hey, someone has to be the disappointment. I'm taking one for the team."

"Leonard stays in the pot because his name is *Leonard*," Rhett says with a cackle.

"The clerk at Prada rolled her eyes at me when she thought I wasn't looking." Lux tosses the last chip into the pile in the center of the table.

"All right, let's do this." Rhett deals each of us two cards.

The rules of the game are simple. Everyone buys in with a small grievance. These are easy to come up with, especially if you're Maeve and consider a guy staring at your boobs for 0.482 seconds a close cousin to murder.

The final rounds of betting move on to higher stakes: leaked sex tapes, cheating, harassment. The winning hand decides the winning grievance. Sometimes it's an obvious choice, like the time some skank tried to blackmail Pierce, thinking he was a stupid asshole who would tolerate getting sucked into drama like that without major payback. Other times, it's all about who will make the most interesting prey.

By the time Rhett flips over the turn, he's folded, but I'm holding an eight of spades and a six of diamonds. There's a seven of diamonds and a ten of hearts on the table. If the river turns out to be a nine, I'm looking at a straight and potentially the winning hand.

Pierce raises the bet. "I caught Isabella texting some guy." He throws three chips into the middle.

Lux gasps. "That bitch."

He keeps his eyes on his cards.

"You actually want to take her down?" Maeve asks.

Pierce shoots her a quick glance before focusing on his hand again. "Not down. Just . . . teach her a lesson."

Maeve shrugs and tosses in five chips. "As much as I would love to see another Ella bite the dust, I'm raising too. Mimi Rabago didn't send me an invite to her party."

Lux scoffs. "You hate Mimi."

"That's not the point. She excluded me to send a message. I want to let her know the message has been received." Her eyes flash with that particular brand of wickedness exclusive to Maeve Wilson. "Along with a message of my own."

I think back over the past week, and the truth is, I've got nothing. Maeve is right. I don't care about this stupid game anymore. I'm tired of keeping track of petty grievances. There are plenty, but remembering what they are is the least of my concerns.

I toss my cards down. "I'm out." I couldn't give a shit if that last card ends up being a nine.

A tiny frown crosses Pierce's face but quickly disappears again. Maeve sighs dramatically, like me pulling out of the game is a personal affront. All eyes turn to Lux. It's her against our two leading psychopaths.

"I'll raise too." She shoves her entire stack of chips into the center and leans back in her chair, a cat satisfied with herself.

Maeve's mouth falls open. "What the fuck, Lux?" A satisfying tongue-twister that spins through my mind over and over.

"Who are you betting?" Pierce asks, the scowl taking up residence on his face again. *Losing* isn't a word he's familiar with.

Lux looks around the table, blinking those giant brown eyes at each of us in turn. She reaches up to twirl a piece of long, blonde hair around her fingers. The six inches of thick gold bangles she's wearing slide down her arm, revealing what look like bruises around her wrist. She quickly shuffles the bracelets back into place before I can get a better look.

"Walker Halifax."

I can't speak for anyone else in the room, but my lungs feel like they've been rammed into a barbed wire fence. Everyone stays quiet, absorbing what she has said.

Maeve's hiss breaks through the silence. "Lux!"

A few seconds pass, which I imagine are full of significant looks and shifting glances, but I can't verify because I'm focused on draining the rest of my cocktail. I have no desire to witness whatever exchange is happening around the table.

Then the weight of Lux's full attention becomes oppressive. "Shit, Heath. I am sooo sorry!" she says.

I set my glass back onto the table and crack my knuckles, turning to Pierce. "You got more whiskey in the kitchen?"

"Help yourself, mate."

"You sure you don't want more Black-Beer-y Smash?" Rhett says with a snicker.

A thumping sound under the table accompanies Maeve's glare. Rhett curses and grabs his leg.

I get up and head for the kitchen, wishing I could keep walking, through the window in the living room and into the night.

"Dude, Walker's back?" Rhett says from the game room. The guy is as quiet as a thunderstorm.

There's more mumbled conversation, but I don't stay to listen. I don't give a damn what they're saying in there. I don't give a damn about Lux's dramatic revelation, either.

I pour myself two fingers of whiskey from the top-shelf stuff Pierce stocks his liquor cabinet with. I toss it back and pour another shot. It follows the first. I refill my glass once more and decide to head back before someone comes looking for me.

Lux is talking animatedly as I approach. This explains why she was so quiet earlier. She knew the only way to keep this secret for the most dramatic effect was to say as little as possible beforehand.

"—airport bathroom is the new Mile High—" She stops abruptly as everyone's eyes land on me.

I sit back in my chair, already eager for this night to be over.

"That's disgusting, Lux." Maeve fiddles with the pearls around her neck.

"Not if you come equipped with tons of hand sanitizer," Lux replies. "Besides, Carter was in Japan for three whole weeks. I missed him!"

"How big of a dick can a guy who wears boat shoes have anyway?" Rhett says.

"Bigger than yours," Lux retorts.

Rhett laughs loudly. "Oh darling, just say the word, and I'll prove you wrong."

"In your dreams." She shoots him a murderous glare.

They've discarded the game. Lux's cards are lying face up where she dropped them.

"You okay, mate?" Pierce asks quietly.

"I'm good." I offer him a grin, then slide a stack of chips in front of me and work on restacking them. The dull clunks feel like the hollow beat of a heart.

"Why is she back, anyway?" Rhett asks.

"Why did she leave in the first place?" Maeve says.

Apparently they have no intention of dropping the topic anytime soon.

"Probably hiding from the law," Rhett suggests.

"Walker wouldn't break the law," Lux says. "I'll bet she's in witness protection from like, the mafia or something."

Maeve rolls her eyes. "More likely she's hiding from the government. You know how she is about stuff like that."

"Maybe she had a stalker."

"Gambling debts?"

Pierce shakes his head. "You lot are a bunch of idiots."

"I'll bet Heath knows why she left." Rhett's eyes bore into me as he takes a sip of his drink.

I'm going to punch that guy before the night is over. I drop the chips onto the stack. *Clunk. Clunk. Clunk.*

"It's probably just some big scandal with her family," Maeve says.

"Oh my god, Heath," Lux says. "What if you have a secret baby out there?"

The last chip drops from my fingers, and I push my chair back. "I need some air," I announce.

It's hot and muggy outside, but it feels one thousand times better than the aggressively air-conditioned flat. I place my hands on the glass partition of the "terrace" keeping me from plummeting to a swift death on the concrete below.

It's important that I remain calm. No matter what's going on inside my chest, the key is to make sure no one can tell.

The murmur of traffic is muted by the height. I wish I could be in the ocean, the crash of the waves the only sound, the feel of icy water lashing against my skin again and again. Maybe I'll still have time for a late-night swim before high tide.

I head back inside, intent on wishing everyone goodbye and getting the hell out of here. Lux, Maeve, and Rhett are all standing and talking when I walk into the game room. They stop abruptly when they see me, the way people instinctively tap their brakes when they meet a police cruiser on the road.

"Let's let Heath decide," Lux suggests.

"Heath doesn't care." Maeve holds a hand out to me, like *See? He doesn't give a shit about anything.*

"What's it going to be, buddy?" Rhett crosses his arms over his chest. The silver chain around his neck glints in the dim light.

"I don't have a fucking clue what you're talking about," I say before draining the last of my whiskey. "But I'm heading out."

"Nooo," Lux whines. "You can't leave yet. We haven't planned our revenge plot."

"I didn't think you'd finished the game," I say.

"We didn't," Pierce says. Judging by his tone, that wasn't his choice.

"We unanimously decided that Walker should be the victim," Lux says. "Playing seemed redundant."

"You decided that," Maeve says.

Lux spins a curl around her finger. "She left all of us. I figured you'd be dying for the chance to get back at her."

"I am." Maeve straightens to her full height, which still puts her a full twelve inches below me. "But it's still fair to take a vote if we're not going to finish the game."

"Fine." Pierce gets to his feet. "We'll take a vote." There's a note of finality in his voice that not even Maeve dares challenge. "Everyone in favor of getting revenge on Walker, raise your hand."

Three hands shoot up around the table. Pierce keeps his eyes on me and slowly raises his own hand, as if he's waiting to see what my reaction will be. All too late, I realize I'm the only one who hasn't voted. They're all staring at me.

I quickly lift my hand.

Maeve claps her palms together once. "Okay, it's settled. Walker will be our next victim." She sits, and Lux and Rhett do the same. They look at me expectantly.

"I'm leaving, but I'll see you guys on the links tomorrow," I say.

"Heath, you can't leave yet," Maeve announces. "You have insider intel."

Rhett snorts and mutters "insider" under his breath. Maeve kicks his shin again.

I prop my hands on the back of my chair. "I don't have anything that will be helpful."

"All the same," she says. "This is a team effort. We need you."

I stifle the sigh that wants to make its way out of my mouth and show her how much it is taking for me to stay here for another second. Instead I pull out my chair and flop into it, brushing my hair out of my eyes.

She smiles her thanks and turns her attention to the iPad she's pulled out of thin air, which is now lying on the table in front of her. I pull my phone from my pocket—not all of us can command thin air—and tap the Candy Crush app.

Maeve drones on and on about the process these things take, a process I think we all have etched deeply into our brains, right between "Always mount a horse on the left side" and "If forced to choose between money and power, choose power. Money can be replaced."

I keep punching the little candies with my thumb. It's nothing like the relief I'd get from being on a surfboard, but until this prison warden has freed me, I'm stuck here with nothing but the next level to keep me from losing my bloody fucking mind.

"Heath?" Maeve is staring at me the way my English teacher used to when I texted during school instead of paying attention to her nails-on-a-chalkboard voice.

"Hey," I say.

"Well? Do you?" she says.

I scramble backward over the past few minutes, but I have no idea what she's been talking about. "Do I what?"

"Do you have any idea," she says in a slow voice, like I'm a toddler, "what Walker's weakness is?"

I knew the essence of what they were talking about, but it still slams into me with the force of a wrecking ball. "Uhh . . . no?" I say.

"You must know something," Maeve insists.

"I haven't seen her any more recently than you have."

"You're not . . . *bothered* by this, are you?" Maeve asks. The concern on her face is . . . concerning.

I force myself to chuckle. "You forget who you're talking to."

"Lothario, my man!" Rhett claps me on the back, reaching around Lux to do so.

"Do you even know who that is?" Maeve asks, glaring at him.

"Despite what you may think, May-eve, I'm not a juvenile dipshit."

Her face flushes until it's the same shade as her lipstick. She hates when he pronounces her name like that. "Just a full-grown dipshit, then."

He flips her off, a grin splitting his face.

Lux sighs and rests her face in her palms. "We're screwed. There's no way Walker will tell us anything."

"I wouldn't be so sure," Pierce says.

"You didn't see her face in the restroom," Lux says. "I thought she was going to scream."

"I meant that I think Maeve has an idea," he adds, nodding at Maeve. She clears her throat. "As a matter of fact, I do."

I twitch my foot where it's perched on my left knee. My fingers drum a quiet beat on the underside of my chair.

"I was thinking," she continues. "What if we invite her to poker night?"

This is met with the same level of silence as Lux's initial announcement was. Eventually Pierce says, "What makes you think she'll come?"

Maeve grins, already knee-deep in her plot. "I'm sure we'll come up with something. If we can get her here, ply her with alcohol, and make her warm up to us"—she twirls her hand through the air like she's bowing for an audience—"we can find out exactly where to strike her."

3

"Snap" - Rosa Linn

Walker

Like any exceptional human being, I start the way I mean to finish. That means I explore the entire Gothic mansion I get to call home for the next few weeks, assess the comfort level of each of the seven bedrooms and their respective beds so I can choose one, and make a game plan for the weeks ahead.

My favorite room is, to no surprise, the library. It's unlike any home library I've ever seen before, and if there were any way to stuff it into my trunk and take it back to Oxford with me, you'd better believe I would have already done so.

The whole back wall on the north side of the house is made of ornately arched windows. The room is also two stories tall, so there is another set of windows that can be reached from the mezzanine that runs around the perimeter of the space.

A huge fireplace takes up most of the east wall. The chimney stretches to the ceiling and features engraved images, which I haven't had a chance to inspect up close yet. Tucked into a corner, there's a spiral staircase that leads to the mezzanine.

Where there aren't windows or doors set into the walls, there are books. In the alcove behind the staircase, running along the entire mezzanine—even on shelves above the doors. I could spend years in here, doing nothing but reading, and still not come close to consuming all of those words.

Every room in the house features thick, dark wood trim that gleams in the light, thick Persian rugs that don't make a sound when you step on them, and ornate gold-framed paintings of people whose eyes follow you around the room. It is more perfect than anything I could have designed myself.

The only problem is the smell. It's still musty and stale in here, and it's too hot to leave the windows open. I didn't bring candles with me, as they would have put me over the weight limit for my luggage. But I've never complained about needing to buy new candles before, and I don't intend to start now.

As I was preparing for this trip, I contemplated the wisdom of hiring a housekeeper for the duration of my stay, but I've survived on my own at Oxford for the past six years. This house may be fifty times larger than my small flat there, but I won't be here much.

My sole purpose for coming to Wesbourne in the first place is to access the in-depth resources on the life and works of G.R. Huntington stored at the Wesbourne Archives. So, much as I would love to spend the next 365 days of my life in this castle from my wildest daydreams, the reality is I'll be spending minimal time within her walls.

Therefore, housekeeper: unnecessary. I may not be able to whip up a gourmet spread for dinner, but since I'll be hunched over a book or my laptop most of the time anyway, oatmeal and coffee will suffice.

I type "candle shop" into the search bar of my phone and scroll through the results. There's a cute one downtown in the artisanal district. It's right around the corner from my favorite coffee shop— back when I had a right to claim things like a favorite coffee shop and *my* bookstore.

Going downtown is a risk, but since I can't imagine Lux or Maeve stooping low enough to buy their own candles, and the guys would rather extract a kidney themselves than set foot inside a store like that, I calculate the risk as low enough to take.

Since my car is still tucked inside my mum's garage, I order another Uber. Getting rides to and from the Archives is going to get expensive fast, so I'll need to swing by to pick up my Audi. She has no idea I'm in town—unless Lux's big mouth has already reached her—but I can't avoid at least one visit. She would be devastated if she found out later.

I have the driver drop me in front of Cafe de Olla. The scent of espresso and freshly baked pastries hits me as I push open the door. This is the scent I want for the kitchen, something to make me think my oatmeal is more exciting than it has any right to be.

I smile at the barista behind the counter, and she returns it, but I can tell she doesn't recognize me. I used to come here every day to get my vanilla chai latte, but when you've been gone for two years, other faces creep in to take your place in people's memories.

After getting my chai, I walk back outside. The temperature is already climbing, even though it's not even noon. I should've gotten my chai iced.

I can't afford to linger. I'm not willing to risk running into someone I know. This coffee shop may be twenty minutes from the Hills, but I have no idea what habits they keep these days.

The candle shop has a bell over the door, which jingles when I push it open. The heady aroma of thousands of candles greets my nose, and I inhale deeply. Shelves upon shelves stocked with candles in various containers line the room. There are ones in hand-painted teacups, amber-colored glass jars, china dishes, and in vintage lidded bowls in every color of the rainbow.

My heart rate increases as I grab a shopping basket and make my way down the first aisle. I'll need to choose the perfect scent and the perfect container for each of the main rooms of the house.

It takes much longer than it should, and by the time I'm ready to check out, my bladder has decided now is the perfect time to announce its full state. Stupid latte.

There's a restroom to my left, so I set my basket beside the door—the universal signal for *I'll be right back to retrieve this*—and slip inside.

As I'm drying my hands, I congratulate myself in the mirror. My plan is already going splendidly. Other than that slight mishap at the airport, I'm starting to think that I worried a little too much about coming home. This isn't going to be so bad after all.

I walk out of the restroom but immediately halt. There's a blonde woman hunched over in the corridor, unloading the contents of my basket into her own.

"Hey!" I yell as she grabs the vintage candy bowl with the "Rainy Day Reading" scent. "Those are mine!" I reach to pull my basket from her grip, and it comes away much too easily. There's nothing left inside.

She's already barreling toward the checkout, my candles peeking out of the top of her basket. I reach the counter as she's setting it down.

"This woman stole my candles," I say.

Amusement crosses the clerk's face. "I'm sorry. I don't remember you purchasing anything today."

"I hadn't purchased them yet," I say. "I set them outside while I used the restroom."

She gives me a sad smile, the biggest contradictory emotion a person can wear. She begins scanning the candles—my candles. "I can't prove who selected them from the shelf first. I'm sorry."

"Don't you have CCTV?" I say, glancing around.

"We don't have any cameras," she says, at the same time as I come to that realization myself.

I glare at the thief. She doesn't even bother looking my way. She's about my height, with a short blonde bob. She's wearing an olive-green tank and black leggings.

"Ma'am?" the clerk says. "You'll need to go find your own candles." She offers a smile that I think is supposed to look sympathetic. "I'm sorry," she says for the third time.

I come close to walking out of the store without a single candle. But since that wouldn't solve anything, I retreat to the aisles, where I begin the long selection process all over again.

The fact that there are people depraved enough to steal from other people's shopping baskets is infuriating. For one brief second, I imagine the looks on the rest of the shoppers' faces as I tell them about what the woman did, the horror and rage they would express matching my own.

I shake the thought away. That way madness lies, and one cannot afford madness when working on one's dissertation research.

I find new candles—although none of the containers are as good as the first ones I chose—and pay the clerk for them. She tries to engage me in conversation, probably feeling bad about the incident earlier, but I ignore her. I add a potted plant to my purchase at the last second. I need a reminder that not everything is about me.

So much for everything going according to plan.

I should have stayed home.

4

"I Don't Miss You At All" - FINNEAS

Heath

I'm late. And judging from the look on Pierce's face, I'd better have a damn good excuse for it. "We almost lost our tee time," he says as I approach him and Rhett on the edge of the golf course.

It's a bluff, and all three of us know it. Pierce has a standing tee time at Ridgewood, and there isn't a single person at the club who would dare give it to anyone else, regardless of whether he shows up or not.

Rhett smacks me on the shoulder. "You look like shit." He's wearing the most obnoxious golf outfit I've ever seen: a lime-green polo covered in toucans and neon-orange shorts.

"Hey." I smack him back. "I overslept."

He exchanges a knowing look with Pierce, which I'm not supposed to see. It's no secret I'm meant to be the dumb underachiever in the group. *Ol' Heath, can't even use an alarm clock.*

What they don't know, and what I have no intention of telling them, is that I barely slept all night. I had just dozed off when my alarm blared, reminding me that I'd agreed to go golfing this morning for god only knows what reason.

Our three caddies are waiting for us, bags slung over their shoulders.

The day is already hot, the sun blazing down on us like it has things to prove. The rolling green hills stretch out ahead of us, taunting me with the reminder that I'm not about to escape any time soon.

Pierce leads us to the first hole. Rhett hits his ball into the trees beside the fairway. His caddie searches for it but eventually comes back empty-handed.

"Damn it," Rhett says. "Did you even look?"

"I'm sorry, sir. I looked as best as I could," the caddie says.

Rhett's scowl grows deeper. "Fucking incompetents," he mutters.

Pierce marks the penalty stroke on our scorecard. "Chill."

Rhett either does what Pierce says or is smoking a joint I haven't seen yet, because as we're walking to the next hole, he slings an arm over my shoulders. "How are you holding up, mate? You know, with Walker back in town?"

My stomach plummets. I desperately hope he's got weed somewhere on him, because I may need it before the morning is over. I meet Pierce's gaze for a beat before chuckling and shaking my head. "Why would that affect me?"

Rhett shrugs but doesn't drop his arm. "Oh, I don't know. Maybe because you were pretty torn up when she left?"

My chest constricts at the memory. It feels like I'm wearing a wetsuit that's three sizes too small. I step away from him as we reach the second hole. "That was years ago."

I scored the lowest on the last hole, so I prepare to tee off first. My caddie hands me the club and offers a few tips. I swing, and the ball flies into the air and drops into a cluster of trees. "Fuck," I mutter, walking toward it. At least now Rhett can't complain about the deck being stacked against him.

My caddie is already picking his way through the trees to find the ball. Rhett and Pierce each tee off, and to no surprise, my ball is the farthest from the hole. After we finish, Rhett circles back for round two of making my day even shittier.

"You still have feelings for her?" he says when we hit the path.

I give him an incredulous look. "Please tell me you're joking."

He throws up his hands. "I'm just asking."

"Of course I don't." I shake my head and wish he'd leave me the fuck alone. I don't want to think about the past. I don't want to think about what happened two years ago. I definitely don't want to think about *her*. I jog up to where the caddies are walking to discuss the logistics of the next hole.

I manage to avoid both Rhett and Pierce as we play the third hole, mostly by not focusing on my strokes the way I normally would. But like clockwork, Rhett brings it up again as we walk to the next one.

"Dude, let it go," I say.

"I just want to make sure you're good with the plan."

"I told you I'm fine last night."

"And then you overslept," Rhett says. "Maybe because you were up thinking about . . . things? Maybe—"

"Maybe what?" I say.

"—having doubts?"

I run my fingers through my hair, pushing it off my forehead. "You're the one doubting me."

"You've been avoiding us all morning," he says. "It's a little suspicious. Right, Pierce?"

Pierce gives a noncommittal grunt.

It's only eleven o'clock in the morning, I didn't hit the surf first thing the way I wanted, and no one is drunk yet—except maybe Rhett, whose key personality trait is "high-functioning alcoholic." What the fuck does a guy need to do to be left alone?

I whirl around on him. "Just let it go, okay?" It comes out sharper than I intend, or maybe exactly how I intend. I don't usually lose my cool, but when I do, things can get ugly fast. I don't want to lash out at my friends, but if they don't drop this bloody Walker business, I'm not afraid to throw a few punches.

He relents, even though his smile doesn't fade. He holds his palms up in surrender. "Fine. No more talking about Walker. We can talk about my love life instead."

"How is the Princess Royal?" Pierce asks.

"God, so demanding," Rhett says. "She wants me to attend all of these events with her. They're just stupid charity things, too. Boring as fuck and only champagne to drink."

Pierce and I exchange a look. I turn away before Rhett spots my stupid-ass grin. I'm glad he's given me up as the topic of conversation, but the guy is fucked in the head.

"Sounds miserable," Pierce says, a definite note of sarcasm in his voice, which Rhett misses.

"You don't know the half of it," he mutters.

Over the next few holes, he complains about his relationship with Princess Beatrice. You won't find me in line to date someone famous, let alone a royal, but there are plenty of guys who would kill to be in Rhett's shoes. Not only is he on his own path to fame as a musician, but dating the princess has cast him in the spotlight for the past few years, which is his favorite place to be.

"Every time I do something she wants, there are another three requests waiting to take its place," he says. He swings, and his ball sails over the fairway.

"God forbid anyone have expectations of you," Pierce says, with the disapproving air that can only come from the oldest child and the CEO of a billion-dollar company. He hands us each dripping bottles of craft beer from the cooler the caddies are carrying for us.

"It's much easier if you disappoint people early." I take a long drag of the cold drink.

"What are you talking about?" Pierce says.

I work on peeling the label from my bottle as he lines up for his shot. "Better that than after they've invested in you."

"It sounds kind of genius," Rhett says before walking toward his own ball on the green.

"Early and often is my philosophy," I call after him.

He gives me a thumbs-up sign as he walks backward.

"That is so messed up, mate." Pierce tilts his head back to guzzle his beer.

"Let's compare our situations." I hand him my bottle so I can take my shot. "You're stuck in relationship after relationship that is nothing short of a mindfuck." My club hits the ball with a resounding whack. "Meanwhile, I get to enjoy the finer aspects of the female population without any of the garbage."

He pushes his Ray-Bans back up his nose and smirks. "I'm sure each of your . . . companions is fully on board with this arrangement?"

I don't know how my dating life has again become the topic of conversation, but at least this time it's devoid of a certain someone who is sure to make me spiral and screw up this entire round. I follow Pierce to where our balls are sitting near each other on the green. "If they're not, they are immediately given a choice."

Rhett's ball sails into the cup. He jams his fist into the air, his own cheerleading squad.

Pierce takes the putter from his caddie and steps onto the green. "Let me guess," he says. "Agree not to exchange numbers or part ways right there?"

I grin and finish the rest of my beer. "Something like that."

"Is that actually how you plan to spend the rest of your life?" He putts the ball into the cup.

I hand my empty bottle to the caddie and line up for my own shot. "I'm only twenty-four, mate." Not all of us were destined to become CEOs the day we were born, much as my father wishes that were the case. My ball also sinks into the cup, and I go to retrieve it.

"I can't imagine it's very satisfying." Pierce tosses the ball into the air, then catches it in his palm.

I keep my eyes on the horizon as we walk back to the path. "It sure as hell beats disappointing someone you care about."

5

"Shameless" - Camila Cabelo

Walker

The Wesbourne Archives is only ten city blocks from the candle shop, but in this heat, my blazer has become unbearable. I wore it to make a good impression for my first visit since coming back, but I'm regretting that choice now. I shrug out of it, drape it over my arm, and wish for the hundredth time that I had ordered a car while I was standing in the checkout line.

My candles clunk together in my tote bag. I'm going to be even more furious if one of them breaks before I get back to the house. One more reason to pick up my car from my mum's house as soon as possible.

I'll spend a few hours at the Archives, then take an Uber over there once it's too late for her to invite me to stay for dinner. Half an hour to do my duty as her daughter ought to be enough.

I turn the corner, and the imposing structure of the Archives looms above me, all Gothic architecture showing off against the bright midday sun. Stained glass fills the tall arched windows reaching for the pinnacle of the building, leading many tourists to assume it's a cathedral. A set of stone steps leads to the front doors.

Quiet hums through the building as soon as the door whooshes shut behind me. It could be a church, paying homage to the sacred texts within its walls. I've never been more grateful to be inside air-conditioning before. Sweating is truly overrated.

The receptionist at the front desk greets me with a cool smile. I wish now that I had endured the blazer. I look like a university student on tour.

"Hello." I smile and hope my accent assures her that I do, in fact, belong here. She sits behind her giant desk like a sentry, barring access to the antique tomes on the other side of the massive arch to all but those blessed with a membership.

I slide my card from my wallet and across the desk to her. "I'm afraid mine has expired, but I'd like to get a renewal, please."

She pulls it toward her and studies it. She looks like she's midforties, her chin-length hair tucked neatly behind her ears. "Of course. Let me get an application for you." She scoots my card back to me and reaches for a file.

I take the pages from her, relieved she hasn't passed me a QR code to scan and asked me to "please fill out the form on our website." I retreat to the chairs clustered near the door and quickly fill out the application.

When I'm done, I take it back to the desk. The receptionist pores over it, making sure I've filled everything in.

"I triple-checked each line," I tell her.

She gives me a tight smile and continues perusing the entire three pages.

I lightly tap my fingers on the desk and refrain from rolling my eyes. *Calm down,* I tell myself. *This will only take a few minutes.* I'll be running my fingers over antique spines soon.

After a small eternity, she says, "Okay. Everything looks good. I'll send this in for you, and you should have your new card in a few weeks."

"Thank y— What?" I say, shifting my tote bag higher on my shoulder. "Did you say in a few *weeks*?"

"That is correct." She taps the pages on the desk to straighten them. I grit my teeth. They were already perfectly straight when I handed them to her. "Our application board reviews them and—"

"I'm sorry." I lean my arms on the desk. "I'm only here for a few weeks before I need to return to Oxford."

If she's impressed to hear where I'm studying, she doesn't let it show. "That's too bad. I'm sure you would have enjoyed a visit while you're here." She takes a few steps away from the desk like she's about to head to the back room.

"Wait," I say. "You don't understand." My voice is coming out breathless. I force myself to inhale slowly and release it on the count of five. "I'm here from Oxford specifically to do research for my dissertation."

She gives me what I imagine is supposed to be an apologetic smile, but it comes out looking like *I don't give a fuck what the hell you're doing here.* "There's nothing I can do. Sorry."

"I just need a renewal." I slide my card back to her. "This one expired less than a year ago."

"I'm sorry," she says, looking anything but. "We're under new administration, and our policy states that foreign applications should expect two to three weeks for processing."

"I'm not a foreigner!" It's an almost-shout. Her eyes widen at my outburst. I lower my voice. "I'm from Wesbourne." I pull my wallet out again to show her my driver's license. "I'm only living in England while I get my master's degree. Which I can't get unless I submit a dissertation."

She gives my license a rudimentary glance before shaking her head. "There's really nothing I can do."

My hands clench the edge of the desk, turning my knuckles white. "Can't you call someone? The chairman of the board? If you give him my name, I'm sure he—"

"Ma'am, please." She holds up her hand. Her nails are short, no-nonsense like mine, and the only jewelry she's wearing is a gold band on her third finger. "I'm going to have to ask you to leave."

The arched doorway behind her leads to worlds of information I *need* to get my hands on. I can already smell the dusty pages and cracked leather. I'm sure I look like a crazy person trying to break into a sold-out concert without a ticket. I lick my lips and turn back to her. "Is there anything I can do to have my application fast-tracked?"

She must decide I'm pathetic enough to take pity on, because her expression softens a bit, but she still shakes her head. "I'm sorry. You'll have to wait."

I squeeze my eyes shut. An extra two or three weeks in Wesbourne with literally nothing to do? The longer I stay, the higher the risk of running into *him* grows. I cannot do it. I take a deep breath and slip my license back into my wallet. "Thanks anyway." I turn for the door.

I'm two steps from the blistering heat outside when she says, "If you're from here, maybe you have a family member with a membership?"

I halt in my tracks, my loafers squeaking on the tile. A tiny seed of hope blossoms in my chest. I thank her over my shoulder and push out into the sunshine. I've already pulled up the Uber app by the time I reach the bottom of the steps.

Let's hope my mum's membership hasn't expired.

* * *

I'm not blessed with a quiet Uber driver this time. As we make our way through the curving streets of the Hills neighborhoods, he gives me a running commentary on everything he sees.

"Oh shit, look at that place. It's like a miniature palace." He's referring to Colombia Castle, which, despite the name, looks nothing like Wesbourne Palace.

"Have you ever seen grass that green? Here's me thinking we're in a fucking drought. Guess that's only for us peasants." He cackles, clearly lumping me in with said peasants. "Do I curse too much? My girlfriend says I do."

I don't answer him, just mentally count off the minutes until we arrive at my mum's house and I can escape this barbarian.

"Holy motherfucker!" We pass Pierce's family's home, set back behind a row of trees and more than one wrought iron gate, but rising high enough on the hill to be visible over all of it. "How much money do you think a person needs to live in a place like that?"

Billions, I want to tell him, just to watch the shock on his face.

After a few more turns, we pull onto the street leading to my mother's home. When it comes into view around the last bend, I heave a sigh of relief. I may not be excited to see my mum, but I sure as heck can't wait to get away from this clown.

He pulls up to the security gate and punches in the code I give him. The gates swing open, revealing the white Spanish Revival mansion I called home for twenty-two years. "You the maid or something?" he says as I open my car door.

I throw him a smirk through his open window. "Just the daughter." I walk toward the front door, relishing the way his mouth falls open. God, I love the effect money has on some people.

Before I make it to the front steps, the sound of another car engine grows close enough to grab my attention. It's the kind of low rumbling that can only come from a fast car.

My heart trips over itself. I recognize that car as easily as the person driving it.

I stop with my foot on the bottom step as Lux climbs out of her vintage Ferrari Spyder. She's like a walking advert for a luxury brand. White car, white dress, white sunglasses perched on white-blonde hair.

"Walker Jean Halifax," she says slowly, in that lilting voice I've missed so much. "In the flesh."

"Hello, Lux." I hitch my bag higher on my shoulder.

She clears the distance between us. Perfectly manicured hands grab my face as she plants a kiss on each cheek. The familiar scent of roses wafts over us like an expensive, hazy cloud.

"You've been a very naughty girl," she says, leaning back to get a good look at me, hands sliding to my shoulders. "And I don't mean that in a good way. How could you have stayed away so long?"

She isn't looking for any real answers. Those are never given in the portico of a house, not even your mother's.

"I've been busy," I say.

"We are going to remedy that, and soon." She drops her hands.

Oh boy. "What are you doing here?" I say to divert her.

She slides her sunglasses off and dangles them from her fingertips. "I was coming to visit your mum, to find out where you're hiding, and here you are."

I try to conceal my grimace. I can't tell if she catches it, because her face retains the same restrained animation as always, like she's waiting for the punchline of a joke. "I'm not hiding," I say weakly.

"You must come to poker night," she says. "It hasn't been the same without you."

This time I *know* my grimace shows. "I don't think so."

"I won't take no for an answer." She twirls her glasses around. The gold Gucci logo catches the afternoon rays of the sun, throwing blinding flashes of light into my eyes.

"I'm sorry, Lux, but it's not going to happen."

"It's been two whole years since you've gotten revenge on anyone—surely there's someone you want to take down."

I briefly close my eyes as a smile floats at the corners of my lips. It has been an eternity since I've dreamed of a revenge plot. I haven't had the resources or the inclination since leaving Wesbourne.

An image of the lady from the candle shop sails across my mind, and I sneer.

"Aha!" Lux says, thrusting her glasses forward. "I *knew* there was someone you wanted to sabotage."

"Not really." As much as I'd love to stink up that woman's car for stealing my candles, the satisfaction of doing so would be completely obliterated by seeing everyone again. Making excuses. Fake smiling. Avoiding him.

"Come on." She grabs my arm. "We'll even give you a complimentary victim. We can ditch the game and move straight to the plot."

I hold back a laugh. Lux would ditch the game for the plot every night. Not much of a consolation trophy.

While seeing her isn't as awkward as I expected, there is nothing that could induce me to attend poker night. Lux has a way of putting people at ease, which is the only reason I can tolerate having this conversation with her right now. Put me in a room with the rest of them, and it would be like watching someone desperately try to unclog the toilet at someone else's house.

I miss them, sure. But not enough to put myself through that.

Not enough to be around him.

"I appreciate the gesture," I say. "But I'm still going to have to decline."

A knot forms between her expertly arched brows. "I don't know what to say when someone tells me no."

I burst out laughing then, and it feels so good, so cathartic. Two seconds later, Lux is joining me, her musical voice mingling with mine in a sound that is so familiar it hurts.

"God, Lux. I needed that," I say when I manage to get ahold of myself. "You have no idea."

"Something tells me it didn't change your mind, though."

I tug the side of my mouth up into an apologetic smile. "No, sorry. I'm only here for a short visit."

It's not technically a lie, since my plan is still to get my mum's card and complete my research on my original schedule.

She purses her lips together, resigned to her own defeat. "You'll let me know if you do change your mind. You still have my number, right?"

How do I tell her that I blocked and deleted all of their numbers after they wouldn't stop texting me? "I have a new phone," I say. It was easier than being haunted by memories every time I opened my photo gallery or saw the way Maeve had organized my apps by color.

Lux holds out her hand, palm up, and I dig my phone from my bag and give it to her. She immediately snaps a selfie, then taps at the screen with her ridiculously long nails—white, of course—before handing it back.

"Even if you don't change your mind, call me and we can grab drinks." She presses two more kisses to my face. "I miss you."

"Okay," I say, even though I have no intention of doing so. Running into her at the airport was a fluke, a strange one-off that I managed to escape by the skin of my teeth. Talking to her on my mum's front steps like nothing happened has been comparable to getting a tooth extracted—tolerable if necessary. Chatting over drinks and explaining why I left? Not happening, no matter how much I miss her.

"Bye," she calls as she slides into her tiny convertible and reaches one long, slender arm up to wave. She blows a kiss, then peels out of the driveway, leaving only car exhaust and rose water in her wake.

If things go the way they should, that will be the last time I see Lux

Colombia-Clarke.

6

"Where Are You Now?" - Lost Frequencies ft. Calum Scott

Heath

Walker fucking Halifax.

She's been gone for two years and still has the ability to throw my entire day out of whack without even being present.

There's a storm rolling in on the horizon, but it looks like it won't last long. As I eat up the streets on my bike, memories chase me. I try to outrun them, but they keep following.

I hadn't noticed Walker before the day Ms. Dankworth kept the six of us after class and accused us of cheating. None of us knew each other before. We attended different private academies for primary school, but Sterling Hall Academy is *the* secondary school for families in the Hills who have something to prove to the world.

That bitch was a nasty English teacher. I remember she used to wear her hair short and frizzy. I still don't know how she managed to get the job at Sterling Hall, but she didn't retain it for long after we came along.

Ms. Dankworth gave us detention for a week and threatened to tank our grades. I wasn't too bothered. I had been cheating, of course, but I knew my dad could pull a couple of strings and get the whole thing overlooked. He wouldn't be happy about it, but it was better than letting the incident affect my grades.

Walker, on the other hand, looked like she might pass out. The girl is righteous to a fault, especially when it comes to things like school and studying. I had the strange inclination to both corrupt and comfort her.

While we were all sitting in detention later that day, Maeve walked into the room and announced that we were taking that bitch down. A spark came into Walker's eyes then.

We plotted our revenge against Dankworth over the next five days while sitting in detention. We all watched over Walker's shoulder as she designed flyers in Canva using a photo of a woman Rhett found on the dark web. We listed her unique skills and specialties as an escort on the page, and in bold numbers at the bottom, she added Ms. Dankworth's phone number, which Lux had stolen from the school's private database.

Then we distributed them. Pierce, at fourteen, called in a favor with his dad's helicopter pilot, who agreed to drop them over the city. I called the headmaster and pretended to be my dad, threatening to pull my support if my son and his friends received a bad grade for something they didn't do. The Lawrence family has made many notable donations to Sterling Hall over the years, so there was no question of whether it would get dropped or not.

Ms. Dankworth quit a week later.

She was our first victim, and we've been friends ever since.

I pull up to the security gate and punch in the code. The gates swing open, revealing a silver i7 in the driveway. He's home, then. I steel my backbone.

I take my time with the bike, checking the tires and fluid levels. I briefly contemplate slitting a hole in his tire, but that would only keep him here longer. Plus, he wouldn't have to look far to find someone to blame for it.

I hear them as soon as I approach the side door. They're in the kitchen, voices raised, tempers high. My muscles stiffen as I place a hand on the knob. Whatever's going on will get ugly. It always does.

The side door opens into a small back foyer area, where we keep shoes and coats. I toe off my trainers, still green from the golf course, and nudge them out of the way. Cami's voice sounds from around the corner.

"—what you want from me!"

"I want you to try a little harder, for once in your fucking life." Everyone, meet my dad, Robert Lawrence.

"I do try," Cami screams. "Just not in the ways you value!"

"Those are the only ones that matter!" he says.

"And that's coming from the guy who professes *not* to be a narcissist."

"If you'd be even a little bit smarter, you would do something worthwhile with your life," he says. The guy probably doesn't even know what a narcissist is.

I walk far enough to be able to see into the kitchen. I have no interest in intervening, but I will if I need to. While I usually bear the brunt of our father's disappointed outrage, my sisters each receive their fair share too.

Cami is standing with her back to the stark white counter, still in her tennis whites. Dad looms in front of her, also in his white polo and shorts, clenched fists at his sides.

"I'm sorry that my mediocre tennis skills weren't impressive, Dad, but I have over a million followers on Instagram. If your tennis friends don't like me, they're in the minority."

"Those stupid social media apps have no value whatsoever." Spit flies from his mouth.

"Why don't you tell Mark Zuckerburg that?" she says.

Before she can react, my father reaches up and slaps her across the cheek. That's my cue.

I have his arms pinned to his sides two seconds later. "Run, Cami!"

Fortunately, she darts out of the kitchen. I may be younger and taller than my dad, but he's an equal match for me in strength. Years of beating up on your kids will do that to you.

He lurches from my grasp. I know his next move, but I'm too slow to avoid it. He spins around and buries his fist in my stomach.

It knocks the wind out of me. I force myself to grab his arm and twist it to the side, even as I'm struggling to refill my lungs. "Don't ever talk to her that way again," I say, pausing for breath after each word.

He shoves away from me, hard. It knocks my hand off his arm. Once he's free, he steps closer. "She's my daughter, and I'll speak to her any way I damn well please."

"You're a fucking sorry excuse for a human," I say.

He laughs abruptly. "I am? *I* am?" He throws his head back and laughs again. The sound is nothing short of chilling.

"Fuck off, Dad."

His laughter keeps rolling. "Where is it you're headed anyway?"

I glower at him. It doesn't take a genius to figure out where this is going.

"Let me guess," he continues, never needing anyone else when he's perfectly capable of carrying on a conversation by himself. "You're about to go to *work*. At least, I think that's what they call it"—he feigns confusion—"even though we both know you haven't worked a day in your life."

My jaw is clenched so tightly it's twitching.

"Am I right? You're headed to that white trash excuse of a job, and you say I'm the sorry excuse?" He shakes his head and laughs again. "You work at a fucking surf shop, son. When are you going to grow up?"

"I'm an instructor." I can't stay silent forever, even if it's the only way to shut him up.

"Right, right. I'm sorry," he says. "An instructor. What kind of qualifications does an *instructor* need? Hmm?"

I have no intention of responding, but the answers still float through my head. *Safety certification. Good surfing ability. Knowledge of advanced techniques. Communication skills. Love of the ocean.*

He only gives me a few seconds to respond. When I don't, he's more than happy to pick up again. "Any ol' Joe Blow can walk in off the street and become an instructor. You were supposed to be more than that! You were supposed to be special."

I've heard it all before. I'm the son he suffered three daughters for, and I turned out to be an even bigger disappointment than all of them put together.

"If you had tried a little harder in school, you might actually have made something of yourself. But you were too busy showboating to do anything worth mentioning."

By showboating, he means lacrosse. He's never forgiven me for our team winning second place at the national championship during my last year at Sterling Hall. *The only trophy worth winning is first place.*

"Do you remember that I had to buy your way into Oxford? There's an entire new wing at St. Hilda's with my name on it because you couldn't even sit the exams."

"You're the one that wanted me to go." I shouldn't engage, but the man is a fucking bully.

"Because I thought university would teach you to grow up! Instead you barely graduate, then come home and waste your degree by playing around in the ocean."

My fist twitches, begging to embed itself in his mouth. But I deny it permission. There's no point. He won't change. Nothing will ever change.

I stare at him, knowing it drives him crazy when I don't say anything. Then I turn and walk to my bedroom.

The guy isn't worth it.

7

"Piece by Piece" - Kelly Clarkson

Walker

My mum is dating someone. It's the first thing I notice when she opens the door. Even the look of shock and then delight at finding me on her front steps can't hide the fact that she is in a relationship and it's new. Of course, they're usually new—not because she's scared of commitment, but because they never last long enough to reach that stage.

Her hair is several inches shorter than the last time I saw her, over a year ago when we met up in London. She's gotten a blowout within the past few days, and there are new diamonds in her ears. The never-fail trifecta.

"You look great, Mum," I say as she pulls me into the house and into her arms.

She smells like cloves and citrus, a scent that doesn't jive with her personality. A new perfume then, too. She's more hibiscus and ylang-ylang. The powder-blue shorts set she's wearing sets off her tanned limbs like she belongs on the runway.

"You didn't tell me you were coming!" she says. "We have so much catching up to do. You'll stay for dinner?"

I start to protest, but seeing the hope in her eyes, I don't have the heart to refuse her. "Sure. But I won't be here for long. I'm doing research for my dissertation."

"Come to the kitchen, and you can tell me all about it." She leads the way to the back of the house. Even though I lived here most of my life, it feels strange to be back, like I'm a ghost haunting my former residence.

The kitchen is huge and still much the way I remember it. My mum is obsessed with copper. The whole arched ceiling is made from ornamental copper plating. Spanning the entire length of the twelve-foot island in the center of the room is a pot rack that holds close to one hundred copper pots and pans. Copper tureens, vases, bowls, and canisters fill every available shelf in the otherwise creamy-white kitchen. The only difference is the addition of tons of new technology.

"Alexa, play something relaxing," she says as soon as we cross the threshold. Music immediately begins streaming from hidden speakers around the room.

I take a glass from the cupboard on my left and walk to the refrigerator to fill it with water. "Mum, what the heck is this?" A large screen stares back at me from the door of the fridge, showing that it's 3:34 p.m., partly sunny outside, and that the Piano Guys are playing "Michael Meets Mozart."

"That's a smart fridge." She leans against the island. "Isn't it cool?"

"What's wrong with a normal fridge?" I frown and take a sip of water. I tap the screen, and a fish-eye view of the contents behind the door pops up. I jerk backward.

"This one shows you what's inside!"

I slowly turn to face her. "So does opening the door."

"It also gives recipe suggestions based on what you already have."

"Mum." I set my water onto the counter. "You have a chef."

She sighs and brushes her dark hair over her shoulder. "Cariño, what's actually bugging you?"

"Nothing," I say. "I just don't like all of this AI stuff. What if the government uses it to spy on you?"

She throws her head back and laughs. "Why would the queen care what I am doing in my kitchen?"

"That's not the point. You don't know who's watching you. It's creepy."

"You worry too much." She smiles and pats the barstool next to her. "Come. Tell me about this research project you're working on. For your dissertation, you said?"

I carry my water around the island and sit down, choosing to ignore the screen, which has a direct view of my face. The sooner I can get out of here with Mum's card, the better. "I'm researching G.R. Huntington." She has no idea who this is, so I move on. "The Archives hold lots of information about his life and works, so I will be conducting my research there."

"My brilliant niñita." She strokes my hair. "Always so hungry for information."

"Is there any chance you still have your membership to the Archives?" I say, holding my breath.

Realization hits her eyes. The light in them dims, and her smile fades. "Yes, I'm sure I have it somewhere," she says quietly, and hops off her stool.

"Mum," I call after her, wanting to assure her that I would have come to see her regardless, but she doesn't turn around. Her footsteps grow fainter as she goes to retrieve the card.

Damn it. Only here ten minutes and already screwing this up. I drain my water and get up to refill it, averting my eyes from the crazy-ass fridge screen. They land instead on a man's watch lying on the counter next to the fridge. It's a gold Rolex, and it looks just like the one my dad used to wear when I was a kid.

Nausea churns in my belly like a tornado. What is it doing here? *The new boyfriend.* He must have one like it. I pick it up, the metal cold and heavy in my hand, and flip it over. Engraved on the back are the words *Every day, around the clock, never forget that you are our rock.*

I drop my glass. It shatters on the ceramic tile floor, water splashing up my legs. I toss the watch back onto the counter like it's hot metal, then pull a glass shard out of my sock. Fuckity fuck.

Moving carefully, I reach for the roll of kitchen paper in the cupboard under the sink. My mum comes back before I have a chance to start mopping up the mess.

She gasps when she sees it. "What happened?"

"I dropped a glass."

"Oh dear." She bends to help me. "Are you hurt?"

"No," I say through my teeth. The room is tilting, and I reach out a hand to steady myself.

We get the water mopped up and the glass dumped into the bin. She fills a fresh glass and sets it in front of me.

I lock my feet on the bottom rung of the stool. "Why is Dad's watch here?"

Her eyes widen, and she blinks at me. "Where?"

"On your kitchen counter, Mum." I nod to where it's lying beside a copper vase of flowers. "I know it's his, so don't pretend otherwise."

She doesn't even bother glancing at it. "Walker, please don't get mad."

"I'm not mad. I'm simply asking for an explanation."

"Promise you won't get upset."

"Why would I get upset?" My jaw locks into place. "Do you have something to tell me that I'm not going to like?"

She bows her head, and her hair falls forward like a curtain, blocking me from seeing the emotions that are ever present on her face. She fiddles with a dish cloth, wiping small circles on the marble countertop in front of her. "Your father and I started seeing each other again."

Something snaps inside me. "You've got to be kidding me."

"Walker, please." She lifts her head and looks at me, those dark brown eyes pleading with me to understand. "He's changed."

I bark out a laugh. "Changed? How many times has he used that line on you?"

"He—"

"How many times will it take for you to see that that's exactly what it is—a line?"

"Can you please try to understand?" she says.

I stand up. My stool rocks backward but doesn't tip over. "How could you possibly trust him again after everything he did?"

I will never forget the sunshine that day, the way it glinted off the hood of his car like it was mocking us. The sound of his suitcase wheels on the flagstones. He still had one of those older ones, the kind you had to tip backward to roll. I can see it hitting the edge of a stone, temporarily jerking him to a stop until he yanked it loose and kept going.

My heart leapt when it happened, just a tiny skip of hope that crashed as soon as he kept walking.

"He's sorry for everything that happened back then, cariño. He's different, too." Her voice becomes more wheedling the longer she talks about him.

I can still hear the way she screamed as she stood in the doorway, yelling at him to never come back. My ten-year-old brain didn't understand what I was witnessing from my upstairs bedroom window, but I knew what the universal sign of a suitcase and screaming match meant.

"How many times is it now? Six? Seven? Or are there more I don't know about?"

"Don't do this, Walker." She tosses the cloth into the sink and walks over to the smart fridge, opening the door and grabbing a blackberry water. I still don't see what makes it "smarter" than a normal appliance.

"I don't want to see you get hurt," I say.

She twists off the cap and guzzles half the bottle before speaking. "I didn't think you were sticking around long enough to see much of anything."

Ouch. I fully deserved that. "Mum." I soften my voice. "You know he's just going to do it again."

She stares at me as she screws the lid back onto the bottle. Then she lifts her thin shoulders and drops them again, like the whole thing is of little consequence. "He might." She nods. "But he might also not. And that, cariño, is what I'm choosing to believe in."

I steeple my hands together over my nose, searching for the words to make her see reason. "How can you not remember what it was like? The tears, all the brie and crackers, the *drama?*"

Sparks flash in her dark eyes. "I know I put you through a lot, but I am still your mother." Her accent is growing thicker as her temper rises.

"He cheated on you, Mum! That's what he does!" I don't care about placating her anymore. I need to stop her from making another terrible decision. "How many times is it going to take for you to see that once a cheater, always a cheater?"

Tears are rolling down her cheeks, but she doesn't bother brushing them away. They plink onto the marble like raindrops. When she looks up at me, there's a sad lift at the corners of her lips. "How did my daughter grow up so bitter? Don't you know that people can change?"

"People never change," I say. "Who we are is who we are."

"He makes me happy, okay?" She wipes her face with the back of her hand. "He makes me laugh." She shrugs, her smile growing more wistful. "I love him. I've always loved him, cariño."

I feel sick. It's a tale as old as time. Only this one has been told so many times, she should have it memorized by now. I certainly do.

Once upon a time, a beautiful and dramatic Spaniard fell quickly, deeply, and passionately in love. Like clockwork, he breaks her heart, which leads to her becoming quickly, deeply, and passionately depressed. The hero of the story usually changes, except in the case of my father. Then the exact same story gets told on repeat.

Her heart has been broken so many times, it's like a repaired clock—it never ticks the same way again.

"Is he here?" I ask through clenched teeth.

She shakes her head. "He's on a business trip." She won't meet my eyes, but we're both thinking the same thing. Business trips are never *just* business. She lifts her chin and slides something across the counter to me. "I think this is what you were looking for?"

It's her membership card to the Archives, the same one I used until the day I turned sixteen and could apply for my own. It also expired seven years ago. My heart bottoms out.

She must read the disappointment on my face, because she says, "This is what you need, no?"

"It is, but it expired, just like mine." I lift my shoulders in a hopeless gesture.

"Then we'll get them renewed," she says with determination.

"It takes several weeks for that. I was planning to be back in Oxford by then."

Tiny furrows form in her brow, and my heart cracks open at her desperation to help me even when I've been so cold to her.

"It's okay, Mum. I'll figure something out."

Her face brightens in a smile, and she walks around the counter to stroke my hair. "I know you will, my beautiful, brilliant daughter. I cannot believe you're home!" She pulls me into her. I relish the comfort of her arms around me. I've missed her and didn't even know it.

We eat dinner together, and it's almost like old times. Neither of us mentions Dad again or why I left two years ago. I fill her in on my studies at St. Anne's, which she pretends to be interested in, bless her, but I can tell it bores her to tears.

I choose not to think about how her heart will get broken this time, maybe as soon as Dad comes back from his "business trip." I also choose not to think about the fact that my last hope of getting into the Archives tomorrow is dashed. I have no choice but to wait until I'm issued a new card.

I should have called them ahead of time, asked to fill out the renewal application online or via email or over the goddamn phone. I should have visited their website to make sure the policy hadn't changed. I should have been more prepared, checked more boxes, done more things.

The should-haves could eat me alive.

My mum hands me the keys for my car and gives me a kiss. "Come back before you leave." She's remembering the last time, when I sent her a goodbye text from my first-class seat en route to Oxford.

"I will," I promise, and walk through the garage door to my car.

My phone buzzes from inside my bag. I wait until I'm seated before pulling it out. There's a text notification from Dr. Riordan on my screen, but when I unlock it, the last app I used is still open. I'm staring at the selfie Lux snapped in my mum's driveway. That feels like an entire lifetime ago.

My thumb hovers over the back button, but I hesitate. I am out of options. I can hide in my giant house for the next two or three weeks, getting absolutely nowhere with my research. Or I can face my demons and try one last option.

I press call.

She answers after the fifth ring, when I'm about to hang up. "This is Lux—you'd better not be spamming me," she says in a singsong.

"Lux, it's me." Then, afraid she won't recognize my voice, I add, "Walker."

"Oh. Em. Gee. I should've bet money that you'd call. I could be rich!"

I cock a brow in the dark of my car and shake my head. Last chance to change my mind. "So rich," I say.

She cackles at this. If I were to bet on anything, it'd be on the fact that she's already three sheets to the wind. Her laughter continues. At least she's amusing one of us.

"Lux?"

Her laughter dies down.

"I was wondering." I take a deep breath. "Is your offer still open?"

8

"Habits (Stay High)" - Tove Lo

Heath

I'm toweling off my hair when the text comes in. It chimes from my bag, but I don't bother digging my phone out. I fish for the keys to my bike instead and wave goodbye to Seeley.

This is my third summer as an instructor at her surf shop. My dad may think it's a deadbeat job, but he doesn't understand that sometimes a person does something because they love it, not because they stand to make a buck from it.

That's not something he'll ever understand.

My F4CC sport bike is parked at the edge of the car park. I bought it two weeks ago, but the thrill is already wearing off. No wonder Rhett is always tripping on something. Even the waves didn't do it for me today.

I straddle it before remembering the text. I unlock my phone and read it, then immediately wish I hadn't.

It's from Lux.

Walker agreed to poker tomorrow night!! It's happening, bitches!!!!

I read it again. The words stay the same.

I read it once more.

Still there.

Okay, then. Looks like Walker is crashing our second poker night of the week.

I had planned to go home after hitting the gym, but I may need something a little stronger than beer and Netflix.

* * *

The club isn't full tonight. The music is loud, but not the deafening roar it is on the weekends. Only desperation drags us losers out on a Wednesday night.

The pickings are slim, but by the time I've had my third whiskey sour, my standards have dropped considerably. There's a blonde sitting on the blue velvet bench to my left. She came in with another girl, but I haven't seen her companion for the past twenty minutes.

She's hot enough. Hair past her shoulders that she's constantly flicking over her shoulder when she thinks I'm looking, which I usually am. Long, tanned legs that stretch out for an eternity from beneath her tiny dress. Heels sharp enough to stab a guy with.

I shift my eyes from her legs to her face and find her already looking at me. I lift my glass in salute. She returns the gesture with a shy smile that is probably meant to look coy.

My phone buzzes in my pocket. Another text in our group thread— Maeve this time.

Pierce, I'm dying for a spicy cocktail. Think you can make something tomorrow? xx

She knows Walker can't handle even the lowest level of spice. I shove my phone back into my pocket. I drain the rest of my whiskey and glance back at the blonde. She's not even bothering to hide her interest now. She takes another sip of her girly-looking drink while keeping her gaze fixed on me.

What the hell.

I stand and walk to her table. I can't even come up with a cheesy pickup line. "Do you want to get out of here?"

She's on her feet before the words are all out of my mouth, proving she's had much less to drink than I have. She grasps my arm as we head for the door, and I order an Uber. Even if I were sober enough to drive, I wouldn't take this girl on my bike.

She slips into the car ahead of me. The back of her dress dips down to her ass, something I would have discovered sooner if I had put my arm around her as we walked. I slide into the car and grab her.

She tastes like the sweet, candy-infused drink she must have had. She knows what to do with her mouth, I'll give her that. By the time the car drops us at the Carlton, I've already had my hand far enough up her dress to know that she's as ready for this as I am.

The clerk gives a nod of recognition as we approach the desk and tosses me a room key. The blonde giggles from where she's tucked under my arm. I've already forgotten her name. Julia? Jenny?

"What, do you like own this hotel or something?"

"Something," I say. It's as far from the truth as me being president, but I'm not in the mood for explanations.

We ride the lift to the fourth floor. If we had a room higher up, I would consider getting it on in the elevator, but ten seconds isn't enough for anyone, even with a boner this size.

We stumble into the room and do the customary removing of clothes while simultaneously grabbing and touching and kissing. She sinks onto the bed beneath me, nipples like soldiers awaiting marching orders.

Her body's perfect. Perfect tits, perfect legs, perfect ass. She's a good kisser, she doesn't say much, and she is rubbing my cock like it's her favorite toy on the planet. I press into her hand and remind myself that this is what I need.

It doesn't take long. She must have come to the club ready for something besides her vibrator, because I will admit to not being at my most gentlemanly tonight.

I hand her the black dress pooled on the floor. She takes it with an actual shy smile this time. I pull my boxers on, but I prefer to get dressed after they leave. There is something about dressing in front of someone that feels more intimate than sex itself.

When she has all of her things, she looks at me and bites her lip. I know what's coming.

"Can I have your phone? That way you'll have my number."

"Sure." I grab it from the nightstand and hand it to her. "But don't expect a call."

She stops with her hand outstretched. "What?"

"Feel free to put your number in if it makes you feel better, but I'm not going to call."

Her hand drops, and she takes a step backward. "What would make me feel better is if you wouldn't be a jerk."

"I'm not trying to be a jerk," I say. "Just honest."

A shrill sound comes from her mouth. I think it's supposed to be a laugh. *"Honest?* Why would you say something like that in the first place?"

"Because it's easier to hear now than in three days when I haven't called."

"You're an ass." She slams the door behind her.

I run my hands through my hair. I don't know why they always get mad. I'm doing them a favor by letting them know what to expect ahead of time, but it's never enough.

I walk to the window and look out over the city. No matter how much I try to control people's expectations of me, they always end up wanting more than I can give them. I thought it made me considerate. Maybe it just makes me a jerk.

My keys fall to the floor when I pull them out of my pocket. As I bend to pick them up, my eyes catch on the photo keychain I haven't been able to take off of my keyring.

Walker and I were in Switzerland when the picture was taken, arguably the best two weeks of my life. Something changed between us on that trip. I ended up telling her about my dad while we were lying on our backs, staring at the stars. Instead of being scared off the way I thought she'd be, she told me she loved me.

It was different with her—easier—like our souls had known each other since the beginning of time.

I should get rid of it. Drop it in the hotel rubbish bin, where there will never be a hope of recovering it. But something keeps me from sliding it off the ring. Idiocy probably, or maybe cowardice. Or maybe I need the reminder that someone once loved me for who I am.

I check the time on my phone before sliding it into my pocket: 12:13 a.m.

Less than eight hours to go.

9

"Do I Wanna Know?" - Arctic Monkeys

Walker

In a stroke of brilliance, I managed to pack every summer clothing item I own and still have nothing to wear tonight. I discard a burgundy top onto a pile that threatens to topple over the edge of the bed with each new addition.

What does one wear to a poker night with former friends one hasn't seen in two years to convey both "I am not the same girl you knew back then" and "Can I pretty please ask a huge favor of you?"

It's too hot for a blazer, and I can already hear what Rhett will say if I walk in wearing one. Which means my top is of utmost importance. It can't be too casual, but it also shouldn't scream *uptight*.

That rules out 90 percent of my options.

I hold up a black sleeveless turtleneck. It's a flattering cut, and I've received compliments every time I've worn it. It will have to work. I'm running out of time before I need to leave for Pierce's flat.

I flip through my skirts and settle on a tweed suspender number that hits midthigh. It will set off the turtleneck nicely. I pair the outfit with my black lace-up boots, a pair of slouchy socks, and my grandmother's diamond necklace.

The mirror tells me I'm presentable, pretty even.

My heart tells me I'm an idiot and going to go into cardiac arrest.

* * *

That sentiment only grows stronger the closer I get to downtown. My hands are sweaty on the steering wheel. I wipe them on my skirt, but they soon grow slick again. I'm going to need alcohol pronto.

I pull into the parking garage of the Atlantis. *Shit.* This idea was so many shades of stupid I'm beginning to question if my brain suffered damaging altitude sickness on the plane ride. What was I thinking?

I park in one of the visitor spots. Only people with too much money put chandeliers in a car park. I haven't been a part of this world for two whole years.

Nothing good will come from panicking. I need to present a cool and collected front. Otherwise this will all end badly.

I take a deep breath and walk to the lift on the other side of the garage, pressing the button for level twenty-two. The doors whiz shut behind me. And then I'm going up.

It takes much less time to get to Pierce's floor than I need to compose my racing heart. I walk to the door I've been through more times than I could possibly count. I wipe my hands on my skirt once more. Then I lift my fist and knock.

The seconds that pass are filled with every possible question.

What if they all hate me for leaving?

What if it's awkward and we don't know what to say?

What if I look like a fool for coming?

What if this is a trap?

What if—

The door opens, revealing Pierce's wide grin. Lux darts into the foyer behind him. She's wearing a short-sleeved belted white trench coat and likely nothing underneath it. Tall white boots snake up her impossibly long legs. Her rainbow has three colors: white, off-white, and cotton candy pink.

"You came!" she sings out, and reaches around Pierce to pull me inside. She squeezes me into her rose-scented embrace.

I let out the breath I've been holding and hug her back. I shouldn't have worried. With Lux present, no one is allowed to be awkward.

She releases me and gives my outfit a once-over. "Cuuteee." She looks at Pierce over my shoulder. "Always our little student."

He puts an arm around my shoulders. His shirt is still tucked into his pants from work, but he's lost the jacket and tie. "It's good to see you, Walker."

I smile and thank him for the invite. I let my eyes land on a painting in the foyer, desperate for something to ground me. It's a modern take on chains being shed.

"Simone Caldwell's *Emancipation*," he says.

Lux rolls her eyes and pulls me by the hand into the next room. "Let's go before he ropes us into an art lecture."

We walk down the hall to the game room. The other three are already sitting around the poker table. The dim lights cast shadows around the edges of the room and on their faces, but I would be able to recognize my former best friends anywhere.

"Walker, what is *up?*" Rhett calls as we walk in. I toss him a wave and a smile, and he holds up his glass in a mock toast. I want to make a comment about his ridiculous black floral-print shirt, which is unbuttoned to the middle of his chest, but there will be time for that later, when I've regained my courage.

Maeve stands when she sees me and comes over for a hug, albeit a less exuberant one than Lux's. She's wearing a typical Maeve outfit: navy-blue silk top with a Peter Pan collar, plaid miniskirt, her family's heirloom pearls, and four-inch heels. I try to read from her expression if she's forgiven me yet, but the only thing visible is her fire-engine-red lips, pulled into that trademark smirk.

I've never seen her lips a shade other than Chanel Dragon, including natural, and though she would vehemently deny it, I secretly suspect she's had them permanently colored. I don't even know if that's a thing, but if it is, Maeve would be the first in line. She is not a believer in redundant actions. Or redundant people, for that matter.

The last remaining figure doesn't look at me. There's an awkward beat of silence while everyone waits to see what's going to happen, but then Lux diffuses it by announcing that I should sit next to her. No one objects, so I slide into the chair beside her, and Pierce sets a dangerous-looking cocktail in front of me. I reach for it eagerly.

"I wouldn't drink that." The voice beside me is quiet, especially given the noise level of the rest of the room. Something flutters inside me at the intimacy of it, as if we are sequestered in a dark corner alone.

I turn my head and look at the one person I vowed to ignore the entire night. Intentional or not, in seating me next to herself, Lux also sat me next to him. My eyes land on his face, and it's exactly the way I remember it, but also different in a million ways that would take me a lifetime to chart.

Heath.

He has on a long-sleeve T-shirt with a faded logo for Pap's Seafood Grill. Waves of golden-brown hair spill out from beneath his backwards ballcap. The braided necklace he never goes without is strung around his neck. My brain registers these things in the nanosecond it takes me to meet his gaze.

Then there are those eyes that will forever haunt my dreams, deep, brown tidepools that will suck me down if I stare at them too long. I grab my drink and take a big gulp. A jolt of tequila hits my tongue, followed by the fire of jalapeño. A sputtering cough rips from my throat, making my eyes water.

"Told you not to drink it," he says with a bemused expression as he lifts his own drink to his lips.

I jerk my head back to face the rest of the table and discreetly wipe the tears from the corners of my eyes.

Pierce winces when he sees me. "Sorry, Walker. I forgot you don't like spice. I can make you something else—"

"It's fine." I pick up my tumbler again and take a tiny sip, just enough to show everyone that Walker Halifax may look like the girl they all remember, but inside she is different. Stronger. Braver. Much more badass.

It will take a very long time to get drunk at this rate, but at least the sipping will keep me busy. And busy is what I need to be if I'm going to keep my mind from straying to the fact that Heath is less than two feet away, close enough that I can smell the ocean rolling off of him, that saltwater-sandalwood-rum combination that used to make me heady with desire—

I yank my thoughts out of that spiral.

Maeve is shuffling the cards. "Antes?" she says, glancing at each of us in turn.

And just like that, my body relaxes. Not entirely. I'm still sitting next to *Heath*, for god's sake. But enough to remember how it used to feel to sit here among my friends, laughing as we plotted the sabotage of our next victim.

Heath shifts beside me. Even after two years apart, my body is still painfully aware of his. Every time he reaches his arm across the table to take his cards or place a chip on the pile. Every time he cracks his knuckles and sends Maeve into a fit of exasperation. Every time he adjusts his hat or fiddles with his necklace.

Everyone submits their first grievance. I spent so much time trying to prepare emotionally that I forgot to prepare for the game. When they all stare at me expectantly, Lux bails me out. "Walker gets a freebie," she says with a wink. "In honor of your first night back."

Unease crawls down my spine at her use of the word "first." It's essential that this is my *only* night with them. Otherwise . . . I don't want to think about the otherwise. "Thanks," I say. "Isn't poker night usually Tuesday?"

Lux twirls a piece of hair around her index finger. "We made an exception when we found out you were in town."

No one mentions my sudden departure. No one mentions the fact that it's been two whole years since we've seen or talked to each other. No one mentions that this is awkward as fuck.

Apparently the MO tonight is "avoid the elephant in the room." I'm cool with that. If I can accomplish what I came here for and leave with my dignity intact, I will consider the night a success. I just need the perfect opportunity to broach the subject.

I lift my glass for another sip. The cocktail is growing on me, even though I have to studiously avoid tearing up every time that jalapeño makes its presence known. Maeve reaches across the table when I set the drink back down.

"Oh my god," she says, grabbing my hand. "You finally stopped biting your nails."

Lux joins her in admiring my short-and-bare-but-clipped-instead-of-bitten nails.

That's not the only thing that's changed.

Play commences, and I end up with a decent hand. It suddenly occurs to me to hope I don't get stuck with the winning one, because the only thing worse than not gaining access to an Archives membership would be getting roped into a revenge plot with these five.

I can't fold yet or Maeve will wig out. By the time we're placing our first bets, I have a game plan. "The lady who stole the candles from my basket." I toss a chip into the pile.

Five sets of eyes fix on me.

"I'm going to need this story," Rhett says.

The key is to keep it boring. I don't want anyone thinking the woman would make an interesting target, regardless of how much I'd like to bring her down myself. "She took them when I was in the restroom."

"What the hell?" Lux says.

I shrug as if to say *People are idiots, what are you going to do.*

Beside me, Heath leans back in his chair, his legs out to the sides, bouncing up and down. His right knee is just inches from mine. I force my eyes to stay above the table. *Do not look over. Do* not *look over.*

"All right then." Maeve turns over the flop.

Within thirty minutes, the game is over, Pierce has won (big shock there), and my cocktail is gone. "I've got some gin in the kitchen if you want a G and T," Pierce says, looking at me.

I smile at him and pick up my glass. It is sweet that he remembers what I like, even if he forgot when he chose his cocktail recipe for tonight. "Thanks." I move to the door. By the time I come back with my new drink in hand, they look like they've been deep in a discussion about something.

I ignore the way my skin prickles as I squeeze past Heath's chair.

"Pierce picked the winner," Lux announces as I sit back down. Everyone looks at me.

I raise my brows and let my eyes dart between Rhett and Pierce across the table from me. "What?"

"Candle Lady!" Lux sings out.

It takes me two seconds to realize that's *my* grievance, and another two to realize this means I'm fucked.

They're all waiting for my reaction. I flutter my fingers above the table in a terrible attempt at jazz hands. "Yay." It comes out as weak as I feel.

Now what? I'm going to get roped into this revenge plot and god only knows what else.

"We should start planning immediately." Maeve is already firing up her iPad. "Walker, you're on research."

That was fast. "What did you do before I came back?" I mutter quietly.

"Drew straws," Heath says beside me, just as quietly.

My instinct is to swivel my head to look at him, but I refrain. He's hardly said anything all night, aside from submitting his own grievances. I pretend not to hear him.

"What am I researching exactly?"

"Weaknesses," Maeve says without looking up from her screen.

"That's obvious," Pierce says. "She must be obsessed with candles if she's going to steal them from someone else's basket."

"Let's stink up her entire house!" Lux bounces in her seat.

A wily grin spreads across Rhett's face. "Back up the sewage."

"Better yet," Pierce says, "go through her AC unit. It's going to be blasting in this heat."

"Ooohh." Lux's eyes light up. Nothing like a little revenge to turn a girl on. "Bitch won't know what hit her."

"What do we put into the unit?" Maeve asks. "Dog feces?"

"Just say 'shit,' Maeve. S-H-I-T," Rhett says.

She smacks him on the back of his head.

"Dead prawns." Heath leans forward in his chair as he says it. "They smell godawful when they start to rot."

"Genius." Maeve looks like she's about to kiss him. There's an uncomfortable twinge in my belly.

I grab our discarded cards from the center of the table and stand a few on end while they discuss best methods for tracking the woman down. The only thing I can supply is a vague description.

They eventually come up with some plan for getting the info they need. I don't find out what it is because I'm too busy trying not to notice the way Heath's hands and legs are twitching. He's leaning into the table, putting both his elbows and his knees into the physical space I've mentally claimed as mine.

Every time I chance a subtle glance at him, he's focused on the card tower I'm constructing. His gaze is a physical weight. My hands tremble at the knowledge that his eyes are focused on them.

All three levels crumble to the table.

He lets out a breath and leans back in his chair. Then, as if he can't handle another second in my presence, he stands and announces his intention to get another drink.

The others all ignore him, but I suddenly feel as empty as the spot on my left. Strings from my heart attempt to follow him, but I snatch them back into place.

"So what are you back in town for?" Maeve asks, like making small talk is something we do.

"Working on my dissertation, actually," I say. Is now the time to bring up the Archives membership? I can't focus.

"Remind me what a dissertation is?" Rhett leans back and balances his chair on two legs.

"A long research paper." Pierce knocks Rhett's chair forward with his foot. "Didn't you have to write one?"

Rhett laughs. "Dude, I never wrote a single paper myself." He turns to me. "You should get AI to write it for you."

I cringe. "St. Anne's has a strict no-AI policy. As do I."

"So what, they'd throw you out?" he persists.

"Uh, yeah." As would pretty much any university in the world.

"What are you writing about?" Lux is the last person to be interested in academics, so she must be trying to make conversation.

"Um, G.R. Huntington?" I don't know why it comes out as a question. "The author?" I squirm in my chair, adrenaline pulsing through my veins. It feels like I've had three shots of espresso.

"Hmm, don't know him," Lux muses. "You couldn't do it in Oxford?"

I open my mouth to respond, but nothing comes out. *This is your chance, Walker. Take it. Tell them about the Archives and how you need to get in. Ask if anyone has a membership they'd be willing to let you use.*

"I need to use the restroom." I bolt out of my chair and leave the room with the grace of a sloppy drunk. I can't sit there anymore, unmoored and adrift.

I find my way to the bathroom down the corridor. I close the door behind me and lean against it, trying to catch my breath. After using the toilet, I give myself a pep talk in the mirror.

"You are going to go back in there and tell them exactly what's wrong. You're going to ask if anyone happens to have a card you can use. No one will, because none of them have any use for an academic institution of any kind. But at least when you lie down to sleep tonight, you can do so knowing that you have done everything within your power to get back to Oxford as soon as possible. You will go to sleep, and when you wake up, you will find a way to get through the next several weeks without losing your bloody mind."

I open the door and almost stumble into a body in the corridor. The oceanic scent of him is so strong, so intoxicating, it nearly knocks me backward. I grab onto the doorjamb.

"Hey," he says.

I forgot how magical Heath's *heys* are. A million different meanings folded into those three letters, all depending on the context and the inflection in his voice. *You okay?* or *I'm sorry* or *It's good to see you* or *You're so sexy, I want to kiss you.* This one seems to be less along those lines and more *What the fuck are you doing here?*

"Hey," I squeak out, like an idiot.

He watches me for a few beats. "Were you talking to yourself in there?" His voice is a slow drag over pebbles.

I jerk a thumb over my shoulder. "In there? Definitely not." I shake my head and beg the floor to swallow me up. I wouldn't even mind landing in the flat below me if it meant I could get out of this situation.

He nods. I can't be positive with the dim lights, but I'm pretty sure there's a tiny smile in the creases of his eyes. "Okay," he says.

"Okay," I say back.

Next comes the awkward "you go that way and I'll go this way" shuffle. By the time we manage to scoot around each other and go our respective ways, him to the restroom and me back to the game room, suicide by shotgun has begun to sound appealing. I'm confident my face rivals Maeve's lips in shade.

They're in the middle of a discussion when I get back to the room. It could be about the candle lady, Pierce's latest girlfriend, or a communist takeover for all I can concentrate. I slink into my chair and give myself a mental shake. I have to shake out of this funk. My future at Oxford depends on it. Hell, my future sanity depends on it.

If I can't get access to the Archives soon, I'm going to get roped into the myriad of plans Maeve is bound to make. Extracting myself will be as easy as separating two flat Lego pieces.

"Does anyone have a current membership to the Archives?" I blurt out.

The conversation halts, and everyone turns their attention to me.

"Sure." Rhett digs his wallet out of his back pocket, then pulls something out and looks at it. "Oh, never mind. It's for the strip club, sorry." He laughs as Maeve swats his arm.

"I think I do," she says. "Let me check." She grabs her purse off the floor, and my heart soars. Could it be this easy?

She locates the card and pulls it out. My heart is racing so fast, it's nearly moving my turtleneck.

Lux must notice my anticipation because she says, "Geez, Walker. Chill."

I let out a breath. "Sorry. I just really need to get in for my research."

Maeve looks up. "Here it is." She studies it for a few beats. "Oh, wait. It expired six months ago."

Disappointment as real as the baize on the table in front of me coats my skin. It wraps around my throat and squeezes. This cannot be happening.

I nod over and over, like a fucking maniac. No Archives, no research, no going back to England where I belong. "Okay. It's okay," I say. "My new card will be done in a few weeks. I'll just, you know, find something to do until then." I grab my gin and tonic and down the rest of the glass. A warm hum steals over my muscles.

Heath walks back into the room as I'm setting my glass down. Our eyes meet. The buzz that started with the alcohol ends with the look he gives me, which goes right through the center of my core. I swallow loudly and avert my eyes.

"Heath," Maeve says. "Doesn't your mum use the Wesbourne Archives sometimes?"

A small frown puckers his brow as he pulls out his chair and sits. "Yeah, she goes there for research for her books." Virginia Lawrence is a semifamous historical fiction author.

"So she has a membership."

I don't like where Maeve is going with this, even if my heart does a tiny skip through my chest.

Heath does that casual lift and drop of his shoulders I remember so well. "I would imagine."

"I don't think you can use someone else's card," I say. That was going to be the second part of my favor of desperation. "They would have to be present too." Short of impersonating Heath's mum, this idea doesn't get me any closer to my goal.

"Isn't it a family-wide membership, though?" Pierce asks.

"Yes, but—" I start, but Maeve interrupts me.

"So Heath can go with you. He still lives at home."

The room stills.

I'm not sure if they're all waiting to see what Heath and I will say to this, or if it's in response to the edge in Maeve's voice when she points out that he still lives with his parents. There's an echoing thrum in my ears, as if I'm underwater and someone's plucking a bass guitar over and over.

"Unless that would be too weird . . . ?" Maeve adds. I'm beginning to wish she would choke on her own tongue.

I want to say that of course it wouldn't be weird, we're both adults, we've both moved on, we're both fully capable of being in the same place without destroying each other or everything around us. Instead, all I can think is *Of course it's too fucking weird.*

I would rather never return to Oxford again.

I would rather walk my mum down the aisle as she remarries my dad.

I would rather peel off each of my finger- and toenails.

I would rather do anything in this world than sit in a room with Heath Lawrence for days on end.

But of course I can't say any of that. So I do the only thing I possibly can in this situation. I smile at Maeve through teeth so gritted they're wearing each other down, and I say in a voice that belongs to a Chic-fil-A worker, "That wouldn't be weird at all."

Then, to prove my point to everyone around this table, including myself, I turn my smile upon the man sitting next to me.

If he notices the falsetto in my voice or the constipated look I'm sure I'm wearing, he doesn't let on. His eyes flick back and forth over my face, reading every single thought in my head.

I don't replenish my lungs with air during the ten seconds that follow my declaration. The room empties of everything but the two of us. The echo in my ears grows louder, until it's practically a scream, while I wait for Heath's verdict.

"Sure," he says when I'm about to expire. "I'm down."

The breath I've been holding leaves my chest in a whoosh, as if someone has punched me in the gut. There's a buzz of conversation around us as everyone starts talking again. I couldn't focus on what they're saying if someone held a gun to my head and demanded it. There's only one thought running through my head.

I think I just agreed to spend the next few weeks locked in a library with my ex-boyfriend.

10

"You're Different" - The Shelters

Heath

I got reamed in the head by my surfboard when I was fifteen. I ended up in the hospital with a concussion and ten stitches through my eyebrow.

This feels a little like that.

I may have said I was fine with this, that I'm down with whatever shit Maeve and the others want to heap on Walker, but that was before she was sitting a few bloody inches from me.

That was before I smelled her fucking coconut conditioner and heard her low laugh at some idiotic thing Rhett said.

That was before she looked at me breathlessly and I couldn't remember what I was supposed to say. Hell, I couldn't even remember my own name.

There's some commotion at the table, and I'm snapped out of whatever funk I've fallen into. Lux has her arms around Walker and is wishing her goodbye. Then Walker is looking at me and saying, "Does tomorrow at ten work for you?" like we're colleagues scheduling a lunch meeting.

I must nod, because she turns away. The next thing I know, she's gone and Maeve is trying to get everyone's attention again.

"That went exceptionally well," she says. "I don't think she suspects a thing."

Pierce gives her a high-five.

Something churns in my stomach. It feels like the beginnings of car sickness.

"It's obvious what her weakness is," Maeve continues.

Lux looks at her blankly. "What?"

Maeve's brows flicker. She's trying to decide if Lux is serious or not. "Hello? Her dissertation?"

Lux bobs her head. "Right."

"So we go for the heart," Pierce says. "Sabotage the dissertation."

"Exactly," Maeve says. "As she was talking, I was thinking."

Of course you were.

"I think we submit a fake and terrible dissertation before she can get hers in." She looks at each of us, waiting for congratulations.

Lux folds her arms. "I'm not writing a stupid paper."

"We'll get AI to do it," Pierce says. "We just need to know the topic she's writing about."

"Which Heath can find out when he's with her at the Archives," Maeve adds.

They both turn to me, looks of anticipation on their faces. "You expect me to do recon?" I say. "I'm just the getaway driver."

"Not this time, buddy," Pierce says. If he also slaps me on the shoulder, I'm going to kill him.

They continue plotting, but I block them out. My head feels like it's stuffed with cotton, muffling everything and making it impossible to think clearly.

Walker was different in a way I can't put my finger on. It wasn't that her hair was a little longer, or that her ears had a second set of piercings. She carried herself differently, like she had something to prove to the world.

When I came back into the room and Maeve ambushed the two of us about using my mum's card to get into the Archives, I thought Walker was going to flip out right there. It was apparent to anyone who cared that she was struggling to keep her composure.

I happen to be intimately familiar with every nuance of her face, including that look. That was the look of a girl who's been backed up against a tree.

"I don't think we should do this." I make the risky decision to interrupt Maeve's planning session. Everyone looks at me like I'm crazy. "It just seemed really important to her."

"Duh." Maeve's expression leaves no doubt as to her opinion of my interjection.

"You don't think it's a little harsh?"

"Heath, that's the number one rule of revenge: hit 'em where it hurts," Pierce says.

I hold up my hand. "All I'm saying is maybe we should take it a little easier on her. She's our friend, after all."

"Friends don't walk away without a goodbye or an explanation. And they definitely don't break other friends' hearts," Maeve says.

And there it is. The thing we've all been dancing around since Lux dropped her bombshell two nights ago.

You don't need to be a psychic to know what they're all thinking. *Poor Heath, had his little heart broken by the love of his life. She didn't even have the decency to break up with him. Now he's a dysfunctional mess who can't handle a real relationship.* Even Rhett is looking at me with something that looks suspiciously like pity in his eyes. The fucking traitor.

"Unless there's something you want to tell us?" Maeve drags the words out slowly, as if I'm a dog that might bite if provoked.

Something I want to tell them. What is she fishing for? The reason behind Walker's sudden disappearance? As if that's something I have any business exploring.

I force my face into a mask of indifference and shake my head. "No, you're right."

You're right, and I'm a bloody idiot.

Pierce and Maeve do their little eye communication thing that only people with an IQ over 120 are allowed to be a part of.

"Then it's settled. That bitch is going down," Maeve says.

There's a chorus of whoops around the table. Rhett announces that he's going to hunt for food in the kitchen. Lux pulls out her phone and fiddles with her hair before taking a selfie. Maeve and Pierce talk in hushed tones.

I should move, get out of here, hit the surf or do something to clear my head. But I can't. I swirl the amber-colored liquid in my glass. Even whiskey holds no appeal tonight.

The memory of Walker's bare wrist comes back. I couldn't even see a scar. She must have had it removed soon after she left. Without thinking, I rub my thumb over the tattoo on my own wrist. Half of the Big Dipper, missing its counterpart.

I expected the awkwardness, the pain, the sadness. I didn't expect the joy. It's stupid, the way my body reacted when she sat down beside me. It was like hitting the crest of a wave and performing a flawless aerial, sheer adrenaline and euphoria.

I should be upset. Angry even. She left two years ago without a single word, a few weeks after we'd all returned after graduation. I had to find out from Maeve, who found out from Walker's mum, that she'd gone back to Oxford.

I tried calling, of course, but she didn't answer. I sent texts every hour until I got a notice that the number had been disconnected from service.

She hasn't posted a single thing on her social accounts in two years.

I used to check multiple times a day. Eventually it lessened, until I forgot to do it at all. I expected her to block me on those too, but she never did.

"You okay?" Lux reaches a bracelet-encrusted arm across the table to touch my wrist.

I give her a goofy smile. "Fine."

"You know there has to be payback for what she did, right?" she says.

I nod to show her that I agree.

"If we don't punish her for leaving that way, what's to stop her from doing it to someone else?" Lux keeps her fingers on my arm. "Consider it community service."

It's sick and twisted, but I don't say anything.

"Lux, what happened to your wrist?" Maeve asks.

Lux immediately removes her hand from mine and pushes her bracelets back down. "Don't kink shame me," she says to Maeve, a wicked smile on her lips. "I told you Carter missed me."

Maeve's brows still convey skepticism, but she drops it as Rhett walks back into the room, carrying more snacks than I knew could fit in one person's arms.

"Did you leave *anything* in my pantry?" Pierce asks.

"I had a blunt on the way over here. I'm starving." Rhett dumps the entire load onto the poker table.

Lux scoffs. "You smoked it *before* coming? Rude."

He winks at her and digs around in his pocket before producing another one. "I also came prepared."

"Is there anything edible in this pile?" Maeve rifles through it with a curled lip. She's intolerant of gluten, lactose, and idiots.

Pierce hands her a package of gluten-free crisps she loves.

"I could kiss you," she says.

"Please don't," he retorts with a look of disgust.

"That stuff will rot your organs." Lux looks at Rhett's snack cache like it's a live skunk. She'd rather die than let anything made in a factory pass her lips.

"You know what we need to do?" Rhett says as he hands the lit joint across the table to Lux. "Host a food-based orgy."

"Fuck me now," Maeve mutters, and bites into a crisp with a loud crunch.

"It's actually not a bad idea," he says.

"It's probably the worst idea you've ever had," Pierce says. "And that's saying something." He snatches the joint from Lux before Rhett can take it back. He inhales, then offers it to Maeve.

She declines, even though she could use it more than the rest of us put together.

I accept it from him and take a long drag.

"Did you guys think Walker seemed different?" Lux asks.

"Different how?" Pierce says, already slipping back into CEO mode as he waits for her answer.

"She had bangs," Maeve says.

Lux leans onto the table. "Not her hair. Something else."

"She didn't talk about any conspiracy theories," Maeve offers. "That was new."

"Do you guys remember when she was so sure people landed on the moon?" Rhett says.

Pierce cocks his brow. "They *did* land on the moon, mate."

Lux cackles. "How are you this high already?"

"What about her theory that the earth is flat?" Maeve says. "We spent an entire weekend trying to prove her wrong."

A thousand memories threaten to surface, but I shove them down into the black hole of my mind. Now is not the time to dwell on them.

This, right here, is what friendship looks like. Not sneaking off to another country without telling anyone you're leaving. Not enacting radio silence while everyone loses their mind trying to find out what happened to you.

Like it or not, they're right. Walker does need to learn her lesson. If I'm the one who has to teach it to her, then so be it.

The faster she returns to Oxford, the better.

11

"i hate u, i love u" - gnash ft. olivia o'brien

Walker

I shouldn't be surprised that he's late. Being on time is as repulsive to Heath as reading a dictionary is to most people. By the time I've been standing outside the Archives for eleven minutes, I have thoroughly regretted not only the decision to come here with him, but every single decision that brought me to this place.

I have no idea what to expect once we're inside—if he ever shows up. Will he want to talk? He's never been big on conversation. Will he linger and make it hard for me to concentrate? I'll have to ignore him if he does, pretend that he's no different from the other scholars there to study quietly.

Of course, the idea of Heath being scholarly in any way, shape, or form is hysterical. The guy couldn't even be bothered to read *Animal Farm*. He skimmed the CliffNotes and somehow managed to pass the exam.

My palms are sweaty again—my new default state—and the knot in my stomach grows by the second. I can't identify every emotion wrapped within it, but anger is in there somewhere.

I check my watch. The guy is now fifteen minutes late. He probably overslept or decided he'd rather surf than show up. Or he forgot.

Apparently I'm the only one who was up all night wondering what kind of idiot agrees to this.

The sound of a rumbling engine cuts through the noise of the pedestrians slowly filling the city streets, bustling in and out of coffee shops and cafes with their morning lattes and breakfast toasties. A sleek black motorbike pulls up to the curb. My body knows it's him before he even comes to a complete stop, in spite of the dark helmet he's wearing.

He removes the helmet and shakes out that glorious head of hair. The sun hits his brown waves, turning them the color of caramel. He runs a hand through it to get it out of his face. My fingers itch with the memory of how luxurious it feels.

Shit.

How is he still able to cause a visceral reaction on my body? This is not good. In fact, this is the worst thing that could happen. I need to stay immune to him if I am to have any hope of completing my research and getting the fuck out of Wesbourne.

Heath walks toward the entrance to the Archives, avoiding every crack in the concrete. I physically feel the exact moment he notices me.

"Hey," he says. My belly croons.

I bury a knife up to the hilt in it. "You're late," I snap.

He shrugs like he didn't just make me wait twenty minutes in the sweltering sun. Because yes, I was five minutes early in case he happened to be as well. Lesson learned.

"Traffic was bad."

I want to bark that traffic is always bad at this time of the morning, but it won't do any good. "Button your shirt," I say instead. "We can't afford to get kicked out before we even get inside."

He keeps his eyes on me while fumbling with his linen button-down.

Enough of his chest is visible to know that he must still be hitting the gym every day. That kind of definition does not come without some serious discipline.

When he has fastened two more buttons—an improvement, but still too few to be decent—he motions toward the entrance. "After you," he says in that low drawl that used to make my belly flip over.

I march to the door. If he's trying to get under my skin, it's working. If he's not trying, it's still working.

The same receptionist is sitting at the desk. If she recognizes me, she doesn't mention it. "Welcome to the Archives," she says.

Heath slides his mum's card across the desk along with his driver's license. She confirms that the addresses on both match and waves us through the huge arch and into the main room.

There's an air of familiarity, but also of something new, like a treasure waiting to be discovered within the history-rich walls. The ceiling soars above us while light filters through the stained glass windows that line the space.

There are books as far as the eye can see. Arch after arch melts into the distance, each one separating another section of Wesbourne history. We have a historical society too, where some of the more important texts are kept. The Archives is focused primarily on published works detailing the life of Wesbourne saints, politicians, kings, crusaders, and other important people.

I scan the rows, letting my fingers trail over the spines of antique books. The smell of this place brings back so many memories. It's similar to the library at St. Anne's, but it has its own particular combination of leather, book pages, and dust.

In the center of each aisle is a table and a few chairs. Some of these are occupied by old men in three-piece suits and reading glasses. They frown at us as we walk by.

Heath remains a few steps behind me. Neither of us says anything, but I can sense him as clearly as I can sense my own head on my shoulders.

I find the section on Wesbourne authors. I haven't studied G.R. Huntington in the Archives before. My interest in his life didn't start until after I was at Oxford. I own a first edition of each of his works, of course, but don't know more than the basics about his life and the influences that made him one of the most famous and respected Gothic horror novelists of all time.

When Heath realizes I'm going to be in this section for a while, he folds himself over one of the armchairs in the corner. I try not to notice the way he manages to look graceful even though his limbs stick out at all angles. Must be the surfer in him. Anyone who can manage to not only stay on a board while it's riding a wave, but also do multiple tricks in the air, has to have at least a modicum of grace.

I continue perusing the shelves. I occasionally get detained by an interesting biography or collection of works I haven't seen before. Wesbourne is a country ripe with authors, and I could spend an entire year learning about each one.

Heath shifts in his chair, and my eyes instinctively leave the pages I'm skimming on the life of Rhetha Barning Willoughby. He has moved so he's facing the front, arms resting on his knees. His phone is in his hands. It looks like he's playing a game of some sort.

I grit my teeth and return the book to the shelf. My toes curl in my shoes as I stop in front of the next section of the bookcase. It's not like I want his help. In fact, I pointedly *don't* want his help. But something about the way he's sitting there, playing on his phone like a sullen teenager, makes me want to scream.

He shifts again. Every nerve in my body stops what it's doing to focus on this movement of his. *Stop that,* I chide them. *We don't care about him.*

My body doesn't listen. Two minutes later, when he moves again—

this time to get up and pace—it launches a full five-alarm fire. When he stops right beside me, my organs threaten to burst into flames.

"Hey," he says quietly. "Finding what you're looking for?"

I shove the book in my hands back onto the shelf. "No," I say, my voice choppy in contrast to his soft tones. "I can't find anything on G.R. Huntington."

"And he is . . . ?"

I turn to look at him, not sure if I can trust the interest in his voice. "He, uh . . . he was a Gothic horror novelist. Pretty famous, in fact. The Stephen King of the nineteenth century."

"Ah." Heath nods in understanding. "And you need him for your research?"

"I'm writing my dissertation on the effect he's still having on horror literature today. Many of our modern stories use techniques he invented back in the mid-eighteen hundreds, such as the use of the—" The horror of what I've been doing sinks in.

I turn back to the shelf in front of me, using my finger to keep my place as I browse the titles.

"You didn't have to stop," he says.

My face heats, but I refuse to look at him. "I don't want to bore you."

He stays quiet, but his eyes probe. Finally I can't take it anymore. I sneak a quick peek at him out of the corner of my eye. "You're not boring me," he says.

One of the things I've always liked about books is that no matter how many times you go back to them, the ending never changes. The bad guy always gets what's coming to him, the couple always ends up together, the treasure is always found.

If only life came with that kind of predictability. We'd all be spared a world of pain.

"I can help you look," he says.

This time I turn my whole head to see him. His face is blank. His dark eyes draw me in like quicksand. He's leaning a shoulder against the bookcase—Heath doesn't stand when he can lean, sit, or lie down. He is the personification of relaxation.

"It's okay." I face the shelf again. Looking at him for too long is dangerous.

"Walker."

I ignore the butterflies that launch from my stomach and flutter their way around my chest. I clear my throat. "I appreciate the offer, but I'm perfectly capable—"

"I know you are," he says. "But I want to help." He kneels and pulls a thick volume from the bottom shelf.

The words in my own book swim before my eyes. I can't make out anything with his tousled head in my peripheral vision. I slam it shut and return it to the shelf, then move several steps to the left, hoping a little distance will clear my head.

"Will this help?" Heath is still crouched beside the bottom shelf, the book in his hands open to the table of contents.

Reluctantly, I return to where he's at. He stands quickly, brushing against me ever so slightly. Fireworks crackle across my skin. I ensure there are at least three inches between us before leaning over his shoulder to see what he's pointing at.

The book is a collection of minibiographies of various Wesbournian authors. G.R. Huntington is listed, of course, but based on the size of the book alone, I can tell it won't give me anything more than the bare-bones version I'm already familiar with. I explain this to him.

"Okay," he says, just like that. He flips to the bio on Huntington. I take this as my cue to return to my own searching.

Several minutes later, he breaks the silence again. "I've read that."

I look over at him. He's still standing, but instead of leaning against the shelf, he's pacing the small area between the bookcases.

"You've read what?" I ask.

"The Disappearance of Emily Blanchard."

It's one of Huntington's more popular works, but I don't remember it on the syllabus for any of Heath's classes. Yes, I read his syllabi. I used to read cereal boxes, too. Multiple times. "What, the CliffNotes?"

His eyes flicker over to meet mine. "No, the book."

"You read a book," I deadpan.

Several beats pass as we hold each other's gaze. "Yep." He drops his eyes back to the page. "I didn't recognize his name when you said it, but I do remember that title."

I reshelve my book without a word.

He returns to the bookcase and slides his own book back in. We continue browsing in silence for several more minutes. When I'm about to break the silence and ask what he thought of the book, he walks off.

Just up and leaves the section without a word.

12

"Lines" - Alfie Jukes

Heath

I don't know how long I can survive this. While the Archives is impressive, with its tall ceilings, dark wooden bookshelves, and old books, there is a definite lack of sunshine and balmy breeze. Not to mention the addition of the one person guaranteed to drive me mad.

I tried to distract myself. Looking at my phone worked for a while, but then she would tuck her hair behind her ear or bite her lip while concentrating on the spines on the shelf. How the fuck is a guy supposed to lose himself in a game when every move she makes is like a siren to his dick?

I hardly slept last night. Sleep became nothing more than a distant possibility the minute I found out I would be seeing her again in a matter of hours. And not just seeing her, but be *alone* with her. There are a few people scattered throughout the aisles of this place, but we are as alone as we would be if we were in the back of my car right now.

I scrub that picture from my mind. I have no business imagining myself alone with her anywhere, but especially not in the back of a car.

I make my way to the front desk. I've been here maybe twice with my mum, both times becoming bored enough that she sent me home with the driver.

"Excuse me," I say to the woman who greeted us earlier. I smile when she looks up from her home design magazine. "I'm looking for resources on a particular person."

"Of course." She puts the magazine down and wakes her computer by moving the mouse. "Who are you looking for?"

Damn it. I should have taken a photo of the bio I was reading. I've already forgotten the guy's name. "He's a famous author? Something with 'Hunt' in it, I think."

"G.R. Huntington?" she asks.

"That sounds right. Gothic horror?" I ask, just to be sure.

"That's him," she says. "We have a special room dedicated to all of the resources we have on him." She stands and makes her way around the desk. "I can take you there."

She leads the way through the arches. When we approach the bookcase I left Walker at, I ask her to wait a moment. Then I motion to Walker to come with us. She pulls her brows down the way she does when she's frustrated or confused.

I want to grab her hand and make her laugh. Instead I say, "Come on."

To her credit, she follows me, but she doesn't hold her tongue. "Where are we going?"

"You'll see." I smile.

Her frown deepens.

The librarian leads us all the way to the back, then down a narrow corridor with several small doors coming off it. She opens one of them and stands back so we can enter.

It's the size of a small bedroom, each wall lined with rows of books. In the center is a large library table and several chairs. An octagon-shaped stained glass window lets in a pinprick of sunlight.

"Let me know if you need anything else," the woman says before closing the door.

"What is this room?" Walker heads to the nearest shelf.

I know how much she likes finding the answers herself, so I stay quiet and wait for the realization to dawn.

Several seconds later, her head whips around. She looks at me for a moment, then turns back to the books. Her fingers quickly skim the spines. She moves to another shelf on the other wall. Her fingers dance upon the titles as she takes it all in.

She stops as suddenly as she started. She stays facing the bookcase, and I picture her swallowing. She reaches to tuck her hair behind her ear. The scent of that coconut conditioner she still uses floats across the room to me. My dick responds by surging against my pants. It remembers all too well what that scent means.

When she turns, there's something in her eyes I can't identify. Caution maybe, but something else too. "Thank you," she says quietly.

I sink into one of the chairs. "No big deal. Let me know if you want any help." I pull my phone out of my pocket again, then proceed to fail the same level twice. This isn't going to cut it. I drop my phone back on the table. She doesn't look up, engrossed in a book the size of a Bible.

Her hair falls across her face, shielding it from my view. A pang reverberates through my chest, but then she sets the book on the table without breaking her concentration and pulls her hair back into a knot at the base of her neck. She's only inches away, and I can practically taste her conditioner now.

My eyes linger on her wrist. I still can't believe she had the tattoo removed. Laser removal is no small deal, and she avoids medical intervention whenever possible. Was she that desperate to wash all traces of me from her life?

She looks up from the page and catches me staring. "What?" She swipes at her cheek like she has remnants of her breakfast there.

"Nothing," I say. "Just wondering if you have a book recommendation for me."

She stares at me without blinking. "Sorry, what?"

"A book?" I say again. "By Huntington?"

"Very funny." She returns to her reading.

"I'm serious," I say. "I liked *Emily Blanchard*. What should I try next?"

Her eyes dart to me. She thinks I'm messing with her, but the truth is, after she left, I was a mess. I was so fucked I was willing to do anything to feel connected to her again. She'd left the book in my bedroom, and I ended up reading it cover to cover. It took me five weeks, but I finished it.

Her teeth inevitably find her lip again. My groin aches as she bites down gently. Eventually she has mercy on me and releases it to say, "Try *The Haunting at 83rd Street*."

Her attention snaps back to the open book on the table, leaving me to find the novel she's recommended on my own. I don't mind. It gives me something to do and keeps me from hauling her across the table and into my lap.

It's thoughts like that that will wreck this entire thing.

I locate the book with ease—there's a whole shelf of all of Huntington's works—and an hour passes as I lose myself in Victorian-era Wesbourne. I have to keep moving around, of course, but I'm surprised at how much time has passed when Walker speaks.

"You like it?"

I look up to find her watching me. I close the book and set it on the table. "It's good," I say.

A tiny smile plays at the corners of her mouth. I would do anything to see it in full bloom. "Can you do something for me?"

She could ask me for a kidney, and I'd cut myself open with a pen knife to remove it. I have to get out of this fucking library. "Sure." My voice catches, and it comes out strained.

"I need to send Dr. Riordan an update. I was wondering if you could take a photo of me in front of all the books." There's a shyness in her voice that I haven't heard in so long.

"Who's Dr. Riordan?"

"My professor."

"You send updates to your professor?"

She hands me her phone. The camera app is already open. "He's supervising my dissertation."

I take the phone and hold it while she positions herself in front of the bookcases. She spreads her arms wide, and a huge smile lights up her face. I snap the picture and hand the phone back.

I try to get lost in my book again, but the moment has been killed. My hands clench around the sides. I close it before I rip something and walk to the window instead. I can't see anything due to the colored glass, but being close to the outdoors makes me feel better.

Who the fuck is this guy she's sending pictures of herself to? And more importantly, why do I want to rip his head from his shoulders for making her smile like that?

13

"Goosebumps" - Travis Scott

Walker

The texts come in during my morning shower. I'm stepping inside the sea-glass-tiled stall when the first ping sounds. By the time I'm lathering shampoo into my hair, five more have followed. When I emerge fifteen minutes later, I have a total of twenty-two notifications.

It's a group thread started by Maeve. It was a mistake to call Lux. I should have asked about poker night via carrier pigeon or hired a blimp. Giving her my new number won't end well.

Sure enough, they're already making plans for today—plans they expect me to participate in. It takes me no time at all to match up who is who and add their names to my contacts. In for a penny, in for a pound.

Maeve: *Fire on 79 tonight? I heard DJ Giovanni is back. xx*

Lux: *Yesssss! I'm so in!*

Rhett: *Sickkk*

Pierce: *I promised Isabella I'd take her out tonight.*

Rhett: *DUDE*

Maeve: *You cannot be serious. After she was texting some other bloke?*

Lux: *Pierceeeeeee!*

Pierce: *It was a misunderstanding.*

Maeve: *You cannot bail on us tonight. I won't tolerate it.*

Pierce: *Fine. I'll bring her along.*

Lux: *Nooooooooo*

Maeve: *Absolutely not.*

Rhett: *You know I love you mate but that might be taking it a step too far*

Pierce: *You guys are the worst. I'll see if I can get out of it.*

Heath: *Hey*

Lux: *Heath!!!*

They continue the verbal barrage, Rhett sending pictures of a guitar he just bought and Lux informing us she has the winning bid on a rare 1976 Hermes bag. There's also a separate thread, which Maeve started seconds after the first one. This one only includes the girls.

Maeve: *We obviously will need to go shopping today.*

Lux: *OBVS x*

Maeve: *Walker, that includes you.*

Lux: *It will be just like old times!!*

Maeve: *Walker?*

Maeve: *I will show up on your doorstep and drag you out of the house myself if necessary. You're coming. xx*

Unfortunately, that last one isn't a joke. Maeve isn't the joking type, nor does she take kindly to people disrupting her vision of something, even if it's just a night at the club or a shopping trip with the girls.

Me: *I need to work on compiling my notes from yesterday. x*

It's not a lie exactly, but it will only take me an hour.

Maeve: *Unacceptable excuse. We'll be there to pick you up in two hours. xx*

Me: *I'd really rather not.*

Maeve: *Do you imagine that will stop me?*

Lux: *Come on Walker. Pleeeaaaseee?*

Me: *Fine. *MASSIVE SIGH**

Lux: Yayyyyy!!!

Maeve: *You won't regret this. xx*

Not true, because I'm already waist-deep in regret. I should never have attended poker night. That was the catalyst to all of this. But if I hadn't, I also wouldn't have gotten access to the Archives yesterday.

True to their word, Lux and Maeve show up at my Airbnb two hours later in a hired car. I had to drop a pin so they could locate it, something I'm sure will eventually come back to bite me in the ass.

As I lock up the house, I can't ignore the tiny thread of excitement weaving its way into my conscience. It's been so long since I've hung out with anyone to do something besides study that I've forgotten to miss it.

"Walker!" Lux says as I climb into the car. "The only person alive who actually talks in semicolons."

We visit several different shops on Boutique Boulevard, the downtown strip littered with designer and luxury labels. The champagne flows freely, the personal shoppers are attentive, and the vintage dresses Lux has to name-drop to get a look at are gorgeous.

Maeve whips out her phone after one assistant argues with her over which Celine bag is more of a classic. She types furiously, adding to a note labeled *Revenge List*.

When Maeve and I both express alarm at Lux's confession that her boyfriend sometimes scares her, she laughs and says, "Guys! I'm not saying he beats me. Just that he has a temper."

I'm sinking back into my former life with alarming ease. I set my champagne down and pull out my phone. It's time to remind myself of the reason I'm here. Vintage Chanel is certainly not it.

Maeve walks over to where I'm sitting, determination in every step. "What are you wearing?"

I glance down at my skirt and vest. "I should think that pretty obvious."

"I mean to the club."

I open my mouth, but all of my excuses choose this moment to desert me. I've tried on multiple dresses at their insistence, but so far I've been able to put off committing to anything.

"You don't think you're getting out of tonight, do you?" she says with narrowed eyes.

"Maeve, I'm tired. I'd rather just stay home."

"That's too bad." She flips through dresses on the rack next to me. "Because I have no intention of dropping you back at that ghastly haunted house until tomorrow morning." She pulls a black lace corset dress out and hands it to me. "Try this on."

I do so with a sinking feeling in my gut. Shopping with Maeve and Lux is one thing. Hanging out with everyone at the club is something else entirely. I don't want to hear their inside jokes from the past two years, ones that I have no reference point for. I don't want to be reminded that I have one foot in and one foot out. I don't want to miss them, to miss this, to miss everything we had.

Because the truth is, I can never get it back, no matter how hard I try or how much I want to. Things can never go back to the way they were before.

I step out of the fitting room in the dress, and Maeve and Lux nearly lose their shit when they see me.

"Oh my god, Walker," Lux shrieks. "That's the one!"

"It's perfect," Maeve agrees. "Guys won't be able to keep their hands off you."

Not sure that's the look I'm going for, but if this dress makes them happy, I'm willing to get it. One of the sales assistants takes it and my credit card.

"Speaking of guys," Maeve says, looking at Lux, "I wonder which bimbo Heath will go home with tonight."

Lux rolls her eyes. "I'm convinced the fewer brain cells they have, the better he likes them."

I guess I'm not the only one who has changed.

They continue discussing the intricacies of Heath's love life, but I tune them out as I sign the receipt.

For reasons I can't explain, I'm one hundred times more apprehensive than I was earlier. It's become an active stomachache, churning and roiling in my gut like a ship during a storm.

We get ready at Lux's house, a big Italianate halfway between downtown and the Hills. It is, of course, decorated in shades of white and pink, and it feels like we're inside a giant strawberry buttercream cake.

We wear our new dresses. Maeve bought an emerald-green silk minidress with a plunging neckline. She looks like a goddess. Lux got a vintage baby-pink taffeta dress with a flared skirt. She looks like a celebrity on the red carpet. I feel drab in black next to them, but they assure me I look extremely dishy.

The guys meet us at the club. Pierce must have wrangled out of his commitment with his girlfriend, because he shows up alone, looking like he just walked out of a cologne advert. Rhett immediately heads to the dance floor, and I only get a glimpse of the back of his red shag jacket.

I don't want to look at Heath, but my eyes refuse to follow directives. They manage to snag not only a look at him, but his steady gaze, too. He's wearing a button-up shirt with vertical gold stripes, haphazardly tucked into blue jeans. His eyes grow a tad wider as he takes in my outfit. The look of hunger on his face gives me a boost of confidence. Maybe I don't look so bad after all.

We order a round of drinks and find an empty booth with a view of the dance floor. The lights and all the seats are red, and the temperature is a little higher than is comfortable.

"This place feels a little like hell," I say to Lux over the thumping music.

She laughs and says, "That's why you need to dance." She tugs on my hand, but I resist. I'm not sure how dancing is meant to cool anyone off.

"You go on," I say. "I'll join you later."

She sails onto the dance floor and is immediately joined by several men vying for her attention. How would Carter respond to this? I take another sip of my cocktail.

"I'm going to the restroom," Maeve says into my ear. "Want to come?"

I shake my head. I have no desire to fight the bodies crowding the floor to get there.

She becomes lost in the throng of people. A quick glance proves Pierce has also deserted us, leaving only Heath and me at the table. We're sitting across from each other, making it obvious we're not together, because within seconds a willowy brunette seats herself next to him.

Something clenches beneath my ribs. She runs her hands through his hair and into the collar of his shirt. He smiles and doesn't push her away, but when she whispers something in his ear, he shakes his head. She pouts, but when she realizes he's not going to be swayed, she saunters off.

This process is repeated several times. By the time the third girl has walked away and my second cocktail is almost gone, I have the courage to say, "You don't need to turn them down on my account." It's such a Heath thing to do, it doesn't even occur to me how presumptuous it sounds.

He lifts his head and smiles. "I know."

That smile would be enough to make my knees buckle if I were standing. Good thing I'm securely planted on this bench with no intention of moving until Maeve and Lux are ready to go.

A waiter brings us another round of drinks, and I accept mine eagerly. The temperature is climbing. Even without the red glow in here, I'm sure my cheeks are scarlet.

I studiously avoid Heath. Yesterday at the Archives gave me practice, but I need to improve my skills.

Rhett is making a fool of himself on the dance floor, but it seems to be working for him, because he is surrounded by fans who only further encourage him. Lux is rubbing her ass on a guy I'm pretty sure is not her boyfriend. I can't see Pierce or Maeve anywhere, but since they haven't returned to our table, they must be out there somewhere.

"Hey," Heath says, breaking the bubble I've erected to keep him out and scooting a little closer. "Wanna dance?"

Whether it's the fact that I'm on my third cocktail or that I'm tired of sitting and watching my friends have fun, I think I surprise us both when I say yes.

He wraps my hand in his as he leads me to the crowded dance floor. There's no way to ignore the sparks traveling up my arm from our point of contact. It's been two years since we last touched, but my body says it was just yesterday.

If he were much taller, I wouldn't be able to reach his head. As it is, my fingers are tangled into the hair at the nape of his neck. It feels as silky as I remember. It's a good thing he's taking the lead in swaying us back and forth, because my brain has become a scrambled mash.

His hands are resting on my hips, and there's nothing sexual about it. It would be like this no matter who I was dancing with. In fact, you could argue he's being more of a gentleman than most of the guys here tonight.

So then why is that the only thing I'm aware of? When I move my hips even the slightest bit, they slide under his palms, leaving the impression that he is dragging his hands all over my body.

Someone bumps into my back, sending me straight into Heath's chest. He catches me with ease, but not before I get a lungful of sandalwood. When I meet his gaze, I find his eyes dark and hooded, his expression impossible to discern.

When the music shifts to a faster beat, I expect him to let go. Instead he tugs me a little closer. Our bodies brush against each other with every move. It's a good thing it's so dark in here, because my nipples are screaming the state of my libido to anyone who will listen.

Rhett chooses this moment to drape his arms across our shoulders, panting like a dog. "You pick your prey yet?" he asks Heath.

Heath gives him a dark look and shakes his head. "Not in the mood tonight."

"Could've fooled me," Rhett says with a laugh. He slaps Heath on the back and whoops his way back to the center of the dance floor.

I drop my hands, and Heath does the same. The moment is broken.

"I'm going to use the ladies' room," I say, as breathless as Rhett. The only difference is, I've hardly been moving.

Heath nods and looks relieved as I walk off the floor.

I have no idea what just happened out there.

But whatever it was, it can't happen again.

14

"Standing in the Dark" - Lawson

Heath

I am the world's most fucked twat.

I don't know what possessed me to ask Walker to dance, but it wasn't sanity, that's for sure.

Maybe it was the alcohol, maybe it was the music, maybe it was that tiny dress she was wearing, designed to drive a man insane. Maybe it was a combination of all three.

I don't know, and frankly, I don't care. I twist the handlebars of my bike and will the car in front of me to speed up. The only thing I want is to get home and crack one off, since there's no way in hell I'm taking anyone to the Carlton tonight. She has fucked me through and through.

The worst part is I can't even fuck her, despite how much I want to.

It's still dark out, but the sun will be up in a few hours. My mind flies back to the feel of her hips under my hands, the way she gently swayed them from side to side. I swerve back into my lane when an oncoming vehicle honks at me.

Damn it. *Focus, Heath.*

I'm not sure whether she realized it or not, but toward the end of our dance, I could feel her nipples through the thin lace of her dress. For a minute there, the only thing I could focus on were those perfect little peaks and what they meant. But in typical fashion, Rhett killed the moment before anything could happen.

The house is dark when I get home. I unlock the kitchen door as quietly as I can, not wanting to wake my mum.

Does Walker still sleep like a fucking tornado, a chaotic jumble of blankets and limbs? It used to take an air horn to wake her.

I'm almost to the stairs when I run into something hard.

"Fuck!" I whisper-yell.

This is followed by a crash. I'm not as close to the stairs as I thought I was, and I've run into the table in the foyer, which sent one of those expensive vases to the floor.

The door to my dad's study opens, and I freeze. Now I wish I *had* gotten a room at the Carlton.

"Heath? Is that you?" he says from the doorway.

"Yeah, just me."

The light comes on, blinding me for a second. My dad is still wearing his work clothes, and they're rumpled. His gaze drops from me to the broken vase.

"What the fuck," he yells. "Do you have any idea how much that thing cost?"

"Sorry." I squeeze my eyes together with my thumb and pointer finger. "I'll pay for it."

"You'll pay for it? With what, your little surfing paycheck?"

"I said I'm sorry."

He steps closer. "That's your problem, son. You're always sorry. But you just keep breaking everything you touch."

He doesn't even know the half of it.

"At least I'm not scamming the government out of their money." I laugh as his face turns red.

"You don't know what you're talking about." The twanging muscles in his neck tell a different story.

"Come on, Dad. Everyone knows you've been committing tax fraud for years. How else do you explain owning a vase that cost a million dollars?"

I should have expected it, but the punch catches me completely off guard. He socks me right in the head, catching my left eye. Thankfully I have enough alcohol in my system to numb the pain a little and enough sense in my head to not hit back.

"Good night, Dad." I start up the stairs.

So much for my plans to have a wank while picturing Walker with her dress hiked up around her waist. The only thing I want to do is sleep.

At least there's one thing my dad is good for.

15

"Fun and Games" - Kelsea Ballerini

Walker

The weekend has thrown me off. My plans included compiling my research notes and making a comprehensive strategy for tackling the resources at the Archives. My plans did *not* include thinking about Heath, the way I felt when I was with him, or how turned on I've been since then.

I tried not to read anything into the fact that he didn't leave with anyone from the club.

When Tuesday morning rolls around, my list for conquering the G.R. Huntington room at the Archives only has four line items. I also have yet to make plans with Heath to go back to the Archives.

Trying not to think about being alone in that room with him only leads to one thing: thinking about being alone in that room with him.

I knew this would happen if I allowed myself to be distracted. This was the risk I was doing everything to avoid. Because now that I've been sucked in, getting out is as easy as escaping quicksand.

Example number one: this text from Lux.

Lux: *Don't forget about poker night tonight! Candle lady is going down!!!!!!!!*

Me: *I'm sorry. I can't make it tonight. x*

Lux: *Walker Jean, if you do not get your butt over to Pierce's we will descend on your haunted house like zombies xx*

I know better than to argue with her. She'll only sic Maeve on my ass. *Fine,* I text back. *I'll be there.*

This time I don't destroy my entire closet looking for something to wear. I choose a buttoned cardigan, houndstooth trousers with rolled cuffs, a belt, and black boots.

When I arrive, only Maeve and Pierce are at the flat. They're mixing cocktails in the kitchen like a married couple. I mention this, and Maeve shoots daggers into my head with her dark eyes.

Lux and Rhett show up soon after, and Lux squeals again like she's seeing me for the first time. How has it only been a week since I ran into her at WNX?

She is shuffling cards when Heath walks in, a faded baseball cap hiding all of that hair. He's wearing cut-off denim shorts, a striped T-shirt, and high-top sneakers—the epitome of casual comfort. My body tenses as he approaches, the opposite of casual comfort. I'm already too aware of every movement he makes.

I chose my seat strategically tonight, placing myself between Pierce and Lux. My thinking was that no matter where Heath ends up sitting, it won't be next to me. I didn't take into account that if he sits across from me, he'll be in my direct line of sight.

Which is, of course, what happens.

He pulls out his chair and drops into it. As he does, I let out an involuntary gasp.

The skin around his left eye is stained a deep purple. I lift my hand to cover my mouth, hoping no one heard my response. The others don't mention his appearance. Either they all already know what happened or they assume he's going to share during the game.

We start to play, but I'm finding it hard to focus. Who gave him the black eye? Heath is the most laid-back and easy-going guy I've ever met. If someone punched him—

Then it hits me with startling clarity.

I should have thought of it right away, but it's been two years. I've forgotten some of the intricacies of his family life. Besides, the rest of us have all moved out and are living on our own by now. What's keeping him there? He's twenty-four years old, after all.

I glance at the cards Lux has dealt me, a king and queen of hearts. There's a ten of hearts already on the table. I actually have a chance at winning this round. If I do, Robert Lawrence will be our next victim.

My eyes can't stay away from Heath's beautiful, bruised face. When I look up, his gaze is already on me. A flashback to Saturday night at the club makes heat climb my neck. I drop my eyes back to my cards and will this night to end quickly.

Pierce serves us an Elderflower Spanish Gin and Tonic. It's actually good, which means I need to pace myself. Alcohol made me stupid the other night. I can't afford to let the same thing happen again.

After Lux unveils an ace of hearts on the table, Rhett opens the next round of betting. "Some wanker side-swiped my car." He drops an entire handful of chips into the center. He must have a decent hand. That one's going to be hard to top. Rhett's car is practically his mistress.

Pierce hisses through his teeth. "Not the Maserati?"

Cartoon smoke curls from Rhett's ears. "The bloody bastard. It's at the Rebel Wrench right now, but they said it will be two weeks before I get it back."

Lux's attention snaps to him. "I thought we don't patronize them anymore." Her tone is coated in ice.

He shrugs. "They're the best."

"Sure you weren't parked in a handicap spot again?" Maeve asks innocently.

He flips her off.

"Just asking, god." She turns to Heath. "By the way, did you pick up those prawns?"

He nods and shifts in his chair. The movement echoes through my own body. "They're on the back terrace, rotting their little hearts out."

"Brilliant." Maeve looks at me and winks. "Your candle lady is going to rue the day she was born."

I give her a weak thumbs-up. I'm failing to see a way out of this mess, no matter how hard I try.

Maeve claps her hands, her favorite signal for garnering attention. "Okay, back to the game," she says, even though she's the one who interrupted us in the first place.

It's Heath's turn to bet. I find the breath lodged in my throat. He has to top Rhett's huge raise. Out of all of us at the table, I'm guessing he's the only one with anything close.

"The guy that cut me off in traffic," he says as his chips hit the rest of the pile.

"Hold up." Rhett raises a palm. "Some guy *cut you off in traffic.*" Asking if Heath's a fucking idiot would've been more subtle.

"Yep."

"So we're just, what," Rhett says, leaning forward in his chair, "going to ignore that bloody shiner on your face?"

"This?" Heath points to his bruised eye and lifts the side of his mouth. "I was hammered and ran into a doorjamb."

"Dude." Everyone is staring at Heath now. "I can practically see the imprint of the bloke's fist on your eyelid," Rhett says.

"Hey," Maeve interjects. "How do you know it wasn't a woman?"

Pierce scoffs under his breath.

She slugs him in the arm.

"Ow." He rubs his bicep.

"See?" she says with a smug smile.

Heath studies his cards. "It's not a big deal," he says quietly.

Rhett scoots his chair back so hard the ice in my tumbler shifts and clinks against the glass. "Not a big deal? What is going on, man? Who was it?"

"Hey." Heath looks him straight in the eye. "Don't worry about it."

"When someone beats up my best friend, I'm sure as fuck going to worry about it." Rhett leans on his hands, a muscle in his jaw jumping. "Tell us who it was."

Heath shakes his head like he can't believe he's friends with these prats. "It was just my dad, okay?"

I count three beats of silence as everyone processes this. Has he not told any of them?

Then Lux, who doesn't tolerate silence when talking will do, says, "Your *dad* did that to you?"

Heath's eyes catch on mine for a split second before returning to the cards in his hand. "Yeah" is all he says.

"Holy fuck," Maeve mutters under her breath. "That's mine. I bet Robert fucking Lawrence." She tosses her chips into the pile.

"Fold." Pierce smacks his cards onto the table.

I follow his lead and toss my cards down too. "Fold."

Like clockwork, Lux and Rhett do the same.

Maeve arches a perfectly groomed brow at Heath. "What's it going to be, bruiser?"

He levels a glare at each of us in turn. "No."

Maeve scoffs. "What do you mean, *no*? This isn't twenty questions."

"You're not getting revenge on my dad."

"Why the hell not?" Lux says, incredulity lining her voice.

"Because if he's going down, it will be because I took him down." He pushes his chair back and stalks out of the room.

16

"Daddy Issues" - The Neighborhood

Heath

The odds of landing alive from twenty-plus floors up aren't high. The odds of landing on your feet are even slimmer. Even so, I peer out over the street below and give it five seconds of consideration.

The balcony-slash-terrace doesn't provide the relief I thought it would. Sure, it gets me out of Pierce's flat and away from everyone's horrified pity, but it only serves to remind me of how far I am from being able to walk away if I wanted to.

Which I do. Very much.

I should've had a better story. *Running into a doorjamb?* What a plonker. While they definitely all believe I'm stupid enough to do it, one would have to be some kind of crazy-ass gymnast to be able to sustain a black eye simply from running into the frame of a bloody door.

I grip the glass partition separating me from what would be a gruesome death splattered on the pavement below, then lean back and stretch my triceps. The surf was good today. I kept an eye on my phone, thinking Walker might text to ask about visiting the Archives, but she never did. I probably scared her off at the club on Saturday.

The door behind me slides open. I brace myself for whatever onslaught is sure to follow. Maeve telling me to get back inside so we can finish the game. Pierce putting his arm around my shoulder and telling me to hang in there. Rhett cracking jokes about getting beat on by your dad.

I know it's her without turning around. The unmistakable scent of coconut wafts on the slight breeze and directly into the part of my brain that makes bad decisions. I stay where I am, hands on the glass. If Maeve sent her out here to chastise me, she'll have to do it facing my back.

Instead of keeping her distance, Walker sidles up next to me and takes the only spot remaining at the wall. She doesn't look at me, just props her arms on top of the glass and gazes out over the city. We stay like that for thirty, sixty seconds? I lose track of time, distracted as I am by the gentle heat of her and the way her scent is tickling my nose.

"This is a great view," she says after a while.

I scan the skyline, the lake visible in the distance, the sun starting its descent. It's actually pretty great, though I'd take the ocean a million times over the sight of the city.

"Do you want to talk about it?" she asks.

She doesn't turn to look at me. Maybe it's easier that way. Did she draw the short straw? Is that why she's out here?

"There's nothing to say." I take off my hat and let the breeze run through my hair before replacing it.

"Okay," she says quietly.

This has always been the thing about Walker. She doesn't push. If I don't want to talk about something, she accepts that. I've missed that.

"I was drunk and said some things that set him off," I offer.

She nods like she understands, even though she doesn't. My dad's an asshole, but at least he's in my life, even if I wish he weren't. She lives with the knowledge that her dad walked away from her.

"He doesn't get to determine your worth."

Her words are soft, but they carry a power punch directly to my heart. I couldn't stop myself from looking at her if I tried. She senses my gaze and meets it with her own. Those eyes that see everything, even the depths of my depravity.

She knows. She has to know. There's no other explanation for what happened. But if she knows, then what is she doing out here, saying things like that?

I turn back to face the skyline. "Try telling him that."

We're both quiet for a few more minutes, letting the sounds of the city wash over us. I can sense every tiny movement she makes, like a seismometer detecting any shift within the earth's crust.

"They just want to help, you know. Because they care," she says.

I take a deep breath and let it out. "It only confirms the image they have of me in their heads."

"And what's that?"

I cut a glance at her. This time she doesn't look. "Poor Heath, can't even stand up for himself."

Her face pulls into a frown. "That's not what they think."

I breathe out a laugh and shake my head. She wouldn't know. She's been gone for two years.

"And anyway, it's not true," she continues. "You're the strongest person I've ever known."

"Come on, Walker. I don't need your pity too."

"It's not pity. It's the truth."

We're facing each other now. "Can you honestly say that you haven't felt sorry for me?" My words come out a little sharper than I intend, but I'm not in the mood for lies *and* pity tonight.

"I don't feel sorry for you, but I do wonder what the hell you're thinking, still living there."

"Yeah, well, that doesn't concern you."

An entire circus of emotions parade across her face. "I *loved* you!"

My breath gets caught in my throat. "How is that relevant?" I croak.

"Because you're implying that the guy I was in love with, the man I thought I would marry, was nothing but a mirage. Do you think I'm so stupid that you could fool me for four years?"

I can't look at her anymore. I pinch the bridge of my nose with my fingers. I can't afford to go there with her. It's too fucking dangerous. "Of course not," I whisper.

Her memory has clouded with time, softening the sharp edges of what she thought of me when we were still together. Being slapped with an alternate reality now is the universe's way of sticking one to me.

There are a million places my mind could go to. For some reason it chooses Switzerland, maybe because I was staring at that keychain the other night. Memories become glossy with time—Walker's recent revelation is proof of that—but that trip was fucking magical.

I took her to the Abbey Library, and you'd think the girl had never seen books before. She walked around like she was on a bloody cloud, her eyes so full of joy it made you happy just to look at her. That night we lay on the grassy bank near the cabin the six of us had rented together. Everyone else was inside, their laughter spilling out through the open window.

We were staring at the stars, and I was pointing out different constellations to her, when she turned her head to face me and said simply, "I love you."

We hadn't said it to each other yet. We'd only been officially together a few weeks. But I didn't need more time. I knew at that moment she was the only thing I'd ever want for all eternity.

Everything that happened later had nothing to do with her and everything to do with her. Not every heart is meant to hold that much emotion. And not every person deserves to be that happy.

We've both turned back toward the city. I let my eyes wander down to the top of her head. She stands a foot shorter than me. I used to love nothing more than bending over to capture that sweet mouth with my own.

She turns then, as though she can read my thoughts. "They're waiting for us inside. Maeve wants to plan the takedown of the candle lady."

"I'll be there soon," I say. I can't go back yet. "Do you want to go to the Archives tomorrow?"

We arrange to meet there in the morning. I'm determined to not be late this time. She slips back through the door, and I'm left with a giant crater where my heart used to be.

A few more minutes pass before they send Rhett to get me. He stands beside me and swings his arm around my shoulders. "You okay, mate?"

Why does everyone keep asking me that? "I'm fine."

He pats my shoulder a few times. The guy's fucking turning into Pierce. I shrug out from beneath his arm. He doesn't notice, just turns and grins at me. "It looks like you're doing a good job of getting her on the hook. It will make the aftermath even more beautiful."

It takes me a minute to figure out who and what he's talking about. Then it crashes in with the grace of a Saint Bernard.

Walker. The revenge plot.

Heath, you fucking bellend.

I've been romanticizing the past when the future hasn't changed. Walker is still leaving in a few weeks. It's time to get my head out of my ass, or she'll be taking my heart on the plane with her.

17

"Toxic Til the End" - Rosé

Walker

I'm not sure what I was expecting to find in front of the Archives this morning, but it certainly wasn't Heath, early and holding out a to-go cup that looks suspiciously like the ones from Cafe de Olla.

"Hi," I say cautiously as I walk up.

"Hey." He returns the greeting with a smile, making those ridiculous dimples pop.

I give myself a mental slap. I have one job and one job only.

He hands me the cup. It's warm. I do my best not to touch his fingers as I take it from him.

"Still your favorite, I hope."

I take a sip, and to my surprise, it's the exact vanilla chai I was wishing I'd had time to pick up this morning. "You remembered?"

He shrugs, like remembering your ex-girlfriend's favorite drink for two years is perfectly normal. "I don't see how you can drink something hot when it's a million degrees outside." He pulls his T-shirt away from his body and lets it snap back.

I know he'd much rather be in the ocean than inside an airless library.

"I really appreciate this." I hold up the cup and incline my head toward the building. "And you coming with me."

He shoves his hands into the front pocket of his linen shorts. "Ready?"

I follow him inside while fighting a mental battle in my head.

Wise Walker: You will not dwell on this for another second.

Mad Walker: But that was a sweet gesture!

Wise Walker: We don't know what that was, but it's too risky to think about.

Mad Walker: But he looks so incredible in that baby-blue T-shirt. And those dimples!

Wise Walker: Those dimples are hereby a forbidden topic of conversation.

This time we head directly to the back room with all of the G.R. Huntington books. Heath picks up *The Haunting at 83rd Street* and settles into the armchair in the corner. Is he really going to read again?

My eyes keep straying in his direction, waiting for him to set the book down and pull out his phone, but he doesn't, genuinely engrossed in the pages. He lifts his head, and I quickly avert my eyes, pretending to consider the bookcase behind him.

"Need something?" he says.

Now that I'm committed to my farce, I move around the table and scan the shelves next to him. "Just thought I saw something over here that looked interesting." I pull a random volume from the shelf and flip through it.

He leans forward in the chair, holding the book in front of him. We've been here for thirty minutes. I don't think I've ever seen him hold still for this long.

As if he can read my thoughts, his knee starts bouncing, causing the book to jostle. I smile at the familiar motion. He's like a giant conduit for electricity, always moving, always pulsing with energy.

Five minutes later, he discards the novel and stands.

"You okay?" I say without looking up. This is the most disjointed and discombobulated research process I've ever executed. I keep hopping from book to book, hardly absorbing anything I'm reading and forgetting to take notes 90 percent of the time. A monkey could write a better dissertation than me at this point.

"Just restless," Heath says. He peers over my shoulder. "Find anything helpful yet?"

"Some," I say noncommittally. The words swim on the page in front of me. The heat of him is seeping through my lightweight top, making it hard to concentrate on breathing, let alone something as complicated as reading.

"I could help if you tell me what you're looking for."

I snap the book shut. He doesn't move back. With the bookcase in front of me and him behind me, I have nowhere to go. "It's hard to explain." I have no idea why it sounds like I've just climbed three flights of stairs.

"Okay" is all he says.

I turn around then, suddenly anxious to get a look at his face. His eye is still a mottled purple, but the edges are tinged with yellow.

"Does it hurt?" I ask. I gently run my finger along the bottom of the swelling.

He catches his breath between his teeth, and I immediately drop my hand. I don't know what I was thinking.

"It's not too bad." He looks at me with something like trepidation in his eyes. "I've had worse."

A memory flits back. "Like your surfing accident?"

His eyes crinkle at the corners. "Pretty sure my mum thought I was dead."

"You *were* out cold," I point out.

"Just a concussion." I don't know if he's even aware he's doing it, but his fingers rub absently over the scar running through his eyebrow.

We all panicked when we received the call that Heath had had a surfing accident. Fortunately, his uncle was there and fished him out of the water after his board nailed him in the head. I don't want to think about what could have happened if he'd been in the water alone.

"Does your mum . . . ?" I'm not sure how to say it without making things more awkward.

"Does he beat her too?"

I bite the inside of my cheek and nod. Mad Walker tucks "can still read my mind" into her dress pocket with a smile.

He scratches the scar and drops his gaze to his feet. "Yeah."

"Is that why you stay?"

"Maybe? I don't know."

"And your sisters?"

"Cami is the only one still living at home. He doesn't usually hit her when I'm around. Julie and Val moved out before it got very bad."

I've met his oldest sisters a handful of times. Juliette is a business lawyer for the family company. Valerie is married to a wealthy philanthropist and sits on the board of several charities. Camilla is only two years older than Heath and used to give us rides sometimes before we were old enough to drive.

"Have you tried convincing your mum to leave?"

"She won't. She's determined to overlook his 'flaws.'"

"Flaws? God, it's not like routinely getting spinach stuck in your teeth."

His chuckle contains 25 percent mirth, 75 percent sadness. "She's convinced everyone is capable of change."

Irritation boils in my gut. There is nothing worse than a woman who stays with a man out of the belief that she will be the one to change him.

"People don't change," I say.

He looks at me then, really looks at me, and a procession of memories choose that moment to whirl through my mind like a kaleidoscope.

Our first kiss in the rain after slipping out the back door of a club, drunk and crushing on each other.

Stargazing in Switzerland and telling him I loved him.

Taking out his family's sailboat until we were sunburned and sex crazed.

Getting coordinating tattoos of the Big Dipper so they synced up when we put our wrists together.

Our first time, on the beach, and washing sand out of my hair for an entire week and not caring.

A shrill ringing slices through the moment like a sharp blade. I jump backward and reach for my phone in my bag on the table.

"Hi, Mum," I answer. Heath picks up his discarded book and leans back against the bookcase.

"Walker?"

I close my eyes. The tears in her voice are as obvious as my hand in front of my face. This can only mean one thing, and I don't want to have this conversation here. Or anywhere. "Mum, can I call you back?"

"I really need to talk to you, niñita." This is punctuated by a loud sniff.

Fuck. At least I'm not in the main part of the Archives. I'm pretty sure phones aren't allowed out there. Heath is still engrossed in his book.

"What is it?" I say, even though I can recite the words with her.

"You were right." *Here we go.* "I caught him on the phone with another woman." She sniffs again. I picture the wheel of brie on the counter next to her.

"I'm sorry, Mum."

"At first he tried to tell me it was his new assistant, but I called Carla. She answered, which can only mean one thing." The last word comes out as a wail.

I don't want to hear this. I warned her it would happen, and she didn't listen. She thought—like always—that this time would be different.

"I confronted him about it when he hung up, and he just grabbed his things and left. Why am I such a fool?" she moans.

"You're not a fool, Mum." I look up to find Heath's eyes on me, a slight furrow in his brow. "But you can't be too surprised by this."

"I should have listened to you, but I really thought he had changed this time, cariño."

"This is what he does, though. He cheats. He's a cheater. You can't change that in a person," I say.

Heath's eyes have softened with sadness. I turn so I don't have to see him. I cannot handle that while having this conversation.

"Maybe you could come over tonight. We could watch *Gilmore Girls* and eat—"

"I can't tonight. I have to study." Eating brie and crying over my dad is the absolute last entry on my list of things I want to do tonight, right after scrub the toilet with my own toothbrush.

"What about tomorrow night?" She sounds so torn up that I hate to do this to her, but the truth is, I've been there for each one of her breakups. They never get any easier, because she never learns from her previous mistakes.

"I don't know, Mum. I'll have to see."

"Okay," she says. "I'm sorry to bother you."

"You're not a bother." I exhale quietly so she can't hear me through the phone. "I'll call you soon, okay?"

After I hang up, Heath looks at me again. I give him the barest of glances before returning my attention to the bookcase. I select a new book from the shelf. It's time to focus on what I came here to do, or I will end up in the exact same place as my mum.

The floorboards creak as he moves across the room, but I don't turn around. I'm not in the mood for this conversation either.

"Hey." He's right behind my shoulder, and his voice wisps across my neck with the slightest of touches. It's his way of asking if everything's okay.

I offer him a quick, tight smile over my shoulder and turn back to the book I'm holding.

I'm fine, everything's fine, go away, please go the fuck away.

He presses two fingers against my back. It feels like a branding iron. I close my eyes.

"Walk, please talk to me."

It's been ages since someone has called me that. I squeeze my lids together even harder. "There's nothing to say."

"Is your mum okay?"

I nod, emotion making my throat thick. "She will be." He's waiting for more, so I say as lightly as I can, "My dad cheated on her again."

His fingers drop from my back. "Fuck. I'm sorry."

I shake the tension from my shoulders. "It's fine. She'll recover. She always does."

"That doesn't mean either of you should have to go through this."

I attempt to swallow the lump of emotion in my throat. It refuses to dissolve. "Yeah, well, that's what happens when you fall in love with a cheater."

18

"So It Goes" - Taylor Swift

Heath

They've written an entire novel in our group thread by the time I get back to the surf shack.

My last client was convinced they were a natural-born surfer, but they couldn't manage to get past the break. Needless to say, I am in desperate need of a drink.

Seeley tosses me a towel as I walk through the door. I catch it in midair, eyes glued to my phone. Am I the only one who does *anything* with my day? It takes me several minutes to get caught up on the chat Maeve started two hours ago.

The texts keep rolling in as I grab my things. Apparently, before I can go get hammered, I still have to help carry out the revenge plot against the candle lady. I completely forgot.

I've spent the past three days at the Archives with Walker, trying hard as fuck to not hard-fuck her on the table. I don't need any reminders of how stupid this is, either. I'm fully aware. It's only my body remembering how good we were together and those fucking noises she made when—

"You good?" Seeley calls.

I glance up from my phone. With my eyes on the screen, I almost walked into a wall. I give her a sheepish smile. "Good. Just have a lot of texts to catch up on." I lean against the counter and unwrap one of the lollipops that she keeps in a jar for customers.

Her own smile is a flash of white against bronzed skin. "I know you're popular. No need to rub it in." She's pulled her blonde hair back into a high ponytail, and it sways as she shakes her head.

"Nah, just a lot of high-maintenance friends." I stick the sucker into my mouth.

"Ahh." She gives me a knowing look.

I return my attention to my phone. The screen keeps moving with incoming messages.

Lux: *I can drive!!*

Pierce: *Lux, there's hardly room for you AND your purse in your pop can of a car.*

Rhett: *I'd offer but mine's in the garage because some stupid prick SIDESWIPED ME*

Maeve: *WE KNOW. Also, how would you fit six people in a Maserati?*

Rhett: *I have a very roomy boot*

44 1865 88105: *My car holds four . . .*

Maeve: *Street parking might be a beast so ideally we'd all fit in one vehicle. x*

Maeve: *Has anyone heard from Heath today?*

Maeve: *You are still coming, aren't you, Heath?*

Rhett: *YO HEATH*

Me: *Yes we can take my car Maeve*

I stick my phone back into my pocket before she can text and remind me to top off the tank with petrol.

"Shiner's almost gone," Seeley says when I look up.

On instinct, my hand moves to my eye. It hardly hurts anymore, and I forgot it was there. "Yeah."

"Be careful walking," she says with a grin. "Don't want you running into any more walls." Unlike my friends, Seeley at least pretended to buy my story about the doorjamb.

"I'll see what I can do. Later, See." I toss her a wave and head to my bike.

As I ride home, I try to prepare myself for the night ahead. Seeing Walker's number pop up on my screen did weird things to my head. She hasn't texted anything in our group chat yet. The normal thing to do would be to save it in my contacts, but that feels dangerous. It's best to not have anything in my phone that could lead to late-night-drunk Heath doing stupid shit.

Everyone is waiting in the driveway when I get out of the shower. Maeve and Walker are both dressed in all black, as planned. What wasn't planned was Rhett's black one-piece and beanie.

"What are you wearing?" I say with a laugh as I step outside.

He glances down at his outfit, which is so tight I can count every muscle in his six-pack. "Why is everyone hating on it?"

"You look like the missing black Wiggle," Pierce says.

"I thought it was a stealth mission," Rhett says. "I'm trying to be inconspicuous."

"We're the ones on stealth," Maeve says, pointing to herself and Walker. "You're supposed to be the normal-looking guy on the street keeping watch. That outfit is going to land us all in jail."

"You look great, mate." I clap a hand on his shoulder. "I had no idea your balls were so small, though."

He socks me hard in the stomach. I double over in shock and laughter.

"Let's go!" Maeve says.

Everyone heads to my Grenadier, which I had the foresight to move out of the garage and into the driveway earlier.

"I was definitely picturing this thing with a bigger back seat." Maeve looks into the back like it's the living room of a crack den. "There are only three seats."

"So sit on Pierce's lap," Rhett says as he hops into the passenger seat.

"I am not sitting in anyone's lap," she says, still standing outside the car.

Lux, Walker, and Pierce are already sitting in the back. We all stare at Maeve as we wait for her to come to the same conclusion as the rest of us.

"Fine," she growls.

Pierce pulls her inside and onto his lap, and we leave.

Lux hacked the servers at the candle shop earlier this week to track down the woman's purchase. From there, she found her credit card, where she was able to access her address. "That, my friends, is because I am a fucking genius," she informs us.

"With a banging bod," Rhett supplies.

"You're forbidden to speak about banging while you're wearing a catsuit," Maeve says from her perch on Pierce's lap.

"Have we addressed whether Candle Lady has dogs?" Walker says.

"Guys, she has a name. It's Rhonda," Lux says.

"She will forever be Candle Lady to me." Rhett gives a chef's kiss.

"If there are dogs, I'm out," Maeve says.

"Good thing we have Walker to pick up the slack, May-Eve," Rhett says.

Maeve smacks the back of his head. "Walker gets the honors of putting the prawns into the AC unit anyway. It's her revenge."

I can see Walker in the rearview mirror. I try to keep my eyes on the road, but they keep flitting back to her every few seconds. She's quiet, but she looks peaceful and happy, like she's actually having fun.

I think about our conversation after her mum called. If there was any doubt in my mind before, it was obliterated that day. She knows. She definitely knows. I don't know how she found out, but it had to be a factor in driving her to Oxford that summer.

What she's feeling or thinking now that she's back and roped into our circle again remains a mystery. She's always been good at hiding her feelings. Let's be honest: we all are. When your lifestyle depends on fooling others into thinking you have it all together, you learn to school your emotions from a young age.

Candle Lady lives in a two-story townhouse painted black. It sits on the corner, and all of the windows are dark like we hoped. After circling the block, we confirm that the AC unit is behind the house, inside a small fenced-in garden. There's an empty spot on the side street, and I manage to squeeze the 4x4 into it without hitting anything.

"Does everyone remember their positions?" Maeve asks for the fifth time.

"Yes, Mum. We got it." Rhett jumps out of the car and adjusts the crotch of his onesie. How many regrets does the guy have by now?

Maeve, Pierce, and Walker all climb out of the back seat. Lux hops over the console and slides into the seat Rhett has vacated. "Give me two minutes to hack the cameras," she says through the open window. She opens her laptop and starts hammering away at the keys.

Pierce grabs the rotting prawns from the boot. They've been sealed inside a bucket for the past week, but they smell fucking horrible if you get too close. He ceremoniously hands the bucket to Walker, who makes a grimace as she takes it from him.

"All right, I'm in," Lux says.

"Places, people," Maeve whisper-yells. She and Walker scurry to the back gate with the prawns.

Pierce positions himself on the sidewalk, pretending to be on a call as he paces back and forth, hands in his pockets. He and Rhett are meant to give us a warning if anyone returns home. Rhett heads in the opposite direction, looking like a fucking twat in that suit. He will be the reason we all go to prison.

I keep an eye on Walker and Maeve. The back gate is locked, so they have to scramble over the wrought iron fence. Fortunately it's not high, and they don't have much trouble getting over it. A giant tree hangs over the pavement running beside the house, and I lose them in the shadows.

I tap my hands on the steering wheel. This plot ranks a little higher on the risk scale than some of our schemes, but I'm confident we can pull it off. My only concern is Walker. It's been two years since she's done something like this, and I hope she doesn't chicken out now.

"Would you stop that?" Lux says beside me. "I'm trying to concentrate."

I still my fingers. She's on an auction site filled with purses that cost as much as a used car. "I thought you were hacking the cameras."

"I did," she says. "And now I'm bidding on this vintage Hermes Micro Kelly Sellier."

"I have no idea what you just said, but okay." I return my attention to the house, but I can't see Maeve or Walker.

I scan the street for anyone who might notice us when a light at the back of the house flips on. "Shit," I say. "Do they have motion detectors back there?"

Lux looks up from her laptop. "I didn't see any when I planted the bug in the camera app."

Realization hits me as the door opens. "Someone's coming outside. Fuck!"

Maeve and Walker are around the side of the house where the AC unit is. They're not going to know that anyone has come out.

And then the dog shows up. A giant beast of a thing runs into the garden to do his business. As he sniffs around for a spot, he must pick up on their scent, because he starts barking and circling the garden.

Seconds later, a dark shape launches over the fence. As the

streetlamp hits her face, I recognize Maeve. Walker isn't following her.

I jump out of the car. "Where's Walker?" I ask.

She ignores me and continues barreling toward the car like her life depends on it. I run to the back gate and am about to boost myself over it when Walker appears.

"Help me!" she says. The dog is right on her heels.

I grab her arms and drag her over the fence. Her pants catch on one of the spires. When it rips free, we tumble backward. The dog is still going ballistic, barking at us as we scramble to our feet.

The back door slams, and someone calls out for the dog. Their voice grows closer. I try to gauge the time it will take us to get back to the car, but when I glance toward the street, the Grenadier is gone.

Those fucking bastards left us here.

"I have an idea," I say to Walker, right before I press her up against the wall. It's more of an instinct rather than a brilliantly formed idea, the way my mouth meets hers in the shadow of the giant oak above us.

Her lips are tender and slightly cool. She parts them for me immediately, like this is a choreographed dance we've both memorized. She tastes like summer: citrus, basil, and peach all clamoring for attention.

I hold her against the side of the house with my body. With my hands, I cradle her face, tipping it up so I can reach it better. My fingers bury themselves in her hair. She groans and moves closer.

I've wanted to do this since she walked into the game room at Pierce's flat. Every time we're stuck in the Archives and she pulls her lip through her teeth, I want to mark her up with my own mouth.

I tilt her head back even further to give me better access. She gasps and twists her hands into my T-shirt. Her gasp opens her mouth even wider, allowing me to explore her easily. I flick my tongue over every surface I can reach, remembering what she likes.

I want more. I want her beneath me, screaming my name as I fuck her senseless. I want her over me, riding me like I'm her ride-or-die. I press into her even further. She moans as my dick digs into her stomach. I would take her right here if I thought she'd be willing. I would—

"What is going on?" Someone is yelling. "Get out of here!" A woman in an open bathrobe is standing on the other side of the back gate, hands on her hips.

I grab Walker's hand and lead her down the pavement. The woman is still yelling after us. I flip her off over my shoulder. At least she doesn't know what we were actually doing there. I give it about ten minutes before she's ready to kill herself over the smell in her house.

There's no sign of my car anywhere on the street. Walker drops my hand, and we walk in silence for a few minutes. I'm trying to figure out if she wants to kill me or not. She was definitely into the kiss, but that could have been the adrenaline. On the other hand, the sexual tension in that archive room has been next-level. There's no way she hasn't felt it. There's no way she couldn't read in my eyes how badly I wanted to flip her over that table.

Before I can make another terrible misjudgment and open my mouth, I spot the Grenadier coming down the street ahead of us. "There they are," I say quietly.

Pierce stops the car beside us, and I open the back door. "This is why I'm the getaway driver," I mutter as I help Walker in.

"You abandoned your post, mate," Pierce says with an unapologetic look back at us.

"Because I was *rescuing* someone." I'm about to hop in when I remember the seating dilemma we had earlier. Lux is still up front in the passenger seat, and Rhett and Maeve are already in the back.

Like she can read my thoughts, Maeve gives me a hard look. "I am *not* sitting on anyone's lap this time."

"You can sit on my lap," Rhett says to Walker.

She winces at him. "Not in the catsuit, Rhett. Sorry."

Which leaves only one option. I climb in and close the door. Walker settles herself on my lap. My dick is still eager to continue what we started, and she must feel it. She's sitting right on top of it, for fuck's sake.

I shift, trying to hide it a little better, but that only makes it rub against her leg. She does her best to avoid looking at me. Her breathing is a little faster than usual, though, and I'm pretty sure it's not still from the dog.

Everyone wants a recap of what happened. I let Walker tell the story, partly because I like to listen to her and partly because I can't focus on anything but the smell of her hair right in front of my nose and the feel of her ass on top of my dick.

She leans forward to look at something on Lux's phone, and when she straightens again, I hold back a groan. If she's aware of my struggle, she doesn't let on. After twenty minutes of what feels like the most intense lap dance ever, we pull into the driveway of my house.

It's close to ten at night, but there's a strange energy buzzing through all of us. Pierce tosses me the keys over the bonnet of the car. He's wearing a strange look on his face. It isn't until I'm gripping the keys in my hand, that rectangular-shaped photo digging into my palm, that I recognize it. He looks . . . apprehensive and guarded.

He must have seen the keychain.

19

"Jealous" - Nick Jonas

Walker

If I didn't know any better, I would say I'm back in the summer before our last year together at Oxford. We'd come home from uni high as a kite, blitzed on being twenty-one. We thought we were indestructible. We were, too, until Rhett and Heath were almost arrested.

We don't talk about that scheme.

The energy here is the same. Everyone is high after our narrow escape from the crazy candle lady. It's still early for a Saturday night. It's obvious that no one is planning to go home.

"We could go to the Quantum," Pierce suggests.

Lux sags. "Carter is there tonight. I'd rather be anywhere else."

"Something going on between you two?" I ask quietly. She shakes her head. Evidently that subject isn't up for discussion.

"Let's go to Paris, baby!" Rhett shouts into the night air.

There is a chorus of agreement. It takes me a second to remember that this is perfectly normal, this jetting off in the middle of the night to another continent.

An hour later, we're ensconced in Pierce's company jet, en route to Charles-de-Gaulle Airport. Rhett comes prepared with a bag of gummies. I accept one when offered. I'm going to need something to keep my mind off what happened with Heath earlier.

Him pushing me up against the wall was a surprise. The way he tasted and how right it felt to be there with him was not. I haven't been kissed like that in two years. It would only take a skip, hop, and a jump for me to end up remembering what he's like in bed, too. And sitting on his lap in the car did nothing to erase that image from my memory.

He was as turned on as I was, although he couldn't hide it as well as I could. I'll admit that the high of having pulled off the perfect plot and escaping the dog made me a little devious. I may have rubbed against him more than necessary, a thrill coursing through my body when I felt him grow even stiffer beneath me.

But looking at him across the plane now, slumped in his seat and messing around on his phone, brings sudden clarity. I left for a reason. Fooling around with Heath may have been one of several options we could have chosen to explain why we were next to Candle Lady's house, but that doesn't mean it needs to happen again. In fact, it should definitely not happen again.

I'm going to have fun tonight with someone I don't have to see again. I won't hold back either. Let Heath see what he's missing out on. And get my head out of the clouds of my own destructive thoughts.

The club we end up at hours later has a floor that looks like broken glass and is lit from below by a blue light. Glass globes dangle from the entire ceiling. The bass thrums so loud it vibrates in my bones.

Rhett passed another joint around as we drove over. I only took a few puffs, but my muscles are already relaxing. I've also had enough caffeine to fuel an entire football team, so I'm not tired in the least. Tonight is going to be a good night.

I let Maeve and Lux pull me onto the dance floor. I'm wearing a dark red sequined dress that I borrowed from Maeve. She's several inches shorter than me, so it hits a little higher than something I'd normally wear. With the addition of my four-inch Louboutins, I'm confident I look hot tonight.

Lux brushes up against me in her skintight white minidress, and we dance together for a few minutes. I am letting myself loose for the first time in forever. I feel free and alive.

Maeve comes up behind me and yells into my ear over the music. "There's a guy checking you out."

I look over at where she's indicating. A dark-haired man in his late twenties is giving me a lazy smile. He looks hot in his jeans and button-down shirt. When I smile back, he pushes off from the wall and walks toward me.

Normally my pulse would be racing, but I only feel a strange excitement humming through my veins. He puts his hands on my hips, and we move to the music. I block out the images of doing this with Heath in a club last week and focus solely on this moment.

My partner's hands snake a little lower, his fingers brushing my ass. I wiggle closer to him until our bodies are flush. He has a gorgeous smile with bright white teeth that belong in a toothpaste commercial. He bends low over my ear and says in a divine French accent, "You are the most beautiful woman in the room."

It doesn't matter that it's not true. I grin up at him and flutter my eyelashes the way I've watched Lux do a hundred times.

The lights are low, flashing on the walls in an ethereal blue shade. There's a spicy woodsmoke scent in the air. I'm not sure if it's the club or my partner. The plush velvet seats around the edge of the room would normally call my name, but not tonight. Tonight I am living on the edge of the world, and it feels wonderful.

The hands on my hips spin me around until I'm pressed against the man. His erection pushes through my dress, and it makes my nipples tighten in response. I've never left a club with a stranger before, but if things progress, I'll consider it.

I slide my ass back and forth over his cock. We're nearly the same height, thanks to my heels. He groans in my ear. I lift my arms over my head, let them sway to the beat, then drop them around his neck, pulling his face close to mine.

He smells good, and I moan when he moves to that sensitive spot behind my ear. I'm close to spinning around and letting him kiss me when I'm yanked completely out of his arms.

My eyes fly open. My shoulder feels like it's been wrenched from its socket. Attached to my wrist is Heath's hand. He is pulling me across the dance floor, his grip so strong that I couldn't resist if I tried. I don't, because we're already stepping onto the carpet of the lounge.

"What—" I turn to look behind me. The guy I was dancing with has already disappeared.

Heath stops in front of an empty velvet bench. I jerk my hand from his grasp and rub my wrist. "What do you think you're doing?" I say.

"I could ask you the same thing." He's close enough for me to see the charcoal ring around his irises. "What the *fuck* were you thinking?"

"I was having a good time," I say. "Until you came and ruined it."

His eyes flash even in the dim lighting. "I just saved you from making a fool of yourself."

I let out a choked laugh. "Excuse me? You're the one who dragged me from the dance floor in front of everyone."

"Because you were practically in the guy's pants."

"Take a look around, Heath. Everyone is dancing like that." I grab a champagne flute from the trays being circulated by waiters and throw it back. Champagne flows freely here, and it's time I took advantage.

He grabs my arm before I can swipe a second glass. "Not everyone was rubbing their ass over my cock a few hours ago."

I look up at him. "Is that what this is about? You're mad I didn't finish the job?"

"I'm mad that you would move from guy to guy like that."

A disbelieving sound makes its way out of my throat. Is he being serious? "Did you think something *happened* between you and me?"

"Of course something happened. I just had my tongue down your throat!"

The space around us stills. I'm aware that there are other people in the room, but they fade until they're nothing but background noise and movement. There's only Heath, angry and panting over me.

"What's happening here, Walker?" he says, softer this time.

A laugh trills out of my mouth. "I'm really high, and I'm trying to have a good time."

"I mean with us."

I'm beginning to regret that weed. I can't seem to clear my head. Is there something happening between us? I can't remember. All I know is that if Heath were to lay me on this bench behind us and crawl over me, I wouldn't try to stop him.

I shake my head. "Nothing's happening. We were doing what we had to." It doesn't feel like the right thing to say, but whatever that is has eluded me.

"I see."

"I was just having fun. Nothing was going to happen with that guy."

"That's what you think. I'll bet you he leaves with someone else in the next thirty minutes."

"You'll bet me what?" I scan the crowd for my former partner, but I don't see him.

"If I'm right, you go surfing with me."

"And if I'm right?"

"What do you want?" he says.

A dangerous question. I give it a few seconds' thought. "You have to read three Huntington books before I leave."

His eyes narrow slightly. "You've got a deal."

We both sit down and order shots while keeping an eye on the club's exit. When a familiar form heads to the door with his arm around a leggy blonde, I sink back into my seat.

"Twenty-three minutes," Heath says after glancing at his phone. "I'm good."

"Is this where you start to become even more obnoxious?"

He honors that with a little Cabbage Patch dance move.

"God, I think you might be as high as me," I say.

He laughs and clinks his shot glass against mine. "I might be. But I'm not going to go gyrate my hips with a stranger." He throws the shot back. "At least not tonight."

"Surfing? Really?" I say, emptying my own glass.

"You're gonna love it." He bumps my shoulder with his.

That's exactly what I'm afraid of.

20

"Cruel Summer" - Taylor Swift

Walker

I think this might be what death feels like. I wake Tuesday morning with a massive headache and breath that smells like those prawns we dumped in Candle Lady's AC unit. Apparently this is what happens when one lets loose.

Guess I can add this to my list of things to never do again.

Getting home from Paris was a blur. After going nearly forty-eight hours without sleep, I crashed as soon as my head hit anything soft. I can't be positive I didn't drool all over someone's chest and would rather not find out.

One thing from the weekend comes back with startling clarity: my stupid bet with Heath. If I had been in my right mind, I would have told him to bugger off. But I was baked as a cake, and now I have to spend my day in the sun instead of the stacks.

I check my phone, thinking maybe the weather will be unconducive to surfing, but they're predicting lots of sunshine and—*gross*—heat. There's a text from my mum, which I ignore, and a text from Heath, reminding me to be at the surf shop at ten this morning.

I groan and flop back onto the bed.

A sudden thought has me lurching upright again, which my head strongly protests against. *I don't have anything to wear.* When I packed my trunk before leaving Oxford, I never dreamt I would be spending the day at a beach. I was actively avoiding situations like this.

I leave early so I have time to pick something up. I opt for a high-neck surf suit. After everything that happened, it seems safer than a regular bathing suit.

The door to the surf shop is propped open when I arrive. It has a straw roof and a handful of colorful signs advertising what's inside. The salty smell of the ocean is more concentrated here. Surfboards are leaning upright in rows against the walls. Brown and gold bottles of sunscreen and tanning oils give off a warm coconut scent.

A tan woman with blonde braids is behind the counter, waxing a board. Best guess, I'd say she's several years older than me, in her late twenties. She looks up when I walk in and smiles. She has a natural beauty, a wide smile, and a toned body. She's a walking advertisement for the shop.

"You must be Walker," she says. "Heath told me you were coming. I'm prepping your board for you."

"Oh," I say. "Thank you. Is he here?"

"He's finishing up with a client, but he'll be done soon. You can take a look around while you wait."

I move to a rack of T-shirts in various pastel shades. They look like something Heath would wear. There is a rotating display of sunglasses and a mirror, so naturally, I try on several pairs. I'm wearing a pair of knock-off Wayfarers when I recognize his voice. I turn, but he hasn't spotted me.

Instead he approaches the counter and leans across it like he's exhausted. He says something to the woman, and she throws her head back to laugh. I can't see his face, but I recognize the smile in his voice as he murmurs something else.

Their voices are too low for me to hear what they're saying. I don't want to move for fear he'll catch me watching, but a strange curiosity grips me.

She's teasing him about something, because he reaches up and tugs one of her braids. She pulls it from his hand and whacks him in the face with it.

There's an uncomfortable knot in my stomach. I try to ignore it and turn back to the sunglasses, but every time they laugh, it only grows in intensity. Are they . . . seeing each other? And if so, why does that cause a painful lump in my chest?

A ping sounds from my bag. It's another text from my mum, asking when I'm coming over. She's still grieving her breakup, and I can't handle that much sadness. Not when it already feels like my heart is splintering like glass in slow motion.

"Hey."

I look up to find Heath walking toward me, floral-printed board shorts dangling from his hips below a washboard stomach that would take hours to map properly. My mouth goes dry, and I swallow. "Hey." I slip my phone back into my shoulder bag and force my eyes away from those abs. "I'm here. Now what?"

"Now we hit the water," he says with that boyish grin I haven't seen on him since coming home. My heart skids across my chest. He used to wear it all the time. Lately, all I've seen is the bottled-up, scrubbed-up, manly version.

He grabs the surfboard from the counter. "Thanks, See," he calls over his shoulder.

I can't keep the smile from my own face, seeing him like this. I hand my bag to the woman behind the counter for safekeeping and follow him out the back door.

The sunshine is bright and unrelenting. It hits my skin with a ferocity usually reserved for tigers and overprotective mothers. Sand immediately fills my sandals, so I reach down and pull them off. I had to purchase them this morning too, because the only shoes I brought along were boots and loafers, both perfectly suitable for studying and completely inappropriate for the beach.

"We'll start with the basics," Heath says as we approach the water. "Paddling."

He connects me to my board with a strap. I try diligently to keep my eyes focused on something—anything—other than the way his fingers are skimming my ankle.

He's tried to get me to do this before, but I always chickened out. I don't relish the idea of being at the mercy of the water and the sun.

"All set." He stands back up. "If you can ride a wave back to shore standing up, we'll go to the Archives this afternoon."

"Deal."

How hard can it be?

* * *

Pretty hard, it turns out.

I manage to get the hang of paddling and even enjoy catching waves lying on my stomach. Standing up, however, is a different story.

"Can we take a break?" I ask when I've fallen off the board for what feels like the hundredth time.

"Of course." Heath jogs back to the surf shop while I remove the strap from my ankle.

I plop down on the beach under one of the striped umbrellas dotting the shore. He returns a few minutes later with several cold cans of lemonade. He hands me one, then takes a long drink from his own.

"This wasn't so bad," I say when we've sat in silence for a few minutes.

He nudges my shoulder. The contact sends tingles down my spine. "Look at you, trying new things."

"It's harder than I expected." I lean back on my hands. "I can see where all of that comes from." I nod at his midsection.

His eyes travel down to his stomach, then over to me. "Walker Halifax, have you been checking me out?"

"When you parade it around like a billboard, what do you expect?"

He tilts his head back and laughs, and the sound wraps around me like a refreshing breeze.

My mind skips back to our first time having sex. It wasn't on this beach, but one like it. It was sunset, and he'd packed a picnic for us. There must be a handbook out there advising men that if they want to get laid, all they need to do is box up a bottle of wine, some good cheese, a few grapes, and strawberries.

It's always been easy with Heath. He's like the water. He adapts to whatever container he's put into. Dress him up in a tux and send him to a ball at the palace, and he will be the perfect gentleman. Give him a tennis racket and a polo, and he'll give you a run for your money on the court. Hand him a stack of books in a stuffy back room of a library, and he will sit and read them like he's a born scholar.

None of it compares to Heath in the ocean, though. He's fluid, one singular muscle, reading the water and responding to it.

What would it be like if I'd never left? If everything that happened hadn't happened?

"Do you ever wonder where you'd be if you'd made different choices?" I say, staring out across the ocean.

He's been drawing in the sand, but I sense him still beside me. "In general? Or are we talking about something specific?"

I let my shoulders drop, faking nonchalance. "Nothing in particular."

He considers this for a minute. "Sometimes. But there isn't much sense in regretting the past, right?"

This sinks into my stomach like a ship slowly going down. Why dwell on the past when you can move on in the future?

"Are you sleeping with her?" My voice comes out smaller than I intend. I clear my throat.

He whips his head around to look at me. "Who?"

"The girl at the surf shop."

"Seeley?"

"Sorry if I'm probing. Just trying to figure out what I was reading back there."

He turns back to the ocean, feet kicked out in front of him, elbows propped up behind him. The sun has already dried his skin, but damp tendrils of hair stick to his neck. He stays quiet for so long that I'm positive he's not going to answer.

I tell myself I'm okay with that. Why wouldn't I be?

Two years ago I left him. I cannot expect him to still have feelings for me. And even if he does, I no longer have them for him.

Which is why I have no explanation for the pinch in my chest.

21

"I'm Home" - Nevertown

Heath

"Are you sleeping with her?"

Gotta admit, Walker's question takes me by surprise. Not only was I not expecting her to question my relationship with Seeley, but I wasn't expecting her to have an interest in any of my relationships, sexual or otherwise.

Her slender legs stretch out in front of her. If I had to guess, I'd say she opted for the long-sleeve surf suit not because she thought she'd get cold but because she thought it would be less sexy that way. I smash my lips together to keep from grinning. God, was she ever wrong.

She doesn't spend much time in the sun, but she has her mum's olive coloring. Her toenails are painted hot pink. It's so out of character for her that I can't help but applaud the tiny fractures in the glass box she keeps around herself.

As if sensing my perusal, she shifts upright and brushes the sand from her arms. I still haven't answered her question. Much as I don't want to talk about another woman when I'm with her, I can't let her walk away thinking there's more between me and Seeley than there is.

"We've slept together, yeah," I say.

Her hand stills for a moment, but she quickly resumes her brushing.

"That explains a lot," she says.

"Like what?"

She brushes the sand from her legs. I ought to tell her not to bother, that the ocean will wash it off within seconds, but I'm completely mesmerized watching her hands skim over her calves. "Sexual tension. Familiarity. The look on her face."

My head spins. "What?"

"It was all there."

"You were there for how long—a few minutes?"

She looks at me over her shoulder. "Trust me, that's plenty of time to read the chemistry between the two of you."

My mouth hangs open, and I must look like I'm a few sandwiches short of a picnic. But she can't possibly think there's anything *substantial* going on with Seeley. "We only slept together a few times."

She nods and starts swirling her fingers through the sand between her bent legs, biting that bloody lip. My cock pulses inside my shorts. Time to get back in the water.

"Seriously." I touch her arm with my fingertips. When she doesn't pull away, I rub my thumb across the fabric of her wetsuit. It's like touching velvet, and I envision the softness of the skin underneath. "It was only a handful of times. It never went anywhere."

"I think she might wish it had," Walker says quietly.

Every encounter I've had with Seeley since the last time we had sex—at the end of last season—spins through my mind like a merry-go-round. We never had a conversation about it, but she didn't give me any reason to think she wasn't as happy about an after-work fuck as I was.

For a few seconds, I let myself imagine it. Laughing together over a shared piece of banana cream pie. Packing a cooler and taking a road trip to wherever the fuck we want. Waking up in the middle of the night, hard as a sledgehammer, and being able to turn to the person beside me in bed instead of stumbling to the bathroom for a tube of lube.

Of course, I can't imagine those things without also imagining the rest. Nagging about the lack of a cap on the toothpaste or the socks on the floor. Screaming matches after I come home later than I said I would. The look of disappointment in her eyes when she realizes I'm not the person she thought I was.

"Not everyone gets the fairy tale, Walk."

"Referring to her or you?"

How did I let myself get roped into this conversation? "Not referring to anyone." I stand up and reach down a hand to help her to her feet. "Come on. We've got to get you upright on a board."

* * *

It takes another hour, but she finally does it. The look on her face as she rides the board is worth every second of uneasiness I felt earlier.

My bet was a little underhanded. It was obvious that douche from the club was only looking for a warm place to stick his cock. The bet was my way to get Walker out of that stuffy library to have some real fun.

Sure, she had fun when we went out with the whole crew, but I never had her to myself those times. Except for when we were dancing, and if my dick is to keep from giving away everything I'm thinking, I need to think about anything but dancing with her.

"That was so much fun," she says after we return her board. "I'm not going to hang up my bookbag, but I would definitely do it again."

The sun has sprinkled freckles across her nose, and I have the strongest urge to lick them as I gaze down at her. "Glad to hear it," I say. There's something in my throat making me sound like a twelve-year-old in the throes of puberty. "Still want to go to the Archives?"

She scrunches up her nose. "I kind of need to. I haven't been the most efficient lately. Will you be okay?"

"I'll survive," I tell her. "Come on. We can shower at my place."

She follows me in her car. No one is home, thank fuck, and I offer my bathroom to her. "The shower's bigger in there," I say. "I'll take the guest bath."

I grab my stuff and head down the hall. If I'm to survive the rest of the afternoon, I need to bash one out in the shower. I'm ready to hop in when I remember to grab boxers. I wrap the towel around my waist and pad back to my bedroom.

The shower's still running, which means I can slip in without Walker realizing I've come back. I grab a pair of underwear from my closet and walk back through the bedroom.

The door is cracked. I swear it's cracked. I never touched that knob.

But I will admit to looking. If one can drink with one's eyes, I did that too. The shower walls are glass, and the open door gives me the perfect view of the mirror.

She's like a goddess. Her dark hair is slicked back and dripping. Her back arches under the stream of water until it meets the curve of her ass. I can still remember the way it feels in my hand: firm but soft, like a ripe peach.

And then there are her breasts. Water sluices over them, the rivulets running down her body. She used to be frustrated because the left was slightly bigger than the right. I would cut off my own arm to find out if it still is.

I snap out of it when my towel starts to slip off, thanks to my cock deciding that the fantasy is about to become a reality. I walk back to the guest bathroom before I can do anything stupid.

When we meet in the hallway fifteen minutes later, I am a perfect gentleman. Now that I've gotten one off in the shower, I can proceed with a somewhat level head.

Walker is wearing an oversized white button-down shirt and a tiny little skirt that showcases the tan she got this morning. Her hair is barely damp. She must have found the blow dryer I hardly ever use.

"Ready?" she says, swinging her bag over her shoulder.

I motion for her to go first, but instead of heading downstairs, she stops directly in front of me. I catch a whiff of my own shampoo. Why does my scent on her make me want to fuck her all the more?

She reaches for my shirt. Every drop of blood in my body heads south.

"You need to learn how to button a shirt," she says.

I suck in a breath as her fingers fumble with the buttons, slipping and brushing against my abs. She leaves the top two undone, then turns to skip down the stairs. I stumble along behind her, already working several of the rest out of their holes.

If I'm to be trapped in that room with her for the next few hours, it won't be in a buttoned-up shirt.

22

"Lose Control" - Teddy Swims

There are several things to note about our current situation.

1) We are late.

2) I am part of the reason we are late.

3) This doesn't bother me at all.

It bothers me a little that it doesn't bother me, but going down that hole feels a little Alice in Wonderland-y, so I am choosing to ignore it for the time being.

Surfing with Heath was . . . fun. I'm kicking younger Walker for not doing it when she had the chance. The thrill of riding that board to shore was almost enough to make me forget about the real reason I'm here.

That, and the intoxicating man next to me.

It would be dishonest to deny that Heath makes me feel things I'd rather not feel. Every time he's around, I get breathless, and my skin starts to feel clammy. That kiss the other night was enough to make my dreams . . . interesting, to say the least.

And yes, I want to lick every inch of those abs when he walks toward me.

We get to the Archives an hour before closing, thanks to our surfing adventures, and I am perfectly fine. Okay, not perfectly fine, because my body is humming with electricity. But nearly fine.

There is no one at the reception desk when we walk in. We glance around, but no one pops out from behind a potted plant. Heath looks at me and shrugs. We head on back.

The library is mostly empty this late in the day. No one pays us any mind as we slip through the aisles toward the G.R. Huntington room. I don't know why I feel like we are doing something wrong, but when Heath bumps into a globe in the center of the aisle because he's looking back at me, I hush him, then convulse into giggles.

He grins and grabs my arm, tugging me along after him. I force myself to focus on the fact that we only have an hour before we need to leave, and not on the fact that my skin feels seared where his hand is resting on it.

We slip inside the room without running into anyone who works at the Archives. "As rigid as they are about their membership rules, I would think they'd take better care in manning their front desk," he says.

"Technically you don't need to stay." I don't want to keep him here if he'd rather go.

"I'll stay," he says simply, and walks toward the fiction shelf.

I take a deep breath and turn my attention to the book I was perusing the last time we were in here. It feels weird in my hands, like it has an energy of its own.

I carry it to the table and pull my study supplies from my bag. Heath turns when I unzip my pencil pouch.

"She's getting serious." He walks over to the table. "Who needs eight thousand highlighters?"

"I do." I uncap a pink one and highlight the sentence I've just written in my notebook.

He sets his novel aside and leans across the table, resting on his hands. "I think you take this whole thing too seriously."

My gaze flies up to his face. A smile is hiding in the creases of his mouth.

"I'm not sure it's possible for a future professor to take studying too seriously."

"I beg to differ," he says.

"Then we'll have to agree to disagree." I return to the book in front of me, but the words are blurring together on the page.

He shifts so he's sitting on the edge of the table. He picks up my pencil pouch and starts rifling through it. "Tell me why you want to be a professor again?"

I pause. "Because I can't imagine anything better than being surrounded by books all day."

"Why not a librarian?" He uncaps and recaps the highlighters in the bag.

I flick the pen back and forth while I consider my answer. "It's not just the books. It's the research."

"Like this?" He raises his brows as he looks around.

"Like this." I look back down before he pulls me in with those eyes.

"Seems a little . . . stodgy." A smile lurks in his voice. He's trying to distract me, and it's working.

"Give me that." I pull the pouch from his hand and look inside. He's switched all of the caps. "You're a child."

A quiet chuckle floats my way as he hops off the table and walks to the armchair. I've read the same sentence twelve times. At this rate, I'll be lucky to finish a page before it's time to leave.

He sinks into the chair, and I'm mesmerized by the way his body folds itself to accommodate the small space. He's all lean limbs and toned muscles. There's no bulk to him, just height and length and breadth.

What was it like to be able to run my hands over that body, to taste it, to inhale it? What did that hair feel like between my fingers, my breasts, my legs?

As if he can sense my gaze, he looks up from his book and meets my eyes. I blink and look back down at the page.

Focus, Walker. God.

Several minutes later, though, my eyes have wandered back to him. His shirt is hanging open—the bastard undid those buttons I so carefully buttoned—revealing the golden-brown chest that distracted me most of the day. He's methodically cracking his knuckles as he reads. He darts a furtive glance at me, then does a double take when he catches me looking. Again.

This is getting ridiculous.

Heat grows between my thighs the longer we sit here. If I don't get out soon, there's no telling what's going to happen.

Remember what he did. Remember what he did.

I take a quick trip to the restroom. When I get back, he's still sitting, arms resting on his knees.

"I need to email Dr. Riordan with an update tonight." It's a senseless thing to say—why would Heath care?—but it's meant to shift my brain into let's-focus-on-what's-actually-important-here mode. I sit back down and find my spot in the book I was reading.

"Is that a requirement?" he says.

I scrawl a note in the margin of my notebook. "No, but he likes to keep tabs on what I'm up to."

There's silence for a few beats. When I glance over, frown lines are furrowing his brow. "Why would a teacher need to know what his students are doing outside of school?" he says.

I recap my pen. "He's more of a mentor."

"It's still weird."

"No, it's not."

"Yeah, it fucking is."

"What is your problem?" Blood pulses right below the surface of my skin.

"I don't have a problem. I just think it's weird that your professor wants to *keep tabs on you.*"

"I told you, he's a mentor."

"I don't care what he is. It's weird."

I stare at him. "Are you—are you jealous?"

He scoffs. "No, I'm not *jealous.*" He imitates my tone.

"Could've fooled me."

He stands and walks to the table. My heart rate kicks up another notch.

"Why would I be jealous?"

"I don't know." I try to swallow the lump in my throat, but my mouth is too dry. "But this is the second time you've gotten upset about me giving attention to another guy."

"I'm looking out for you. As a friend." He leans down so he's only inches away from my face. Electricity crackles in the space between us.

"We're not friends."

"Damn right we're not." His hand is in my hair before I have time to react. He pulls me up at the same time as he moves his mouth over mine.

The taste of him hits me like shock waves. He tastes like popsicles and the ocean and *Heath.* He tastes like all the best moments of my life rolled into one delectable dessert. He tastes like home.

He parts my lips with his tongue, and I give him access to everything he wants. He groans when I slide my tongue across his. Our teeth clash together as he tries to go deeper.

He walks me backward until the bookcase stops us. He presses into me, his body firm but soft, a wall of gentle heat. He slides one hand from my hair to encircle my neck, all while keeping his mouth firmly on mine. His thumb flicks back and forth across my jugular notch. I whimper at all of the sensations he is dragging out of me.

I bury my fingers into that glorious hair I've been dreaming of and gasp when he moves his mouth to my neck. He nips at my skin and sucks on my earlobe. His other hand travels to my hip, anchoring me against the wall. I cry out when his teeth sink into the space behind my ear.

"Shhh," he murmurs. "You don't want anyone to find us."

Remembering where we are should bring me to my senses. Instead it cranks my libido even higher. "Getting it on in the library has always been a fantasy of mine," I say breathlessly as his mouth works its way across my collarbone.

This drives him into a frenzy. His hand moves from my hip to the hem of my skirt, skimming it over and over with his thumb until I'm ready to beg him for more. Finally he slips it beneath the fabric. I moan as he reaches my lace undies.

The heat of his hand flows through me as he cups me, using the base of his palm to create friction right where I need it most. I keep my hands in his hair as he works me over, tilting my head back and scooting books on the shelf behind me.

"Walker, god," he says, as breathless as I am. His fingers fly over the buttons on my shirt, stopping halfway down to tug my breast out of both bra and shirt. He settles his mouth over it while he continues his ministrations between my thighs.

I buck against him, and he chuckles. The sound is muffled by my breast filling his mouth. He has both hands beneath my skirt now, tracing light circles through my tights and panties.

"This skirt was extremely misleading," he says.

"How so?" I pant. I'm thanking my lucky stars I wore a skirt and not trousers today.

"I thought I only had underwear to get through. I hope you're not particularly fond of these tights." He punctuates this sentence by digging his fingers into the fabric and pulling, tearing them both along the seam.

I gasp out a laugh, which dissolves into a moan the second his fingers reach me.

He rubs his thumb back and forth over my folds, tantalizing me to the brink of madness. Slowly, he slides it further in. He kisses me again, then pulls back. "God, are you this wet for me?"

I let out a breathy chuckle. "Who else would it be for?"

"I don't know. That old guy over in the poetry section?"

I bite his lip, hard. He responds by thrusting his fingers deep inside me. I cry out from the intense pressure. He curls them and strokes me until I'm near combustion.

"Walker, baby," he pants in my ear. "I need to be inside you, like right now."

I don't know if he's simply stating a fact or asking for permission, but I do not have the brain power to focus on conversation. "Please," I whimper.

I've become my mother, and I don't even care.

His fingers slide out from inside me, slick and dripping. He pulls a foil from his wallet, unzips his shorts, and unrolls the condom within seconds.

Then he's back, pushing those fingers back inside until I don't think I can take it anymore. "Heath, please," I whine. "I need more."

He hitches my leg around his waist. Then he presses the back of my other thigh with his fingers. "Now jump," he says.

I do, wrapping both legs around him. He takes another step toward the bookcase, so I'm firmly ensconced between two walls. He pauses at my entrance. Every muscle in my body tenses, waiting for the moment he claims me.

When he thrusts his entire length into me, I throw my head back and cry out his name. He shifts me down onto him so that he's seated inside as far as he can go. Then he holds me in place while pulling out a few inches and slamming it home again.

I'm already coiled so tightly, it only takes a few more thrusts before I break. I cling to his shoulders as the climax rips through me, sending me into a shower of sparks. With a groan and one final thrust, he falls apart.

23

"Over You" - Daughtry

Heath

Is it possible to get a glimpse of heaven while still on earth?

Walker is in my arms. We're on the floor of the small room at the back of the Archives. I have no idea where our clothes are. Sometime between pressing her up against the bookcase and now, we both lost every shred of clothing and sanity.

She stirs her head on my chest, looking up at me with those giant brown eyes, eyes I used to dream about. A gentle smile lifts the corners of her mouth, like she's tripping on happiness right along with me.

My stomach roils in disgust when I think about the photos I snapped of her open notebook when she went to the restroom earlier. I don't deserve this. I don't deserve anything close to this. But I'm sure as fuck going to hang on to it while I have it.

"Hey," I say, tucking her hair behind her ears.

Her smile grows, letting me know she's okay. We used both condoms in my wallet. I hope she's not sore tomorrow. I'm not sure how much sex she's been having in Oxford. Thinking about her having any sex in Oxford makes the jealousy rear its head again.

She exhales a contented sigh and draws circles on my stomach. After the third one, I grab her hand. "That tickles." I entwine our fingers.

She presses her lips to my abdomen. "I know."

A phone rings. She lifts her head and stares at her bag, then groans. She gets up and pads over to her things. I get a healthy view of ass and tits as she's going.

"Oh my god," she says, staring at her phone screen. "How—?" She moves to the door and opens it a crack. It's dark in the rest of the building. She turns back to me. "They've closed the Archives."

"Shit." I get to my feet and pull my shorts on, then grab my T-shirt from the chair. "I'll go see if it's locked."

Using my phone as a torch, I make my way to the front door, which is locked as predicted. Fortunately they don't employ a night security guard, but if they did, at least we could be out of here in a matter of minutes.

When I get back to the room, Walker is dressed and staring at her phone like it's the last hope for humanity. She looks up when I come in, her face begging for good news.

I give her a lopsided smile and shake my head.

"Ugh." She groans and flops backward into the chair. "What are we going to do now?" I'm thinking, trying to come up with a plan, when she says, "Wait a minute. Did you do this on purpose?" She stands up and comes closer, her finger pointing at my chest.

"Do what?"

She pauses, the wheels spinning in her head. Whatever she's thinking, it can't be good. "You seduced me so that we'd get locked in here."

I grant her a mocking smile. "Caught me."

Her gaze turns venomous. "I knew it!"

"Walk, I was kidding."

She turns away, pacing the room as she concocts her crazy theory. "It bothered you that I said I needed to email an update to Dr. Riordan.

You got jealous, so you planned this whole thing so that we'd be locked in and I couldn't email him tonight after all."

I shove my hands in my pockets but don't say anything, waiting for her to finish.

"You're trying to sabotage me," she says. "That's why you've been distracting me every time we're in here. I haven't been able to focus on anything, and it's all because you've been fucking with my head."

"Are you done yet?"

She whirls around on me. "No, I'm not done! What else have you done? Did you tell everyone to pick my revenge during poker so I'd be obligated to go along and spend time with everyone? Is the plan to keep Walker from doing any research so she has to stay forever?"

"You're insane."

She slaps her palms against my chest. "Tell me the truth."

I grab her wrists. "Why would I want to sabotage you?"

"You know why!"

"Okay, yeah. I do think it's weird that your professor wants you to keep in touch. It's summer holiday, for god's sake. Don't you ever take a break?"

"This is my *dissertation*," she says. "My grade hinges on it. You know this, Heath. You, of all people, know how important this is to me."

"Of course I do." She's not wrong in suspecting me, but not in the way she thinks. "So why would you think I want to sabotage that?"

Our eyes meet, and I see the answer lying there.

"It's kind of your MO, isn't it? Destroy Walker?"

I drop her wrists and press my fingers into my eye sockets, wishing I could will myself out of this room and literally anywhere else. "Of course it's not."

"You've done it before. What's once more?"

"That's not what—"

"How could you do that to me?" she screams. Tears are streaming down her face. My heart splinters at the sight.

I shake my head, trying to get the words right, but everything's a jumbled mess. "I was scared, okay?"

"*You* were scared?" She shoves her hands against my chest. "How do you think *I* felt? I loved you, Heath. I thought I was going to die because I loved you so much. I gave you everything. Everything! Do you know how many other people I've done that for?" Her eyes are wide, maniacal. "None! No one else."

I close my eyes. I don't want to do this. "I know."

"You know? You *know*?" She paces to the window. Wildcat Walker is breaking out of her cage.

"Walk, please—"

"Why did you do it? Was I not enough for you anymore? Were you bored, or restless, or just wanted to experi—"

"I wanted you to find out."

The wind rushes from her sails. The lines of her shoulders sink as she takes this in. "What?" It's a tiny, disbelieving whisper. That single word hurts more than all the others she's hurled at me.

"I know it's messed up." I tug on my hair. Stupid fucking wanker.

"'Messed up?'" she parrots. "What kind of fucked-up game are you playing?"

I sink into the armchair and rest my head in my hands. How do I even go about explaining when I don't understand any of it myself? "I was scared of where things were going. I was scared of disappointing you. I didn't want to wake up one day and find that you no longer liked who I was."

"So you cheated?"

I drop my hands and look up at her. She's all fire and brimstone. I don't know what to say anymore. Defending myself is stupid.

I am guilty.

"How could you do that?" she says quietly.

My mouth hangs open for several seconds as I search for the right words. "I told you, I was scared."

"Then you have a bloody conversation, Heath!" She pushes against the table, and it scoots several inches across the floor. "You don't go and sabotage the relationship."

"I know that now," I say.

I'll never forget the day I discovered she was gone. I'd planned to confess everything, knowing it would be the end of the best thing in my life. When I went to her house, her mum said she wasn't home. I tried calling her, but she wouldn't pick up.

No one else had heard from her either. The police said we couldn't file a missing persons report until she had been gone for forty-eight hours or there were signs of foul play. All we could do was sit back and wait.

I must have sent her a hundred texts that day. All of them went unread.

The next morning, Maeve called to say that she'd talked to Walker's mum. Apparently Walker had decided to return to Oxford early. I was relieved to know she was safe, but it didn't answer any of the million other questions churning around in my head.

Does she know?

Is this her way of breaking up with me?

Is she coming back?

"Do you want to know how I found out?" she says.

I really, really don't, but I deserve to listen to this.

"I came over to your house. I'd picked up pad thai and was going to surprise you."

A sharp pain ricochets through my chest.

"I wasn't even suspicious when I saw the car in the driveway," she continues. "I thought it was some friend of Cami's." She laughs at this, like it could possibly be funny. "Idiot that I was, it never crossed my mind that it might be my boyfriend's secret lover."

I push myself out of the chair and cross over to her. "It was only the one time, I swear."

She backs away from me, like she can't stand to share the same air anymore. "I don't care if it was one time or twenty. You cheated on me."

I exhale, long and slow. This is my mess to clean up. "I am so sorry, Walker. I've wanted to tell you I'm sorry since the minute I did it."

The look on her face is devastating. She looks like a broken toy, all the parts spilling out of her with no hope of repair. "Just leave me alone."

"Walker, please—"

"Go." She points to the door. "Now. Please." Her voice hitches on the last word, and I know she doesn't want me to see her cry.

"Okay." I walk backward to the door. "I'll find a way to get us out of here."

"Just go." She closes the door.

The lock clicks into place behind me.

24

"Partners in Crime" - FINNEAS

Heath

If it wasn't clear before now that I am one of the universe's biggest fuckups, there should no longer be any doubt.

Once Walker has locked me out and the Archives staff has locked me in, I don't have a lot of options. Fortunately my phone is still in the pocket of my shorts. I pull it out and call Pierce.

"What the fuck, mate?" he says by way of greeting.

"Uh, hey," I say.

"Where are you guys?"

I pace the area near the reception desk. "Funny you should ask, actually—"

"I knew it," Rhett yells in the background. "You owe me two grand."

"Listen," I say. "Walker and I are stuck inside the Archives—"

"What do you mean, you're stuck?" Pierce says.

Another hoot of laughter comes through the phone.

"We got locked in when they closed."

"Fuck," Pierce mutters. "Any idea how to get out?"

"We can bring some body oil," Rhett shouts.

"Shut the fuck up, Rhett," Pierce says. The background noise grows

159

quieter as he leaves the room.

"I'm looking for a window we can climb out of. Problem is, most of them are pretty high." I consider all of the ones in the front area, but unless I can find a ladder, there's no way we'll get up there. "I think we can manage to find a way up. It's coming down outside that I'm worried about."

"You said Walker's with you?" he says.

I picture her in that tiny room in the back, alone with her anger. "Yeah, she's here too."

"Is she *right* there?"

"She's not *right* here. She's—busy," I finish lamely.

"Maeve wants to know if you have anything yet."

"I'm working on it."

"I'll let her know," he says. "If you guys can climb out through a window, I can have a ladder outside. The other alternative is breaking the glass of the doors."

I'd rather avoid a run-in with the police tonight. "I'll find a window."

"Okay," he says. "And warn Walker, will you? Maeve is on a rampage tonight. She's out for blood after the two of you blew us off."

A surprised laugh comes out of my chest. "What?"

"It's Tuesday, mate."

Fuck. We forgot about poker night.

There's a window in one of the back rooms above a bookcase full of odds and ends: books, reams of paper, plastic spoons, and a pair of women's pantyhose that I don't want to know the origins of. The space is only for staff members—a lunchroom, judging by the microwave sitting next to the watercooler.

The bookcase feels sturdy enough. I climb to the top and shove on the window. It opens with a creak, letting in a gust of muggy air. I inhale several lungfuls before climbing back down.

The easy part is over. The hard part will be convincing Walker to come out.

She doesn't answer when I knock on the door. "Walker," I call. "It's me." I halfway expect a "No shit, doofus," but there's only silence on the other side.

I slide down to the floor. There's no rush. It will take Pierce close to an hour to get a truck and ladder and drive over here.

"Walk, I'm sorry," I say. I scoot my fingers under the door. I can only get the tips of them out on the other side. "I get it if you can't forgive me. It was a shitty thing to do. The worst, actually."

Nothing. Maybe she's fallen asleep.

"Pierce is coming to get us out. I found a window in the back we can climb through." When she still doesn't say anything, I lean my head back against the door. I must doze off, because when the door opens, I jolt upright.

She's standing in the doorway, eyes hooded and mouth flat. "Let's go."

I lurch to my feet, still groggy from sleep. "I never should've—"

"Don't talk."

Things don't get any less awkward in the back room as we wait for Pierce's call saying he's outside. She's studiously ignoring me, and I can't blame her. If some other asshat treated her the way I did, he'd be lucky to be alive after I got my hands on him.

I still distinctly remember beating up Ryan Watkins at a party sophomore year of high school. He tried to have sex with Walker in the bathroom. It took a nice round of plastic surgery to fix his face after Pierce and I were done with him.

Another memory surfaces, and this time I laugh out loud. Walker's brows pull into a frown, but she keeps her eyes on her phone.

"Do you remember Alastair Eaton?" I'm leaning back against a table that has seen better days.

She doesn't respond.

"Stupid glasses, came up to my elbow, always tucked his shirts in?"

I may as well be talking to a rock.

"He thought rats were smarter than humans?"

She doesn't even blink.

"He pronounced 'resonate' as 'resignate'?"

"You mean my first boyfriend," she deadpans without lifting her gaze.

I exhale a laugh. "Yeah. Kid couldn't walk straight for a week after we finished with him."

I expect her to laugh, or at least smile, in remembrance. The guy had stolen her virginity on a fucking sofa, then used her for sex for the duration of their short-lived relationship.

"Is there a point to all of this?" she asks, looking up from her phone. We've left the lights off to avoid alerting anyone to our presence. Even in the shadows, her form is as familiar to me as my own.

"No," I say. "Just remembering that I'm not the first guy to screw you over."

She crosses her arms. I try not to look at her boobs but am not entirely successful. "At least Alastair never cheated on me."

It's supposed to hurt, and it does, but I also can't help but be grateful that she's talking about it instead of running away.

"True," I say. "Want me to track him down? Maybe he's still single."

I can't be sure because of the darkness, but I think her mouth tilts upward.

Pierce arrives with the truck soon afterward. I help steady Walker as she climbs up the bookcase.

"Get your hand off my ass."

I reluctantly comply, already knowing what I'll be dreaming about tonight.

Everyone is waiting for us outside.

"God, Pierce," I mutter as I make my way down the ladder. "You had to bring the entire circus."

Maeve is standing at the bottom. "Hope you're ready for your punishment," she says with a wicked grin. Maeve is scarier than my dad when someone breaks the rules.

"I think I've been punished enough," Walker says, arms once again crossed over her chest.

Maeve's laser focus darts between the two of us. "I'm not going to pretend to know what's going on here, because frankly, I don't care. Poker night is a ritual. And you two dishonored it."

"We're not a cult, Maeve." No matter what punishment she decides to heap on our heads, it won't be anywhere close to as bad as the cold shoulder Walker is determined to give me.

"Rules are rules, Heath," Maeve says. "Right, guys?" She turns to look at Pierce, Rhett, and Lux standing behind her.

Pierce rolls his eyes once she's facing the front again. He mouths something that looks like *Just go with it.*

"We decided that your punishment will be carrying out the next revenge," she says.

Walker's face is as impassive as ever.

"Our victim is Randall Cromley," Pierce adds, stepping up beside Maeve. "He took Maeve out a few times, then ghosted her."

"He's obsessed with his hair," Maeve adds, disgust edging her voice. "That should've been an immediate red flag."

"You two are going to break into his apartment and fill his shower head with Lifesavers." Lux steps forward and dumps a giant bag of clear candies into my arms. "He turns the shower on, and boom—he's a sticky mess."

"No matter how much he showers," Rhett says with a malicious gleam, "mate won't ever get it off."

I exhale and turn to Walker. She's still ignoring me, so I turn back to everyone else. "Okay. Doesn't sound too bad."

"There's one more thing," Pierce says.

The side of Maeve's mouth quirks upward into a smirk you don't want to be on the wrong side of.

"You two have to test it," she says.

25

"Someone You Once Had" - ROSIE

Walker

I'm going to kill Maeve.

I'm sitting next to Heath in his car, and the tension in here is so thick it feels like I'm in a vat of vanilla pudding. Pudding that smells like sandalwood and orange.

I tried to block out the memories of the Archives last night. The dark circles beneath my eyes this morning prove how unsuccessful I was.

Getting mad at Heath is stupid. He cheated on me two years ago, and I've known about it all along. But the way he tried to write it off as self-sabotage only makes me angrier.

It doesn't matter if that's why he did it. The fact is, he slept with a long-legged blonde who drove a cherry-red sports car. It's so cliche I want to gag.

He reaches over and hits the play button. Classic rock fills the car.

I turn it off.

I feel his sideways glance, but I keep my gaze firmly fixed out the window. Rain has been drizzling down since I woke up this morning. It's a dull, dreary rain, the kind that makes me want to curl up in the library with a book. Not sit in a car with my cheating ex-boyfriend with a bag of candy at my feet.

"Hey," he says.

I hate that it makes my heart soften. I cinch my internal armor tighter.

"I'm sorry, okay?" he says. After he realizes I'm not going to respond, he adds, "Can you please talk to me?"

We're crossing the bridge now. He came to pick me up from the manor. It was yet another of Maeve's stipulations.

"Damn it, Walker." He smacks the steering wheel with his palm. "What do you want from me?"

I turn toward him. Anger tightens the lines of my face. "I want you to suffer."

He looks at me with wide eyes, darting them between me and the road. His mouth is open like he's going to say something, but the seconds tick by before he does. "I *have* suffered." He returns his gaze to the road as we navigate through several stoplights. "More than you realize."

I want to scoff. Whatever he went through, it's not enough. It will never be enough.

"You don't believe me? Ask Pierce or any of the others. I was a mess after you left."

"I don't know why," I mutter.

"Because I loved you!"

"You did the one thing you knew would break me!"

He's quiet, absorbing my words or counting the cars on the road or dreaming of the surf, I don't know. Finally he says, "I didn't want to break you."

"Now you tell me."

"Walker, *fuck*." His voice is quiet. "I only meant to give you a reason to break up with me."

I tuck my eyebrows low on my forehead. "Do you realize how fucked up that is?"

"I am aware, yes," he says, eyes straight ahead. "In case you haven't noticed, I'm pretty fucked up myself."

I don't want to feel his pain, but the memories come back anyway. His dad breaking his arm when he was fifteen, knocking him unconscious the summer of graduation, giving him a black eye a few days ago. It's enough to fuck with anyone.

"That's no excuse," I say, even though I'm not sure I believe it.

"I know it's not. And I've beat myself up every day since then, believe me."

"You got what you wanted, didn't you?" I toy with a thread on my sweater. It's already eighty-five degrees outside, but I need to be fully covered today.

"What do you mean?" he says.

"We broke up. You said that's what you wanted."

"I never expected you to . . . *leave*."

The hurt in his eyes cuts through my heart, adding to the wounds already there. "What did you think was going to happen?"

He digs his fingers through his golden waves. "I thought you'd get mad, we'd argue. I thought you'd break up with me for sure, but I thought we would still be friends. If I had known you'd leave and not come back—"

"Well, I did, so we can put it behind us, right?" I brush my hands across my brown trousers, trying to remind myself that we are grown adults who are capable of having a serious conversation without yelling and screaming at each other.

He nods slowly, like he's not sure he wants to agree. "Yeah," he says softly. "You're right."

We drive the rest of the way in silence. When he slows the car in front of a three-story townhouse, my heart rate picks up.

"You have the key?" he asks.

I nod and pat my pocket. Maeve gets a copy of the house key of any guy she sleeps with in case they screw her over. She makes a mold of it while they're in the restroom, somewhere she ensures they always end up by daring them with drinks.

Heath reaches over the center console to grab the bag of Lifesavers on the floor. His arm skims my leg, and even though there is no skin contact, the touch scorches my every nerve ending.

"We're sure he's at work?" I say as we approach the house. The rain has darkened the sky so it feels like dusk instead of morning.

"Maeve says he leaves for work by eight forty-five." He checks his phone. "It's nine thirty now."

"Okay, let's do this," I say.

The front door unlocks easily with Maeve's copy of the key. Heath closes the door behind us, and we both stare around the front room in silence. Blankets, beer cans, pizza boxes, takeaway containers, gaming consoles, and a stuffed panda bear lie strewn from wall to wall. Across the lake of debris, the staircase leads upward.

"Why are men such slobs?" I pick my way over a purple thong, pillow, and an empty crisps can.

"Hey," Heath says right behind me.

We make it to the stairs without losing our lives, but whether we've caught any deadly diseases remains to be seen.

The second floor is in slightly better condition. "How did Maeve ever sleep with this guy?" I nudge aside a pair of briefs in the hallway with my foot. I'll have to throw these boots away.

"I'm guessing he never brought her here. Otherwise she'd have torched the place."

We locate the primary bathroom, if the bras and panties hanging from the shower door and littering the floor are any indication.

"Either this guy is a cross-dresser, or it's obvious why he ghosted

Maeve," Heath says, removing a pink-and-red bra from the handle of the shower door with a pencil he found on the vanity.

"Think Maeve still wants cameras in here?" I hitch the bag on my shoulder higher, three pinhead cameras tucked safely inside.

"Too bad if she doesn't. I hope to god she regrets this," he says. He reaches into the shower and unscrews the metal head.

We get to work opening the individually wrapped candies.

"They could've at least unwrapped these for us," I say as I drop yet another one on the floor. It lands on top of a questionable-looking sock. I reach a gloved hand down to retrieve it. The gloves are necessary for fingerprint reasons, as well as preventing any number of diseases, but they make removing small plastics impossible.

"Here." Heath holds out a hand for the candy. I ignore the thrill that races up my arm as our fingers touch through the gloves. He holds the Lifesaver to his mouth and tears it open with his teeth.

"That was just on the floor," I say.

"If this place is going to give me E. coli, trust me, it already has."

When we can't fit another Lifesaver into the shower head, Heath fastens it again. He turns the knob, and a stream of water hits the back of the shower.

"Great," I say. A sick feeling churns in my stomach. It's not aided by the pigsty we're stuck in. "Can you just stick your hand in, make sure it's sticky?"

He looks at me over his shoulder. "You know that's not what she meant."

"She'll never know." I am not getting into that shower.

"It's Maeve," he says, tugging his shirt over his head. "I'm not taking my chances."

I avert my eyes from the lines of muscle scrawled across his shoulders, but they inevitably crawl back. He keeps his back to me as he waits for the water to heat up. I should be grateful; that chest is not kind to me. I long to turn him around and trace all of it the way I did at the Archives.

He bends over and strips off his shorts and boxers. I steal a quick look at his ass before he steps into the shower and closes the door.

I act within seconds, having no clue why I'm doing it, except possibly a fear of Maeve too. I drape my clothes over a shockingly empty towel rack. I am not trusting that floor with anything but the soles of my shoes.

Heath spins around when I open the door. His eyes travel the length of my naked body as if he's never seen it before. He doesn't say anything, just moves back so I can get in.

I step into the spray, letting it hit every inch of me. I'm not giving Maeve any reason to say we didn't complete the assignment to her satisfaction. The water's warm, and I close my eyes as it washes over me. I run my hands over my breasts and stomach. We won't know until we're dry if it works or not, so why not enjoy it until then?

I open my eyes to find Heath watching me, his gaze hungry with need. His cock has sprung to life, and his fingers are clamped around it. For several seconds neither of us move, held in a trance as the water sprays over us.

Then I slowly move my hands back to my breasts and squeeze. His eyes follow my movements. His own hand moves back and forth over his dick. I draw my fingers to my nipples, pinching and rolling them, encouraging them to form hard peaks.

He responds by picking up the pace. His hand pumps up and down, his breathing growing more ragged. Keeping my eyes locked on his, I slide my fingers down over my stomach. When I reach my hips, I grab onto the shower bar beside me with one hand. With the other, I reach between my legs.

A serrated breath heaves out of Heath's chest. His rubbing becomes erratic, more jerky than before. He must be getting close. I touch my clit, letting my head fall back against the shower wall, and moan. I stick two fingers inside myself. The heat grows stronger.

I open my eyes again when he lets out a strangled groan, in time to watch him release all over his hand. He rubs the cum all over his cock like lotion. The sight is so primitive, it unlocks something inside me. I move my own hand faster, driving it deeper to where I need it most. Every time I open my eyes, he is watching me, a dazed expression on his face. I can't tell if he wants me to continue or if he wishes he could finish me off himself.

I don't find out, because seconds later my own orgasm hits. I cry out and press against the shower wall, thrusting my hips forward as the waves rock through me.

When it's over, I blink up at him. He licks his lips, but I don't think he has any intention of kissing me. In fact, I don't think he has any intention of doing anything.

I reach over and turn off the shower, keeping my eyes locked on his. We stay like that for several seconds, still soaking up the aftershocks of our orgasms. Then he turns and steps out of the shower. He waits and holds the door while I get out. Neither of us says a word as we slip back into our clothes. The stickiness is already making its presence known, and I get dressed as quickly as I can.

When I've finished, Heath has already dug the cameras from my bag and is installing one inside the power outlet over the sink. It only takes a few more minutes to get the others set up in the hallway and bedroom.

The ride back to the manor is quiet. I long to know what he's thinking, but his face reveals nothing. The rain continues drizzling around us, a soft *tap-tap-tap* that only makes the silence inside the car feel louder.

When he pulls up in front of my Airbnb, I hesitate. I'm not ready to go inside, not ready to say goodbye to him for the rest of the day.

I fiddle with the door handle. "After we wash this candy off, do you want to visit the Archives? I assume you won't be surfing with the rain . . ." My voice trails off as I motion out the window.

He looks out, then pulls his phone out of his pocket, checking something on the screen. "I can't today. I already made plans."

That feeling in my chest is not pain, I tell myself, it's relief. Spending time with him would be one of the worst possible decisions I could make.

"Okay." I grab cheerfulness by the arm and force it into my voice. "Tomorrow then?"

He nods. "That's fine."

I climb out of his car and walk toward the house. We need distance between us, or bad things are sure to happen. What happened last night in the Archives—or god, what just happened in stupid Randall the Pig's shower—cannot, under any circumstance, be repeated.

This is good, I remind myself. Distance means we're moving on.

But none of that keeps me from wondering who he has plans with.

26

"Broken" - Jonah Kagen

Heath

Traffic crawls as I make my way downtown, and I wish I'd never agreed to meet Cami for lunch. She's been bugging me since the weekend. I've been putting her off, but after everything that has happened with Walker, it will be good to cool things off between us.

Especially since Maeve has also taken to irritating the shit out of me, texting me several times a day to see when I'm going to get Walker's notes to her.

My sister is even later than I am, which isn't a surprise. She operates on her own time. My guess is she hasn't looked at a clock since she was in school.

I follow the host to the table Cami reserved for us. It's a two-top near the center of the restaurant, where a massive tree grows out of the floor and into the ceiling. They've created a compelling illusion, but since we're thirty-some floors up, I hope no one is convinced that it's real.

Growing up the sides of the tree is a massive amount of green ivy. It climbs all the way to the branches, making this place look like it walked right out of a Walt Disney movie. No wonder Cami picked it.

My old-fashioned is half-gone when she finally shows up. Her hair is flowing around her shoulders like a veil of gold. Loose, rust-colored pants hang from her hips, and she's wearing a crocheted top that's practically two triangles tied together with string. I've seen bikinis cover more.

"They let you in here like that?" I say, pointing as she sits down.

She laughs. "They know I'll post a selfie in front of their plant wall. That alone will be responsible for the next 25 percent of their fiscal profits."

Cami is a social media influencer, whatever the hell that is. She compares it to being a socialite like Lux, with flashier labels so the masses feel like they have a shot at becoming her.

She orders a virgin martini, and at my questioning look, says, "I'm on a health cleanse this month. No booze."

Last month she only ate orange foods. The month before that she sipped every meal through a straw. I have no idea why she chooses to torture herself like this, but she seems happy.

When the server sets the drink down, I say, "You realize the only reason to drink a martini is for the alcohol, right?"

Cami takes a sip and makes a face. "I'm going to agree with you on that one." She pops an olive into her mouth. "But we're not talking about me today."

Fuck. I should have seen this coming.

She points her toothpick at me. "I heard something."

I give her my best bored expression. Past experience tells me she won't drop this no matter what I do. My best option is to let her talk and get it over with as quickly as possible.

"Someone said Walker is back."

"Yep," I say.

Our server returns right then, and we both place an order. My sister's requires multiple steps and a "Can you repeat that back to me?"

"Cami," I chide quietly.

"What?" she says after the guy walks away. "I told you I'm on a cleanse." She takes another sip of her martini. "A little bit of oil would ruin everything."

I check the time on my watch. One more hour, and I can excuse myself.

"How's Taylor?" I say.

"Uh-uh." She shakes her head. "You are not distracting me. I want to hear all about Walker."

"Sorry to disappoint you. There's nothing to tell."

"Bullshit," she says, loud enough for patrons at the next table to glance over.

Sorry, I mouth to them. I give Cami a look that says *Behave, or I walk.*

She shrugs, completely nonplussed. "Have you seen her?"

"Who? Walker?"

She stops with her glass halfway to her mouth. "No, Queen Celia." She takes a drink and lowers it back to the table. "God, Heath. I'm beginning to think you're not over her after all."

"I am," I say. "And I have."

Our server returns with a plate of hummus and pita crisps, both of which he assures Cami twice more were made without oil.

I bite into a crisp and fight a smile. There's no way in hell they're oil free.

Cami crunches into one as well. "Spill," she says with her mouth full. What would her Instagram followers say if they could see her like this?

"I told you, there's nothing to tell."

"And yet you haven't stopped fidgeting or checking your phone since I got here."

I didn't realize I was doing either. But the truth is, as much as I don't want to remember everything that went down with Walker in the past twenty-four hours, my body is not as willing to let the memories go. That scene in the shower with her may be the hottest thing I've ever done.

I exhale and dunk a crisp into the hummus. "We slept together."

Cami chokes and reaches for her water. "You *what*?"

"I'm not going to repeat it."

"Wait, back up," she says. "How long have you known she was back in town?"

I do a quick calculation in my head. "Two weeks."

"And you're just now telling me this?" she shrieks.

"I told you, there's nothing to tell."

"You just said you slept with her."

Her voice isn't as low as she thinks it is, and the couple at the next table gives her another look. She doesn't even notice.

"So?" I take a drink. "I sleep with a lot of people."

"Yeah, but none of them have broken your heart before."

It's still raining, but I wish we were outside. It's too cramped in here, even though the room is two stories tall.

"I've moved on. It's no big deal," I say.

"Then why are you rubbing that tattoo like it's going to kill you if you don't get it off?"

I drop my hand. Why does she have to be so bloody aware of everything?

"Heath, what is going on?" She sheds the hippie, cool-girl act and turns into my big sister again. Her fingers close around my wrist.

I meet her gaze. "I don't know," I say. I rub my eyes, wishing I could rub the memories out as easily. "I've been taking her to do her research, and we're reconnecting, and it's just—" I sigh. I'm not sure what else to say.

"Are you finally going to tell me what happened between the two of you?"

I debate this. Cami won't breathe a word to another soul, but I'm more worried that she'll think less of me once she finds out. But what's the sense in hiding the truth? It's all going to come out eventually, and by then it will only devastate her more.

Our plates arrive from the kitchen—a boring-as-fuck salad for her and a steak for me. I wait until her mouth is empty before saying, "I cheated on her."

She doesn't choke this time, fortunately, but the look on her face is nearly as bad. "You're fucking kidding me."

"I wish."

"Heath, seriously. WTF?" Saying the actual letters out loud instead of what they stand for should be a key indicator someone is spending too much time on social media.

"I'm a dick." I spear a piece of steak and pop it into my mouth. Let her think the worst of me. It's not like it isn't the truth.

"Is this because of Dad?"

I pause my cutting to frown at her. "Why would it be about Dad?"

"Because he's the fuckup that fucked us all up?" she says.

I shake my head and return to my plate. "It has nothing to do with him."

"You can't let him destroy your relationships like that."

"Cami, I told you. He has nothing to do with this." I jab at my food.

She crams a massive forkful of spinach into her mouth. "You're giving him space in your head," she tells me. At least I think that's what she said. It was muffled by her chewing.

"I don't need your new-age mumbo jumbo," I say.

She shakes her head, furiously trying to empty her mouth so she can talk again. "You should go to therapy. You'd be surprised at how much healing you can find there."

"I told you I don't want that crap."

"There's this guy over on the west side who—"

"Cami, I mean it. Cut it out."

She exhales loudly. "Fine. I won't push you." She takes a long drink of water. When she sets the glass back down, she has a funny look in her eyes. "By the way, I'm moving out."

It's my turn to choke. I set my knife down. "What?"

"Taylor got a three-bedroom. We're going to make it work," she says. I can tell she's struggling to meet my eyes.

"That's great," I say. "I'm happy for you." She should've moved out a long time ago. Now he won't ever be able to put his hands on her again.

"You're not upset?"

"That you're getting away from the bastard? Hell no."

Her expression grows more animated, and she reaches for my hands across the table. "You should move out too. You surely have enough to get your own place by now."

"It's not that." I pull away. "I'll do it eventually."

She picks up her fork again, but only to swirl spinach through the dressing pooled on the bottom of her plate. "Why do you do this?"

"Do what?" I say.

"Not allow yourself things."

I sit back in my chair. "I allow myself plenty of things, trust me. Have you seen my new bike?"

"Not the things you really want. Walker, moving out, being yourself."

An uncomfortable feeling grows in my chest. "I don't know what you're talking about."

"It's just another form of self-harm, Heath."

"Is that what your therapist told you?"

"I care about you. You know that, right?"

"What's your point, Cam?"

She drops her fork and steeples her hands in front of her. "If you let Dad convince you that you don't deserve good things in life, you're letting him win."

I frown while I consider this.

"Walker wouldn't have broken up with you if you hadn't cheated."

Why does she think I did it?

"You two could have been happy together," she says. "You broke up with her because you thought you didn't deserve her."

"Are you done psychoanalyzing me now?" I lift my drink to my lips, but it's no longer cold. I flag the server down for another.

"Heath, come on. You know I'm right."

"Let's say you are." I lean forward on the table. "I broke up with her because I'm fucked in the head. But the point remains: I'm fucked in the head, and sooner or later, she would have broken up with me anyway because of it. This saved us both from wasting more of our lives on each other."

Cami gives me a droll expression. "So you're planning to be alone forever?"

"Who knows? Maybe."

"God, Heath. He screwed you over more than I realized."

"At least I'm not the queen." The server hands me a fresh drink, and I take several long swallows. "I can't wait for the day the government finds out what he's been up to."

"How much do you think he's evaded?"

I swirl the stirrer around my glass. "Ten, twenty mil?"

She scoffs. "It has to be way more than that."

"You think?" I say, glancing up.

She fills me in on a few things I was unaware of—how much Dad's income has increased since the pandemic, how his foreign bank accounts have doubled in number, and how he paid less in taxes last year than any other year to date.

"Juliette knows a lot more than me," she says. "But good luck getting her to talk."

Anger bubbles up inside me, like it does every time the conversation turns to our asshat of a father. "One of these days," I mutter and finish my drink.

"Make sure you're prepared to deal with the fallout," she says.

"He needs to learn that he can't always win."

"Don't let him take you down with him." Cami gives me a stern look. "And I'm not talking about the money."

My face says, *I hear you loud and clear. You can stop talking about it now.*

"I need to go." She stands and drapes a slouchy bag across her body. "Give Walker another chance."

"I'll think about it." I press a kiss to her cheek.

"More importantly." She pats my chest. "Give yourself one."

27

"Bad" - James Bay

Walker

Now that I've scrubbed that stupid stickiness off of me, and texted Maeve to let her know that, yes, her plot worked, I have nothing to do. Technically this isn't true, since I could spend some time compiling the few research notes I've taken, email an update to Dr. Riordan, or read one of the thousands of books filling the manor's library.

The problem isn't that I *have* nothing to do. The problem is that there's only one thing I want to do, the same thing I should avoid at all costs.

I find my mind wandering to Heath as I do menial tasks around the house. Putting the trash bag into the outdoor receptacle, applying a fresh face of makeup after my shower, throwing a load of laundry into the washer, doing the few dishes that have accumulated in the sink.

Who are his plans with, and what do those plans entail? Maybe he has a standing date with Seeley to hook up every time they can't surf. I can't blame him. Our last real conversation was me yelling at him for cheating on me.

My phone buzzes on the counter, and I pull my dishwashing gloves off so fast I tear a hole in one finger.

It turns out to be unnecessary, because it's just my mum. Again. I've been ignoring her texts because I'm a terrible daughter. But she's been spiraling since my dad left her—*again*—and I don't want to deal with that.

I'm about to lock my phone without responding to her, but my mind keeps circling back to Heath, even though he's a destructive idea. The guy cheated on me, for god's sake.

Maybe soaking up a little of my mum's heartbreak will be good for me, make me see reason. After all, if I'm not careful, I'll end up just like her.

* * *

The rain leaves my hair a frizzled mess by the time I arrive, but there's something comforting about being back in my old home while the rain streaks the windows. My mum pulls me into a Chanel-scented hug. At least she's back to her signature perfume.

"You could have at least texted me back," she says.

"I'm sorry, Mum. I've been busy."

We both know it's a lie, but she has the grace not to point it out.

"Come on. I'll warm up the brie." She heads toward the kitchen.

I roll my eyes and follow her. "You know, Mum, you could consider turning to something besides food when you're sad."

She halts in her tracks and turns to look at me over her shoulder. "Like what?"

"Oh, I don't know. Therapy, exercise, getting out of the house. Healthy options."

She tuts and keeps walking. "I go out. Be glad I haven't become an alcoholic. Besides, therapy isn't fun. Eating is." She holds up a wheel of cheese and shakes it in the air, a devious smile on her face.

I sigh and shake my head. If she's refusing to see reason after fourteen years, I may as well quit trying. At least she's not depressed anymore. Maybe she's had time to process it, or maybe she's finally learning to cope like a mature adult.

She pops the brie into the oven and fishes the pepper-and-rosemary water biscuits from the cupboard. I fill a glass of water from the spooky, AI-run fridge and try not to think about how many things the government is able to discover about my mum through the bloody thing.

Once the cheese is warm, we grab everything and take it to the living room, which faces the front of the house. It's never been my mum's go-to for entertaining, but after every breakup, this is where we end up, thanks to the huge gas fireplace spanning the entire south wall. A set of arched windows overlook the front driveway, where the rain is still pelting the concrete. Several sofas line the edges of the space, bedecked with pillows.

We grab our favorite throw blankets and settle the tray between us on the sofa. I have to admit, there's something comforting about following our ritual, even if I'm irritated that Mum hasn't learned a better way to cope after all these years.

"So how are you doing?" I hope she can't read how uninterested I am in her answer. Asking usually opens a can of worms that takes thirty minutes to clean up.

"I'm good." She dunks a biscuit into the gooey cheese. "Even better now that you're here."

"You're not still sad?"

"I am. I miss him a lot. But you don't want to hear about all of that."

My chest deflates. "Mum, I want you to be okay."

"I'm getting there." She smiles and brushes her hair from her eyes. "Tell me about you."

I take a bite of my own cheesy biscuit before answering. The familiar combination brings up so many memories. Tears, tissues, binging TV shows. "My research is going well, although not as quickly as I had hoped."

"You found a way to get into the Archives, then?" she says. I'm surprised she remembered.

"Uh, yeah. A friend had a card."

"Who? Maeve?"

Crap. The point was to forget Heath, not talk about him. "No, um . . ." I start. "Heath, actually."

Mum pauses with a biscuit over the cheese and stares at me. "Heath?"

"He was the only one with a card." I shrug, hoping she reads it as *No big deal.*

"And?"

"And what?" I brush crumbs from the corners of my mouth.

Her dark eyes take in everything I'm not saying. "How is that going?"

"It's fine. Have you read any good books recently?"

"Walker."

I toss the new biscuit I picked up back onto the tray. My appetite has vanished. "What? What do you want me to say? You want me to tell you that I slept with him and that I'm starting to have feelings for him again? You want me to say that I'm miserable unless I'm with him?"

"If it's the truth."

I turn to look out the window. Is it? I don't even know. Besides the sex part, of course.

She reaches across the sofa to touch my hand. "Cariño, you can tell me anything, you know. I'm your mother."

I give her a small smile. "Thanks, Mum."

"Does he know why you left?"

I tug my hand away and tuck my hair behind my ear. It's still damp from my shower earlier, which makes me think about the previous one with Heath. My face heats. "He does now," I mutter.

When I texted my mother from the plane to let her know I wasn't coming home, she freaked out. I called her after I landed to reassure her. She wouldn't let it go until I explained why I went back.

"Let me guess," she says. "You're struggling with how to feel about him after all this time."

I bite my lower lip. "I'm still angry, but there are all these other feelings I can't name."

She nods slowly and tucks her feet under her. "You never processed these things before. Being back here opens everything up again."

"Yeah, I guess."

"You still love him, don't you?"

The words cause an ache in my chest that feels like a bruise when you press on it. Sharp, visceral, raw. "I don't know." It comes out high-pitched and childish. "How can you love someone after they hurt you that badly?"

"Oh, niñita. The human heart is a funny thing. You'd be surprised at the things it's capable of."

"But I don't want to end up—" I stop.

"Like me?" she supplies.

I drop my gaze to my hands, which have been fiddling with the tassels on my cashmere blanket.

"Cariño, listen to me. You are not me. And not every man is your father."

"He's already cheated on me once, Mum. That proves he's a cheater, just like Dad."

"One mistake shouldn't define a person."

"I would be a fool to think he'll change."

Her chin lifts, and she sets the tray onto the coffee table. She begins tidying the sofa by folding the throw blankets and arranging pillows. "I see."

"Mum," I say when my words echo back to me. "I didn't mean it like that. I don't think you're a fool."

She glances at me over her shoulder. There's a spark of anger in her eyes. "Yes, you do."

"I—"

She's right. I've always considered her a fool, ever since my father left her the first time and she fell apart. When she took him back six months later, I was happy. I thought our family would finally be okay. But when the entire cycle repeated itself not long after, I realized she was an even bigger fool than I thought.

"You think I'm foolish for believing your father can change." She folds a blanket in half and drapes it over her arm. "And I probably am. But I'd rather be a fool for taking a chance on a man than be a fool for never giving him one in the first place."

"I did give Heath a chance. He used it to cheat on me."

She sits beside me on the sofa. "Heath is a good man, Walker."

I bark out a sharp laugh. "That's what you said about Dad, too."

"Your father is a womanizing manipulator. I knew that the first time I met him."

I jerk my head to the side. "Then why do you keep taking him back? Why did you even date him in the first place?"

"For the same reason any woman loves a man like that. We believe we can inspire them to change."

"You're not really selling your case here."

"My point is that Heath isn't like that, love." She rubs her hand across my knee. "He's one of the good ones."

"How can you be so sure?"

"I saw the two of you together. There was no mistaking how he felt about you."

My mother, ever the optimist. "And yet he cheated on me."

"No one's perfect, cariño."

"I'm not asking for perfection." I shake my head, and my hair falls back into my face. I push it away again. "Just loyalty."

"Some people are capable of change. Others aren't."

"What makes the difference?"

She ponders this for a moment, staring at the rain still running down the tall windows. "I don't know. Something fundamental about them, maybe."

"But how do you make someone change?"

She chuckles, a husky laugh that has men throwing themselves at her feet, all of them dirtbags. "You don't. You can't."

I flop back onto the sofa cushions. "Great. Nice sentiment."

She pats my leg. "You can't force someone to change, but you can inspire them."

"And how do you do that?"

"You believe in them. Those who are willing to change, will. Those who aren't, won't."

28

"Boys" - Alfie Jukes

Walker

There is something to be said for having an entire three floors to yourself. I love Oxford, but sometimes I want to pull out my hair when Mrs. Greenwich bangs on her ceiling from below, mistaking my flat for that of my heavy-metal-playing next-door neighbor, or when the couple upstairs is having yet another go in their bed, which should be fastened to the wall.

I take my time coming downstairs, enjoying the feel of the smooth wooden banister beneath my hand and the plush carpet runner under my bare toes. I'm going to miss this house when I leave. And I'm going to miss my mum.

Our conversation on Wednesday made me question a lot of things, namely my propensity to define a person based on one action. Does a single lie make a person a liar, or an accident make a person a killer?

She's right about these things being multifaceted. Slapping labels on people because of something they've done isn't right. But neither is intentionally cheating so that your girlfriend will break up with you.

Heath and I visited the Archives on Thursday, but it was so awkward and painful that I told him I had other things I needed to do the rest of the week. We left after only two hours.

I've spent the last two days staring at the notes on my computer screen and wandering the rooms of this house, wishing for a secret passage to get my mind out of all the places it wants to wander to.

Namely, Heath.

Things have been weird between us since we had sex. Not just awkward, but tense, knotted with friction. I can't tell what he's thinking. He's put up a wall that I don't have a clue how to scale.

I end up in the library, scanning the shelves for a book enticing enough to delve into for the rest of the day. My phone buzzes in my pocket.

Lux: *BEACH DAY BITCHES!!!*

Oh boy.

The responses immediately start rolling in.

Maeve: *I'll plan an itinerary. x*

Maeve: *Which house?*

Rhett: *FUCK YES*

Pierce: *I'll check my schedule.*

Lux: *Villa Rosita! xxxx*

Maeve: *Perfect. Can everyone be ready in an hour? We can miss the noon traffic that way. x*

Rhett: *I was born ready baby*

Maeve: *Oh god.*

Rhett: *Pierce, I will drag your ass out of the city myself.*

I wait a few minutes to see if Heath will respond. The beach isn't usually my preferred way to spend a Sunday, but I had a lot of fun surfing earlier this week. Besides, it's summer, and I should be enjoying myself.

Me: *Count me in. x*

Lux: *YAY!! I thought we were going to have to strap you to the top of the* *car! xx*

Heath: *I'll be there*

My heart does a strange little dance around my chest. I send Lux a separate text.

Me: *Do you have a bathing suit I can borrow? x*

She's both taller and thinner than me, but our boobs are roughly the same size.

Lux: *I have enough suits to outfit an entire runway show, love. Of course you can borrow something!! x*

Me: *One is fine. Not planning on walking the runway any time soon.*

Lux: *All the same, I'll pick something extra special! *wink* xx*

That wink makes me nervous. I will have to steer clear of Lux and any matchmaking fantasies she tries to enact.

I'm tingling with excitement as I pack. The sunscreen slips out of my hands and onto the floor. It's been forever since we've all hung out on the beach, and I'm looking forward to it more than I would have thought possible a few weeks ago.

I grab a few G.R. Huntington books and stuff them into my bag. I can do a little research-based reading while we're there. It's like writing a vacation off on your taxes.

By the time my bag is packed, a three-page itinerary is sitting in my inbox, and Lux and Maeve show up in my driveway as I'm dragging my suitcase downstairs. I offer my car as long as I don't have to drive. Maeve says she'll do it (naturally), and Lux volunteers to play DJ, since she has the best taste in music. Her words, not mine.

"Remind me again why you didn't get the e-tron?" Maeve says as she slips into the driver's seat.

"I will never drive an electric vehicle." I shudder. "Someone could operate it remotely."

Lux and Maeve look at each other in the front seat and burst out laughing.

"God, I've missed you, Walker," Lux says as she connects her phone to the Bluetooth.

Lux's grandfather owns at least six vacation homes, several of them on the beach. The only requirement for his family members to use them? Spend an hour with the old man doing whatever he wants. It's creepy as fuck, but the perks are pretty sweet.

"What did he want this time?" Maeve asks as we pull out of the driveway.

"A game of checkers and a shoulder massage," Lux says, eyes on her phone. The choir voices at the beginning of "So Long, London" echo through the car speakers.

Maeve makes a disgusted sound. "Gross. You had to *touch* him?"

"That is typically how one gives massages, yes," Lux says.

"Is that how you got that?" I ask, pointing to a deep purple bruise near her shoulder.

Her fingers brush over it instinctively. "No, Pops isn't violent."

The car is silent for a few beats, then Maeve says, "So who is?"

Lux doesn't say anything.

"Lux?" I say.

She flashes that breathtaking smile at both of us. "No one, silly. I just happen to be exceptionally clumsy."

This is a lie. Lux is the most graceful person I know, fluttering around like a ballerina butterfly. But she clearly doesn't want to talk about whatever is going on, and I'm not about to press her.

Maeve, however, does not have the same reservations. "Is it Carter?"

Lux's head snaps sideways to glare at her. "Is *what* Carter?"

Maeve keeps her eyes on the road. "Did he give you that bruise?"

"Of course not." Lux scoffs and turns toward the window. Less than a minute later, she spins around, anger already forgotten. "Tell us everything about you and Heath."

I blink in the face of her sudden attention. "Uh," I start, "there's nothing to say?"

"No way." Maeve shakes her head, flashing me a look in the rearview mirror. "That's not going to work. We've got an entire hour ahead of us to dissect every little thing between you and Heath."

Oh god.

Kill me now.

* * *

When we pull up to Villa Rosita an hour later, I've managed to keep the details of what happened between Heath and me to myself. Lux and Maeve don't know that he cheated or that we had sex. They do know that I am struggling to determine my feelings for him.

This last piece of info was dragged out of me with the precision of a professional. Maeve should consider a career in interrogational torture.

The beach house makes the mansions back in the Hills look like dollhouses. It's a humongous three-story affair made of white stucco and wide pillars, with balconies holding potted trees in front of every window.

The front of the house is surrounded by stone pools of various sizes, all of which are filled with turquoise water and look like they've been placed there by Mother Nature herself. An arched stone bridge allows us to cross to the sprawling six-car attached garage.

The guys are already here. Pierce doesn't believe in driving in the vicinity of the speed limit when your car can go over two hundred miles an hour. Maeve, on the other hand, has an unnatural fear of being pulled over.

Our itinerary allows for several hours of relaxing before the caterer brings tonight's dinner. Everyone scatters to their assigned bedrooms (again, courtesy of Maeve) to change into beach-appropriate clothing.

Lux gave me a Christian Dior tote full of swimsuits and told me I'm welcome to wear whatever I like. I end up choosing a simple navy-blue bikini with a tiny floral print. It's alarming how well it fits my body and my style.

I look in the mirror and freeze. Maybe I should have opted for my surf suit. The strings holding this thing together suddenly seem as thin as threads.

The back of the house opens onto a huge stone terrace that juts out over the ocean. Part of it is under the roof of the house, and gauzy white curtains tied to the pillars flutter in the breeze. The terrace is as large as the main floor and holds two swimming pools, a hot tub, several gazebos, a tennis court, half a dozen umbrella-covered tables, and a handful of scattered sofas and chaise lounges.

But, beautiful as the house may be, the main attraction for everyone is the beach, which can be accessed via a set of stone steps leading from the terrace.

I descend the staircase. It twists its way down, large-leafed plants obscuring my view until I reach the bottom. The magnificent white sand and the rolling waves of the ocean stretch out like a painting.

My bag is heavy with several Huntington tomes and my sunblock, and I hitch it higher on my shoulder. There's a cluster of candy-striped umbrellas a short distance away. I move toward them, my sand-logged sandals slowing me down.

The guys are already messing around in the water, a short distance from shore. Maeve and Lux must still be inside, probably meticulously slathering on their tanning oils.

I fish my sunscreen from the bag and start applying it to my legs. I may be blessed with my mother's Spanish skin, but with how much time I spend inside, it isn't familiar with the rays of the sun. Better to be safe than sorry.

I'm applying the lotion on my shoulders when a shadow falls across me. Heath is standing on the other side of my chaise lounge.

"Need some help?" he says.

I didn't even hear him approach. "Sure," I say, before I can think better of it. I hand him the bottle.

A few torturous seconds pass as he squirts the sunblock into his hands. Then his warm fingers are on my back. He rubs in large circles, the way he has a hundred times for me before. Something about this time feels different, though. Maybe because the last conversation we had was an argument.

Or maybe because a million things have happened to us, and we're no longer the same people we were.

"All done," he says. I try not to shiver as he gives my back one final swipe. He hands the bottle back to me, and my fingers accidentally graze his. It feels even more intimate than him rubbing my back.

My eyes flit up to his, but he's wearing sunglasses, and I can't read his expression. "Thank you," I say quietly.

In the distance, Maeve calls something to the guys. Until she arrives, for these few trapped seconds, it's only Heath and me, holding onto the same sunscreen bottle and staring at each other.

"God, I would kill for a cocktail right now." Maeve dumps her bag onto the chair next to mine.

The moment is broken, and Heath releases his grip. I quickly look away and stick the bottle back into my bag. By the time I finish, he's already on his way back to the water.

"What was that?" Maeve asks. She's wearing high-waisted red gingham bottoms and a matching bandeau top. A pair of huge cat-eye sunglasses obscure her eyes.

"What?" I reach for one of the novels in my bag.

She motions between me and Heath's retreating back with a rolled-up magazine. *That.*

I recline in my chair. "Nothing."

"That was not nothing," she says.

Lux, thank god, chooses that moment to join us. "Isn't the weather *glorious*? Tell me I'm a genius for suggesting this." She dumps three totes onto the sand and spreads her arms wide. Her silk kimono opens to reveal a white bikini with braided gold straps that look like chains. Her giant floppy hat hangs so low I can't even see her face.

"You're a genius," I say.

"If only we had something to toast with." Maeve groans, forgetting the interrogation she was about to put me under.

Lux unpacks her bags. "The liquor cabinet is stocked."

"I would hope so," Maeve says. "I'm just too lazy to go in and fetch anything."

"Pierce!" Lux calls.

He's tossing a football with Rhett, classic perfection in his striped trunks and Wayfarers.

"We need booze," she calls.

He throws the ball back to Rhett and heads our way. "What are we drinking?" He stops directly beside Maeve's chair.

"Anything that will make me forget I'm outside." She swats at a bug crawling on her arm with her rolled-up magazine. "I'm getting eaten out here."

"That's because you're wearing a tablecloth," Pierce says. "They think they're at a picnic."

She whacks him with the magazine. He laughs and runs up the beach toward the house.

Maeve pulls an iPad out of her bag. "We need a real vacation," she says. "I'm thinking Rome, Golden Triangle, or Nice. Thoughts?"

"You are the only person on the planet who plans a vacation while on a vacation," Lux says. She has shut her umbrella and is lying on her back, eyes closed to the sun.

"It's not a vacation. It's a day trip," Maeve says, already distracted by something on her screen.

"I vote Rome," I say. "An air-conditioned museum sounds amazing right now."

"I was dreaming of a hot romance with a Frenchman, but Italians are sexy," Maeve muses.

My gaze travels to the water, where Heath is surfing and Rhett is doing something that I think is supposed to be body surfing, although I can't be sure. He looks an awful lot like a cat trying to skateboard.

I should read. I pull my book onto my lap, but Lux and Maeve are arguing the merits of the French and the Italians, and the sun is so bright, seeping into my pores, and Pierce comes back with our drinks, complete with little umbrellas, and it's all just so much.

I wish I could bottle up this feeling right here, the way my heart feels so full, like I've found my place in the world and don't need to wander anymore. Which is nonsense, because I've already established that Oxford is my place in the world, and if I can spend the rest of my days there, I'll be the happiest girl on earth.

So why have I never experienced this kind of bliss in Oxford, the kind that threatens to overwhelm me when I'm with these people? Even sitting here under the brutal sun with bugs flying around and sand stuck between my toes, I think I'm happier than I've been any time in the past two years.

Maybe it's not the setting that counts so much as the people beside you.

I open my book. I need to read if I want to justify this beach trip, because it feels like cheating on my research project to be here. Tuesday is the earliest I'll be able to get back into the Archives, so I should make the most of the time between now and then.

I try. I really do. But there is too much going on for the book to hold my attention. One bare chest in particular continues stealing it away.

Heath drops his board onto the sand and takes the beer Pierce is holding out to him. His skin is slick, and the sun hits all the angles of his muscles, highlighting them as he tilts his head back and drains the beer. Droplets of water glisten at the ends of his hair.

I drag my eyes back to the page in front of me, the same one I've tried to read eight times. I finally absorb enough to allow myself to flip it, but my attention is soon focused on the figure moving toward us.

He's like a god walking across the beach, the sun at his back, lighting him from behind. I hold my hand up to shield my eyes. He drops to the sand beside me and takes my other hand. My book closes and drops between my bent knees as he places something in my palm.

I bring it closer for inspection. It's a tiny clamshell tinted varying shades of purple, like coffee rings on a book. "It's beautiful," I breathe.

He grins at me, and then he's gone, just like that.

I wrap my fingers around the shell as he retreats to the water. Maeve's gaze sits heavy on me, but I ignore her and return to my book.

Heath brings me three more shells over the next hour. He used to do things like this all the time, before everything changed and he was no longer the person I knew or loved.

The guys get restless as the afternoon comes to a close. My phone buzzes from the bag beside my chair. I pull it out to find a text from Dr. Riordan, asking how my research is going. I have yet to send him my notes, partly because I'm embarrassed by how few there are, but mostly because I've forgotten.

My mind couldn't be any further from Oxford.

"Volleyball!" Rhett calls to us as he runs past our chairs to the court further up the beach.

Maeve and Lux leave their things and follow him. I open the text message to respond to my professor. The cursor blinks back at me, reminding me how difficult it is to focus on anything but this moment. It's like being in a different universe. Maybe the sun has that effect out here.

Before I can type out anything beyond an apology, Rhett returns. He bends over and tosses me across his shoulder like I'm nothing more than a small child. I laugh in surprise and toss my phone onto the chaise lounge as he bolts across the sand with me.

Heath directs a stormy look at Rhett when we arrive at the court. Everyone else is as blissed out as I am, encouraged, I'm sure, by the alcohol that's been flowing and the gummies Rhett passed around earlier. We divide into teams, and it hits me.

I *miss* them. I miss this.

Oxford is wonderful, but it doesn't have this. It will never have this again. Which means I have a choice to make: School, with all of its books and academia and security for the future. Or my friends, my life, my heart, in all of its tripped-out happiness.

The choice seems blatantly, painfully obvious.

If only it were that easy.

29

"Skin" - Rihanna

Heath

I'm going to rip that smug bastard's head off. If Rhett's grin were any bigger, his face would split in half. When he sprints across the sand with Walker flung over his shoulder, his hand on her fucking ass, I crumple the empty beer can in my hand without even remembering I'm holding it. I fling it to the side, and it hits the sand with a soft pop.

The volleyball game sucks. To no surprise, our team loses. It's hard to pay attention to the ball when Walker is standing in front of me wearing a fucking bikini that leaves little to the imagination.

Memories of her body beneath me in the Archives don't help either.

The sun is setting when we walk back to the house. Lux jumps on Pierce's back for a piggyback ride, and Maeve yells at me to quit being a superstitious twat when I avoid the cracks in the wooden steps. A sushi chef has laid out a giant buffet of at least twenty different kinds of rolls on the sprawling dining room table. We load our plates and move to the terrace to eat.

Lux moans as she pops her last piece into her mouth. "God, I'm going to die a happy girl," she says, her mouth still full.

"Why don't we do this more?" Pierce asks.

"Because there's more to life than sand and mosquitos." Maeve smacks her hand against a bug on her arm.

"You know what would make this day even more perfect?" Lux says. Without waiting for a response, she adds, "Jetting off to Singapore for dim sum." She leans her head back against her chair and closes her eyes.

"I'm down," Rhett says from the pool, where he's floating on a huge inflatable peacock. "Singaporeans are hot."

Pierce shakes his head and chucks a can of beer at him. "When are you going to grow up?"

Rhett catches it effortlessly and cracks it open. "Ready for me to take Isabella off your hands already?" He grins wolfishly as he tilts the can to his mouth.

Pierce lunges for him, knocking him off the float. They hit the water with a splash.

"Idiots," Maeve mutters. She turns to Lux. "Singapore sounds fun, as long as I'm back for the board meeting on Thursday."

Lux squeals and squirms in her chair. "It's going to be so much fun. Walker, Heath, you in?"

Walker is sitting on the other side of the table, and I've felt her gaze on me throughout the day. Hesitation dances in her eyes. She hates disappointing people, but she feels guilty about not studying.

"I have to work," I say, even though I can spend as much or little time at the surf shop as I want.

Walker's eyes dart to me before returning to Lux. "And I should study."

"Wait a minute." Lux looks at both of us in turn. "Is this so you can stay behind and hook up?"

Walker couldn't possibly look more mortified. "Definitely not," she says.

"Pooh." Lux's pout is applaudable. "I could use a juicy scandal."

Walker and I share another glance. A quiet "thank you" hides in her eyes. She wouldn't be thanking me if she knew I sent those pictures of her notebooks, after getting sick and tired of Maeve's nagging. There were only a few, so I doubt she'll be able to do much with them.

"Where's the scandal?" Rhett walks toward us, leaving a trail of water behind him. He cracks open another beer and guzzles it.

Pierce towels off his hair as he approaches. He snags the last piece of sushi from Maeve's plate and pops it into his mouth.

"Hey!" She elbows him in the gut. "I was going to eat that."

He lurches out of the way before she can slug him again.

"Who's up for a friendly little game of *Mario Kart?*" Rhett asks, hands in the air.

"No!" Maeve says, standing up. "We're watching a film tonight. It's on the itinerary."

Rhett gives her a dramatic eye roll. "No one wants to watch your boring movies, Maeve. They're not even in color."

They start arguing, Lux joins in, and Pierce acts as mediator. Then the four of them migrate to the house, leaving me and Walker alone in the silence. She makes no move to get up, so I stay in my seat.

I don't know if this was an intentional plot on their part, giving me the opportunity to siphon info from her, but I'm not thinking about that tonight. Not when I'm alone with her for the first time in days.

"Wanna take a walk?" I find myself saying.

She looks up like she's surprised to hear my voice. "Sure."

I follow her down the steps to the beach, allowing myself only two peeks at that fine ass. Okay, maybe three.

Dusk has fallen, so everything is bathed in shadows. Away from the noise of the group, the ocean becomes a presence of its own, the waves crashing onto shore, then retreating to build up again.

"It's beautiful," Walker says. "I always forget how peaceful the ocean is."

I want to ask if she's forgotten anything else, like how good we were together, but I don't.

We walk the strip of sand between the water and the rock face beneath the house in silence. This may be the thing I miss the most. Walker doesn't need words. She never has. She's one of the few people I know who doesn't feel the need to fill every moment with speech.

We turn around after half a mile to head back to the house. My pulse kicks up as we approach. I don't want this night to end. I don't want to say goodbye to her.

The stars are already out and twinkling their hellos. I drop to the sand and recline onto my back, hands behind my head. A few seconds later, she joins me.

The heat of her soft body brushes against me, even though we're not touching. We lie there for a long time, not saying anything, watching the stars. Well, she's watching the stars. I can barely concentrate on breathing, she's so distracting.

"What's your favorite sound?" She breaks the silence at last.

The crash of the ocean is amplified by the lack of other noises. It's an obvious choice, one she expects me to make. "Guess," I say.

"The ocean."

I turn my head to face her. She does the same. I let the corner of my mouth pull upward. "Nope."

She narrows her eyes. "You're lying."

"Swear to god."

She tilts her face back to the sky. I keep my eyes on her profile, that straight nose, those angular cheekbones. The bangs are new, but I like the way they add definition to her features.

"Rain?"

"No."

"Campfire?"

"Nope."

She snaps her fingers. "Coffee maker."

I chuckle quietly. "No."

She *hmphs* and bites her lip. My groin tightens. "Music?"

I shake my head.

"A train whistle?"

"No."

"Thunderstorm."

"That's yours," I say.

"It is," she says dreamily. "Best sound ever."

There's a weird pressure in my chest, like my rib cage is two sizes too small for my heart.

"City sounds," she says, turning to look at me again.

I frown.

"I didn't think so," she says, returning her gaze to the stars, "but I'm running out of ideas. Just tell me."

"You really want to know?"

She doesn't say anything right away, like she can read the warning in my words. Then she slowly turns to face me. "Yeah," she says, her voice soft.

I exhale quietly. I should've gone with the ocean when I had the chance. Carefully, as if she's a bird who could fly away from me at any second, I reach a hand toward her bare stomach. She's warm and as soft as velvet. She lets out a barely audible gasp.

"My favorite sounds," I whisper, "are the ones you make when I touch you."

Her eyes waltz drunkenly over my face as I gently stroke circles on her belly. When my fingers skim the top of her bikini bottom, the gasp switches to a soft whimper.

"That, right there," I say, leaning even closer. "All those tiny little noises you make." If I could record them for my own personal soundtrack, I would.

I let my fingers dance along the seam of her swimsuit, enjoying the way her eyes stay locked on me, like I'm solely responsible for ensuring she has everything she needs.

When her breathing switches to almost panting, I find the string on the side of her bottoms and give it a little tug. The knot comes apart in my hand. Her breath hitches as I reach to do the same on the other side.

A small moan escapes her lips as I slide my palm back across her stomach, allowing my fingers to dip below the waistband of her newly unfastened bikini. I tear my gaze from her face and let it fall on the rest of her magnificent body.

She's not curvy, but she has a softness to her edges that makes me weak at the knees. Gripping the bikini bottom in my hands, I pull it down and disentangle the strings. When it's lying in the sand between her legs, I allow myself a full view.

She looks different here in the moonlight than she did in the Archives. Luminous, radiant, like a goddess of the sea.

I run my fingers over the area that was covered by her swimsuit seconds ago. She stifles a groan as they glide over her folds without slipping inside. I long to swallow all of her sounds, but if I kiss her, I won't be able to see or hear everything this is doing to her.

I shift more fully onto my elbow, giving myself more room to explore. When heat pulses from her, I know she's wet enough. I slip one finger between those soft folds, and she arches her back and gasps. I smile and press against her clit.

She bows in half again. I imagine the amount of sand she's going to be finding in the crevices of her body. My cock goes rigid in response. I reach down and spread her thighs further apart, then slide two fingers deep inside her. She groans as I start pumping them, in and out, in and out. How anyone could not find this the most incredible sound in the world is beyond me.

My fingers are slick with her, and they make a smacking noise as they ram into her over and over. I lean down to press a kiss to her stomach. But one taste of her skin is not going to be enough.

I trail kisses down until I reach my hand. I continue thrusting my fingers in and out, adding a third, just to watch her arch that back again. I use my free hand to lift her ass. Then I lower my head between her legs and get a taste of her.

Her pussy is like honey on my tongue. She cries out as I suck her clit, my fingers sliding deeper than ever. I tilt her hips up higher, and she wraps her legs over my shoulders, giving me unadulterated access to everything I want.

She's spread so wide, and she's oozing sweet juices all over my face. I want to bury myself here and never come out. Using the hand holding her up, I circle her anal opening with my pinkie. She bucks against me. I clamp down on her with my mouth and feel her tighten around my fingers. She throws her head back and cries out as her climax rips through her.

* * *

If the others know what we were up to, they don't say anything when we get back to the house. Walker says good night to everyone, avoiding my eyes, and heads to her room. Her absence hangs in the air after she leaves.

I hang around long enough for one more drink and a game of pool with Pierce before calling it a night. On my way to bed, I pause outside Walker's door, but something keeps me from knocking. I spend the night tossing in my own sheets, haunted by the scent of her still on my hands.

The next morning, during breakfast prepared by another chef Maeve hired, we hear a banging on the front door. We exchange glances around the table, but when no one claims to be expecting a visitor, I offer to investigate.

I open the front door, revealing Carter Fitzgerald-Smythe standing outside, wearing a pink polo and suede espadrilles. His coiffed hair adds three inches to his height. I have no idea what Lux sees in the twat. He gives me a single irritated look before pushing past me and into the house. "Lux!" he calls.

"Hey." I grab his shoulder before he can take more than a few steps.

He whirls around on me. "Where is she?"

"Lux." I keep a hand on Carter. "Visitor."

She walks around the corner. "Carter? What are you doing here?"

He yanks his shoulder from my grip and grabs her wrist. After tossing another dirty look at me, he drags her into the room beside the foyer.

Everyone sticks their heads around the corner to see what's going on. "What do we know about this douchebag?" I ask.

"Not much," Maeve says. "She won't tell me anything."

Raised voices float from the room Lux is in with her boyfriend.

"I'm going to throw him out on his ass." Pierce heads toward them.

Before he can do that, Lux comes into the foyer. She gives us a half-assed smile and says, "I'm going to ride back with Carter. You guys can stay as long as you want. Just make sure to lock up when you leave."

Maeve protests, but Lux won't be swayed. She goes upstairs to pack and returns a few minutes later with her luggage. Rhett and I each grab several bags, since her prick of a boyfriend makes no move to help her.

"Talk to her," I whisper to Walker as I head for the front door.

When I get back from loading her bags into the wanker's orange McLaren, Walker gives me a hopeless look. "I tried," she says.

Lux follows Carter out the door. The rest of us exchange glances.

"That prick is going down," Pierce says.

30

"Play With Fire" - Sam Tinnesz ft. Yacht Money

Walker

The beach fucked with my head. It also fucked with my plans, but since there's little to be done about that, I focus my energy on regaining my mental clarity.

It doesn't help that I'm still worried about Lux. She responded to my texts saying everything was fine, that Carter had just been in a bad mood because he thought she was coming home the night before, but it does little to ease my anxiety.

It also doesn't help that I can't get the scene with Heath on the beach out of my head. Every time I close my eyes, he's there, moving between my thighs. Every time I open my eyes, he's there, reading that damn Huntington novel in the back room of the Archives.

I pluck my poet's blouse away from my chest. Did it get warmer in here?

I have to fix this.

"God, I can't seem to wake up." I stifle a large and very fake yawn.

Heath looks up from his book. "Want me to grab some coffee?"

I pretend to ponder this. "Do you mind?"

"Not at all." He thumps the book shut and drops it onto the chair. "I'll be right back."

There's a tiny moment when he pauses and I'm afraid he's going to kiss me, or something equally terrifying, but then he walks out the door like the thought never crossed his mind.

I now have around twenty Heath-free minutes to get as much research done as possible. I grab the three most promising books from the shelf and set them on the table. Opening my notebook to a clean page, I start scribbling as fast as I can.

I'm on my third page of notes when a quiet rap sounds on the door. Standing in the doorway is the last person I expect to see.

"Dr. Riordan!" I jump up.

He's young for a professor, midthirties maybe, but seeing him outside of his lecture hall makes him appear even younger. His thick black hair curls over his forehead just enough to give him a boyish look.

A blinding grin—white against brown skin—stretches across his face as he takes in the room. "So this is where you've been holed up."

"This is it. An entire room dedicated to G.R. Huntington."

"Wow." He pulls a volume off the shelf. "Incredible."

"What are you doing here?" I say. "I had no idea you were in Wesbourne."

He looks up and smiles, then reshelves the book. "I just arrived. When you didn't text me back, I decided to come see for myself what you are up to."

Something ticks inside me, maybe Heath's warning that Riordan's too invested in my work. I did forget to text him back on Sunday. "I've been kind of busy."

"I can see that." He walks the perimeter of the room, stopping to look at various volumes.

My face heats. I didn't mean I was busy studying, but there's no reason for him to know I've been spending as much time with my friends as I have at the Archives. "Do you have a membership here?" I ask.

"Oxford professors get honorary one-day passes." He stops right in front of me. "Can I see what you have so far?"

"Of course." I reach for my notebook. "I've mostly been reading." *And surfing. And getting even. And having sex.*

He takes a few minutes to read over my notes. "This is really good, Walker." He rests his hand on my shoulder as he looks over the last page. "I'm excited to read your dissertation."

"I still have a lot to do," I say.

He tosses my notebook back onto the table. "It's important to not overdo it." His hand slides across my back to my other shoulder, and he starts giving me a massage. "Are you enjoying yourself too? It can be easy to burn out on a project like this."

"I—" An involuntary groan slips past my lips. Something about this feels wrong, but he's my professor, for god's sake.

"You are very tight." He kneads my knots with his thumbs. "That comes from bending over a book too long."

Or from trying not to fall back in love with the guy who broke my heart.

"If you want, we can go somewhere, and I can work to relieve all of this tension," he says quietly.

Go somewhere? "I'm not sure that would be at all appropriate, Dr. Riordan." I'm hoping the use of his title will remind him of where he is and who he's with. I pull away and turn to face him. "Thank you, but I'll be fine."

His smile returns, and he leans both hands on the back of the chair I vacated when he entered. "I don't think you understand how worried I was about you, Walker. You are one of my brightest students. Talent like that shouldn't be wasted."

"I can assure you, it's not." I take a few steps backward. Where is

Heath when I need him?

"And yet, you understand that I feel it my duty to make sure." He scoots the chair under the table and takes a few measured steps in my direction.

I try to back up, but the bookcase prevents me from going any further. I step to the side instead.

"Allow me to help you." He reaches a hand toward me. "I only have your best interests at heart."

I retreat to the other side of the room. "I prefer your help from a distance, sir."

He tilts his head backward and chuckles. "You misunderstand. My help will be mutually beneficial for both of us, I assure you."

"I don't know what you're driving at, sir, but you're making me uncomfortable."

Something snaps in him. He takes several long strides toward me, the smile vanishing from his face. Before I have time to dart out of the way, he's right in front of me, his hands clamped down on my arms.

"Things will only get more uncomfortable if you don't accept my help." Spittle lands on my cheek, and I turn my face away from him. His cool fingers pull it back. "We both know how important this work is to you, hmm? And we both know how much of it is riding on my assistance."

Cold, hard dread sinks in my stomach. Is he threatening my grade?

"What do you want?" I spit out. How did I ever find this man attractive?

He gives me a placating smile, as if I'm a misbehaving child who needs to be corrected and it pains him to do it. "Nothing much. Nothing you won't enjoy giving, I'm sure," he says into my ear.

"Get away from me, you sleazebag." I shove at him. His off-white dress shirt and tie hide his considerable strength. He doesn't even budge.

"Now, Walker, it doesn't need to be like this." Garlic and onion emanate with his breath, likely from the ranch pretzels he accepted on the flight over.

"Oh yeah?" another voice says. "Then what does it need to be like?"

Before Riordan has time to react, Heath grabs him, spins him around, and punches him in the nose. Blood spews from his face and onto the front of Heath's T-shirt. Riordan doesn't even have time to draw his arm back before Heath slams his fist into his face again.

"Heath," I say. "Stop!"

He throws a glance my way, and it's long enough for Dr. Riordan to land a punch in his stomach, knocking the wind out of him.

I gasp and cover my mouth, not wanting to see this but unable to look away.

Heath rears back and socks his fist into Riordan's gut. The older man stumbles backward into a bookcase. Several books slide off the shelf.

"Stop it!" I say again, but neither of them is paying any attention to me.

Riordan feigns a blow, and Heath ducks to the side. There's a snap as Heath's fist connects with Riordan's jaw. "Don't *ever* touch her again," he growls.

Dr. Riordan slumps backward over the table. At first I'm worried Heath has knocked him out, but eventually he stirs and groans, clamping a hand to his face.

The security guard chooses that moment to enter. He takes one look at the three of us and jerks his thumb over his shoulder. "Out. All of you."

"But I need to—" I start.

"Ma'am, you're going to have to leave."

"Please. I wasn't even involved," I say.

He shakes his head and motions to the door once more. "Out. Now."

I squeeze my eyes shut for two seconds, then turn to the table for my notebook.

The security guard hauls Dr. Riordan to his feet and ushers him to the door. "You two," he says to Heath and me. "Get your things, and let's go."

We follow him from the room. He takes all of our names, and I understand belatedly that it's to ban us from reentering.

"Please, sir," I say. "I need access for my research. I promise—"

"I'm afraid the rules are the rules." His stoic look doesn't change. "You won't be able to come back for a whole year."

"You don't understand—"

"Walker, let's go." Heath leads me through the front door by the arm.

I jerk away from him once we're outside. "This is your fault!"

He looks at me like I'm crazy. "I just saved your ass from that predator, and you wanna talk to me about whose fault this is?"

"I had it handled," I snap.

He blinks and crosses his arms over his chest, then looks down at me and laughs. "You had it *handled*?"

"Yes," I hiss.

"He had his hands on you. What do you think would have happened if I hadn't come back when I did?"

"I don't know," I say, crossing my own arms, "but we'll never find out because *I can't get back in there.*"

"Unbelievable." He turns away and shakes his head at the sky, like the answers to my absurdity lie up there. "Don't you carry pepper spray or something?"

"I had no reason to think I'd need it. He's my professor!"

"I warned you he was bad news." Heath steps closer as a man in a tweed suit walks past us. The guy throws a wary glance in our direction, as if we're wild animals who can't be trusted to behave properly when released.

"Congratulations. You were right," I say. "I'm not giving you a trophy. You had us thrown out!"

"That was an unexpected consequence." He runs his fingers through his hair.

"One that you might have considered had you stopped to think before slamming your fist into the guy. How the hell am I supposed to finish my research now?"

"We'll think of something, okay? I promise." He reaches for me, but I step away. "I'm sorry. I didn't think about what would happen. I was focused on getting him away from you."

"You cost me a lot more than he did." I stare at a pair of turtledoves on the pavement picking at a hamburger wrapper. "Did you know he's married? Dr. Riordan?" I squint up at Heath. "Do you think there are any men left in the world who don't cheat?"

This has the effect I hoped for. He pinches the bridge of his nose and mumbles something under his breath that sounds like "For fuck's sake."

"This couldn't have been an isolated incident," I say. "I wonder how long he's been preying on students."

Heath kicks at a loose pebble on the pavement. "We need to report him."

"*We* are not doing anything together."

"Hey." He stretches his hand toward my face. "Don't shut me out now."

I jerk away like he's burned me. "Don't touch me."

His face crumples as if he'd been expecting something different. Did he think I would just put this behind me after he cost me my research project? "Walker, please," he says quietly. "I want to help."

"I've seen what your help looks like," I say, "and I'm not interested."

I head in the direction of my parked car, glad I turned down his offer of a ride this morning, not because I would've ridden back with him, but because it packs less of a punch when you walk away to stand at the curb and wait for your Uber.

I should be grateful for Heath's help. He did keep Riordan from doing anything worse. But his impulsiveness ruined everything.

31

"One Way or Another" - Blondie

Heath

Since beating up Walker's professor, I've thought of around a thousand different ways I could have handled the situation besides the way I did—not that any of that helps me now.

I rummage around in the garage until I find my skateboard behind a moving carton labeled "Cami's Stuff - Hands Off!" in thick black Sharpie. She really is moving out.

Board in the back of my car, I head to the skate park. The waves are too choppy to surf safely, and I need a way to clear my head. Wide gray clouds stretch their way across the sky, hanging low like they'll dump rain any minute.

I rub my right hand over my fist on the steering wheel. My knuckles are swollen and bleeding. I didn't think a guy who sits behind a desk all day would be so hard to knock down.

I can still smell the bay rum he was wearing, the fucking bastard. It can't be the same five-hundred-dollar cologne my dad wears, but it smells just like it, that sickly Caribbean scent that makes me want to hurl.

I should've knocked him out just for that.

The skate park is empty when I pull up. The impending rain has scared everyone off. Before I can think better of it, I pull out my phone and send a text to Walker.

Hey, I'm really sorry for what happened earlier. If there's any way I can make it up to you, please let me know. xx

Then I unload my board from the trunk and head to the half-pipe. Better to do something with my hands than to sit in the car and stew over everything that went wrong.

Skating doesn't have the effect I hoped for. My brain can't shut out all the things grappling for my attention. I wipe out three times before deciding I've had enough.

The sky opens, and rain pours from the clouds. I'm drenched within seconds. Hauling my board back to the car, I toss it in the backseat. While I wait it out, I check my phone for any new messages. Knowing Walker won't have texted me back doesn't keep me from hoping.

She hasn't, of course, but there is one from Maeve in the group chat that doesn't include Walker.

Maeve: *Heath, status update on the Walker situation?*

I laugh out loud at the coincidence of her text, my heart lurching with the reminder of what I'm supposed to be doing.

Me: *I had her thrown out of the Archives*

It takes several minutes for a reply.

Maeve: *You did what?*

Rhett: *Ouch mate! #score*

Lux: *Whoa Heath. What happened? Rhett, don't use hashtags like that. Ever x*

Me: *Her professor showed up and tried to make a move on her and I punched him in the face*

Rhett: *#DUDE #what #a #ledge*

Maeve: *You realize this complicates things, right?*

No, Maeve. I had no fucking clue.

Me: *Yep*

Maeve: *I'm working with what you've sent me so far, but I'm going to need more. Can you send me her most recent notes? x*

Me: *She doesn't want to see me*

Maeve: *Why the F not?*

Me: *Because I beat up Dr. Wonderful and got us kicked out*

Lux: *She got mad at you for protecting her?*

Me: *Yep*

Bubbles appear next to Maeve's name, then disappear, only to return again a few seconds later.

Maeve: *Just so we're clear, you need to get back into her good graces. The game isn't over yet.*

Me: *I know. I just don't have a plan yet*

Maeve: *Well, figure it out. And do it soon. I need to get this paper sent in before she leaves. x*

I toss my phone onto the seat beside me and start the car. Easy for Maeve to say. Not all of us are devilish geniuses with how-to manuals for wrecking everyone in our back pockets.

My stomach rolls at the thought of deliberately sabotaging Walker. Doing it accidentally was bad enough, but to try to get her in trouble with the university?

I don't even know what I want anymore. Walker would be off-limits, even if she did want to talk to me. I don't want to take her down, even if she left without telling anyone.

What does Maeve expect me to do? Walker doesn't want to see me. We're both banned from the Archives. Accessing her notes and helping her with her research will be as easy as robbing a bank.

And like that, I have a plan.

32

"Crazy in Love" - Sofia Karlberg

Walker

I hate the internet. No matter how credible a source seems, there's never any definitive way to verify the information, not unless you also have the book they are referencing. And I don't plan to be in Wesbourne long enough to have several dozen books shipped to me just so I can double-check the info.

I should be on a plane to Oxford, but the last thing I want to think about is packing up and heading back. This manor is cozy, especially with the rain the past two days, and I'm not that eager to return to Mrs. Greenwich and her five cats.

I hunch over my laptop and try to gain as much information online as I can. I've enacted security measures to keep anyone from tracking me. The threat of internet and government stalking is real, but I'm not going to become one of their victims.

I have a lot of studying to make up for, and I can't afford to be distracted by poker nights and beaches and revenge plots and Heath bloody Lawrence. My phone is safely ensconced in my bedroom so that I won't be tempted to pull up his sparse Instagram profile and scroll through a handful of pictures of him with his surfboard, abs on display and ready for my next fantasy.

The search for information on G.R. Huntington's childhood has been a dead end. Everything online is a regurgitation of the same facts. What I need is that obscure biography from the Archives that I didn't have a chance to finish before we got thrown out. I search eBay for another copy, but the only one available is in Australia. I go ahead and order it, but it will take two to three weeks to arrive at my Oxford flat.

I push back from the table in frustration. This is useless. I can circle the same sites over and over, but they're never going to tell me anything I don't already know.

Why the bloody hell did Heath have to punch Riordan and get us banned?

I had one mission in coming here: complete my research. Instead I got roped into one revenge plot after another, taking last-minute trips to the beach and fucking *Paris*, and spending valuable time playing poker when I should have been studying.

This is what happens when you take your eyes off the prize.

I head upstairs to pack my bags. There is no reason to stay in Wesbourne a minute longer. I will book a ticket on the first flight out of here.

I'm nearly to the top of the stairs when a faint buzz echoes through the house. I push the breath from my lungs and walk back down to the first floor. Whoever it is can be sent away.

I open the door to find a sopping wet Heath on the other side. His long hair is sending rivulets of water down his face. His shirt is barely buttoned—as usual—and the rain has plastered it to his chest. I move to close the door again, but he stops it with his hand.

"Walker, please. I have something for you."

I raise a brow at his empty hands.

"It's in the car. I didn't want to get it wet," he says.

I cross my arms over my chest, wishing I'd worn something besides the tiny shorts peeking out from beneath my sweatshirt.

"If I go get it, will you please not close the door on me?"

I study him for a few more seconds. His face is earnest, like a puppy's, his eyes wide and hopeful. Irritation at my weakness for him rises.

"Please leave," I say.

"Walker, I promise you, you will want what I brought." He holds up a finger. "I'll be right back." He darts back into the rain like he fully expects me to stand here waiting for him.

I'm about to step back inside, but he's piqued my curiosity. Without making the decision to, I'm still holding the door when he returns with a big box in his hands.

"Can I—" He nods at the doorway.

I scoot backward so he can come inside, already kicking myself for letting things progress this far. How can I throw him out now, and in the rain, no less?

He sets the box down on the foyer floor. Kneeling beside it, he opens the flaps, then leans back so I can see the contents. I come a little closer and stare at the books.

"I hope I got the right ones." He rocks back on his heels. "If not, I can go back."

I drop to my knees next to the box and lift out the top volume. It's the biography I just ordered from eBay. I set it down beside me and reach into the box again.

I recognize the next one too. I made copious notes from it before we got thrown out on Tuesday. The rest of the box holds more books on Huntington.

"Did you . . . *rob* the Archives?"

Several beats pass as Heath studies me, like he's trying to decide how to answer. "Tell me you're not going to get mad about that too."

"That depends," I say as I pull out another biography, "on whether you got caught or not."

"I went through the window last night. No one saw me."

I grab the towering stack of books before it can topple over. "What are you waiting for? Help me bring these in."

We move his loot to the large trestle table in the library. There are over twenty books here. I wipe dust from one of the covers with my hand. "I can't believe you smuggled all of these out."

"Yeah, that part was a little harder than I anticipated."

I keep my eyes on the volume beneath my palm while I gather the courage to say what I need to. "Thank you." It comes out hushed.

Heath is staring at me as if he wants to say something but can't form the words.

"I didn't know what I was going to do." I need to fill the silence between us.

He steps closer to the table, only a handbreadth away from me now. My body pulses with the desire to touch him, forbidden fruit that he is.

"If I say I'm sorry, will you believe me?" he asks.

"For what?"

His breath leaves him in a rush. "Everything."

I'm not sure how to tell him what he wants to hear. "I know you didn't mean to get us kicked out."

"That's not what I asked." He reaches out to touch a strand of hair that has strayed from the messy bun on top of my head.

A tightness hitches in my chest, making each breath twice as difficult as usual. The sound of the rain on the window fills the room, creating the effect of being underwater, the rest of the world blocked from sight and sound.

"I don't know what you want me to say," I whisper.

His fingers skim over my jawbone, a freight train across my nerves. "I want you to believe I would never do that again."

I swallow, but the lump in my throat is here to stay. "Punch someone?" My voice hikes upward.

"Cheat on you." He punctuates his words by inching his fingers past my hairline and into the roots of my hair. Goosebumps break out across my skin.

I open my mouth, intending to answer him, but he reaches out a tentative thumb to touch my bottom lip, and all thoughts flee my mind. He gently draws it downward, and I tremble as the saltiness of his skin hits my tongue.

"Walker." His voice is raspy, and it grates along my sensitive nerves like nails along my spine. My eyes flutter shut. There's too much of him. I should resist, but I'm tired of fighting so hard against what I want.

He turns us so I'm pressed up against the table, and then his mouth is on mine. His thumb is still on my chin. He uses it to pry my mouth open further for deeper access. I moan as he rediscovers every inch, hungry like it's been a century since he's had a taste of me.

He arches me over the table until I'm afraid my spine will snap from the pressure. Then, with a suddenness that steals my breath away, he pulls back and drags me by the hand to the sofa. I let him lead me, hardly able to keep my feet pointed in the right direction, let alone direct my thoughts into any semblance of order.

He pushes me onto the cushions, and I land on my back with a quiet thump. The leather is soft beneath my hands. I scramble backward as he crawls over me. I can't stop the slow grin that spreads across my face.

"What?" He stops directly above me.

"Nothing." My smile grows.

He narrows his eyes and growls, then tugs me further down by my waistband. "Fucking shorts," he mutters. "Nothing but a tease."

My breath catches as he shoves a hand up the front of them from the bottom, his calloused palm rough against the skin of my thigh. His fingers wrap around my hip and sink into the soft flesh there. "I nearly ripped that wanker's head off when I saw him put his hands on you," he says.

I shiver at the molten look in his eyes.

He notices, and an evil grin crosses his face. "What would you have done if I hadn't come over today? Dusted off your vibrator?" He runs the tips of his fingers inside the top of my panty line.

I buck against him, eager for more.

"Patience," he murmurs, and leans down to press his lips against the skin he exposed by rolling my shorts down an inch. A moan escapes me as his warm breath heats me to boiling. With his other hand, he slides a finger inside the crotch of my shorts and panties, running it back and forth until I'm sensitive enough to burst.

In a move characteristic of his short attention span, he pulls away from my waist and pushes up my sweatshirt. Too late, I remember I'm not wearing a bra. A stifled groan slips past his lips when he sees my bare chest. "Fuck."

He leans down and takes my breast into his mouth. I suck in a breath when his teeth close around it. A bright flash of pain later, he draws back and stares at his handiwork. "That will leave a mark. When it does, I want you to remember that no one touches you but me. Got it?"

Chills race each other down my spine as I meet his gaze. I nod.

"I want to hear you say it."

"I'm yours," I whisper. Then I reach up and tug his head down to mine. He falls onto me with a grunt, and the air rushes from my lungs.

He reaches between us and unbuttons my shorts. A few seconds later, he yanks them off and tosses them across the room. My panties follow. When his fingers find their way inside me, I try to arch my hips, but the weight of him pins me to the sofa. He chuckles against my mouth when he realizes I can't move.

"What do you want, baby? You have to tell me." His voice is sandpaper against my heightened nerves.

"I want you." I try desperately to find friction against him.

"I can't give you what you want unless you tell me," he murmurs against my neck.

"Please," I beg.

"Tell me."

"I want you as deep as you can go."

He mutters "fuck" and fishes a condom from his pocket. "What else?"

Words flee my mind as he rolls it on. When he's ready and poised over me, I brace myself, but he's not going to give me anything else until I tell him exactly what I want.

"Hard," I say around a whimper.

A low growl emanates from his chest. "What else, baby? Fast? Or slow?"

I take a few seconds to consider. "Slow."

He groans as his eyes roll back in his head. "Fuck." He drags the word out like I've asked him to deliver the moon. Then his eyes snap back to mine with an intensity that makes me swallow.

With a slowness that makes me ache to scream, he eases into me, taking me inch by inch, like it's a competition to see how long he can drag it out.

"Okay, maybe not that slow," I say through clenched teeth.

A gasping laugh bursts out of him. He picks up the speed by a fraction. "My god," he says once he's fully inside. "This will never get old."

He pulls back out with excruciating languidness. It takes an eternity for him to thrust back in, but when he does, sparks ignite behind my eyelids. A cry slips out of my mouth. He repeats the movement, and this time I'm sure I'm going to expire before ever reaching climax.

After half a dozen more thrusts like that, I say, "Please, Heath. I need more."

He makes a low noise against my neck, then wraps my legs around his hips. He drives into me with a ferocity that sends me bumping into the arm of the sofa. He yanks me further down and does it again. We find a natural rhythm, our bodies slapping together like a symphony.

As the pressure inside me builds and my climax hovers on the horizon, I have a sudden moment of clarity, where I see the truth for what it is.

It doesn't matter that I've spent the past two years hiding from him or the pain he's caused me.

Nothing has changed.

I'm as in love with Heath as I ever was.

33

"If You Love Her" - Forest Blakk

Heath

It's still raining when I wake up. One of those old canopies hangs above us, the curtains creating a cozy cocoon around the bed. The room is dark except for a few candles flickering on a dresser across the room.

Walker stirs on my chest. When she tilts her face up to me, I lean down and brush my lips across hers. She smiles through the kiss, and I pull back. Her hand traces the ridges of my stomach, causing goosebumps to prickle along my skin.

I've lost track of how long we've been here. We must have left the library hours ago, only to fall into bed and start again. She's always had this effect on me. When I'm with her, the world halts on its axis long enough for her to become the only thing in my universe.

I capture her hand with my own, braiding our fingers together. I lift them to my lips and press a kiss to the back of her hand. She inclines her head, and I already want to lose myself in the fragrance of that coconut-scented hair again.

I stroke her wrist with my thumb, her skin puckering beneath my touch. "Why did you have it removed?" I say quietly.

Sadness flickers in her eyes. "It hurt too much to look at it."

I move my arm so that my wrist is visible. Half of the Big Dipper is sprinkled across the skin there. She slips her fingers from mine and traces over the black ink. I long to know what thoughts are swirling through that brilliant mind of hers, but she doesn't say anything else.

"Remember when we got them?" I ask.

"Mmm," she murmurs into my chest.

"You were terrified," I say.

"I hate needles."

She only managed to get through the whole thing because I held her face between my hands and talked about anything I could think of. "I plied you with Bart Simpson jokes." I laugh at the memory.

She smiles against my skin. "You are a ridiculous human being."

"Do you . . . regret it?"

"The tattoo?" she says. When I don't answer, she tilts her head back to look at me. "You mean us?"

I wince, wishing I could take the question back. Now that it's out there, I don't really want to know the answer.

She slides her hand up my chest until it rests on the side of my neck. "Sometimes."

I close my eyes. I deserve it, fucking bastard that I am. But hearing her say that she regrets being with me, that she looks at our past and wishes it gone, sends a guttural pain through me. "That's fair."

"Not all of it though," she says. "The days I spent with you were the best days of my life."

I picture us dancing at the Gentleman's Ball, blissed out and happy at eighteen.

Or shopping at the farmer's market after deciding we had what it took to be world-class chefs. That night ended in the fulfillment of several strawberry-fueled sex fantasies we shared.

Witnessing the awe spread over her face when I took her to the

Abbey Library in Switzerland.

My stomach dipping every time she laughed at something Lux or Rhett said.

Feeling her pulse quicken when I skimmed my fingers across her collarbone.

Her running across the sand to throw herself into my arms.

"We had some good times," I say.

"The best times."

Focusing on this for too long isn't going to lead anywhere good. I search for a subject that doesn't venture into too-delicate territory. "How long before Pierce and Maeve hook up?"

She laughs, and my stomach does that familiar little drop at the sound of it. "Never."

"You don't think so?"

"They're too much alike. Besides, Maeve is nothing like the Ellas."

Pierce has a tendency to date the same make of girlfriend, with only slight variations to the model. I've lost track of all of them over the years, but I do know that they're always blonde, always leggy, and if you blow in their ear, they'll thank you for the refill. Strangely, they're always named something that ends in "ella." Stella, Bella, Isabella.

"The guy knows what he wants," I say.

"Considering his lack of success in any relationship, I'd venture to disagree."

"What about Rhett and the Princess Royal?"

Walker snorts. "That will never happen."

"Why not?"

"You think the queen is going to let her marry someone like Rhett?"

"True." Adding Rhett to the royal family would be like adding a lit match to a barrel of whiskey. I fight the urge to purr as Walker strokes her hand lightly across my stomach. "What do you like about Oxford so much?" I say to distract myself.

Her fingers pause before continuing their leisurely stroll across my skin. "The books. The quiet. The smell." A dreamy quality has taken over her voice. "Everyone's dedication to learning."

My throat tightens as I listen. Everything she's describing sounds torturous. I spent four years there, and I would rather slice off all of my toes than return. There's not enough air, not enough ocean. But it has one thing Wesbourne doesn't.

"Maybe I can go back," I find myself saying.

Her whole hand goes slack against my stomach. She cranes her head, letting me into that dark gaze. "To Oxford?"

I lift one corner of my mouth. It's a ridiculous idea, but I'm ready to be ridiculous for her.

She pushes herself up on her elbow. Her hair falls over her shoulder, hiding her face. I reach out and tuck it behind her ear.

"You hated it there," she says.

I nod, because there's no sense in denying it. The four years I spent at St. Hilda's were tolerable only because the six of us were in the same city together. "It's not my favorite place in the world. But if you're there—"

Her face crumples, and she drops my gaze. "You would be miserable there. You know you would."

"I could—"

"The ocean is over an hour away." She shakes her head. "You'd never survive."

"I just want to be with you."

Her eyes flicker up to mine again, and there's so much sadness in them that a physical ache grows in my gut. "We'll think of something," she says.

I tighten my hold on her hip. "I can't stand it if you leave again." My voice is hushed, but the words need to be said. The first time nearly destroyed me. I was the one who drove her away, and that knowledge made it ten times worse.

She draws lazy circles around my belly button. "Do you ever think about joining your uncle in Australia?"

The question takes me by surprise. I haven't thought of Declan in a while, definitely not since Walker's been back in town. "Not recently, why?" Where is she going with this?

She shrugs, fingers still tracing my stomach. "It sounds like you."

I'm not sure what this means, if she's saying moving halfway around the world sounds like something I would do or that Australia sounds like a place I'd like to live. "Declan's great, but—" The man was like a father to me, teaching me to surf when I had nothing else to live for.

She waits, biting that full bottom lip of hers. My cock stirs at the sight.

"Why the fuck would I be thinking about Australia when I can't think of anything but you?"

That lip trembles, and I long to sweep it up, kiss it until it's twice the size it is now.

"My research is practically done, Heath."

"I know." I've avoided dwelling on it, but only because living in denial seemed like the only path to survival. Now it looms large in front of me, demanding my full attention. "I know," I say again.

"Maybe I could stay?" she says, like she's offering a sacrifice.

I shake my head, like she did when the roles were reversed. "I can't let you give up your dream for me."

She sinks her head back onto my chest, her fingers still at last. We stay like that for several minutes. A tiny bead of moisture drops onto my skin, and I tug her up to me. Her eyelashes are damp.

"Don't cry." I use my thumb to wipe the tear from the corner of her eye. "We'll figure this out."

Walker sniffs loudly. "I don't even know what I want. Being with you is great—it's always been great. But there's a voice in my head telling me I'm only going to get hurt again, that I should protect myself while I still can. But then I look at you, and I know that the only place I'll ever be truly happy is where you are, and it just sucks all of the breath out of my lungs." She takes one shuddering inhale. "I can't breathe, Heath."

Her words fill me like helium and pop the balloon at the same time. She still thinks I'll hurt her. She's still not sure she can trust me.

"Listen to me." I cradle her face in my palm. "If there's one thing you can trust, it's that I won't hurt you again. I swear it."

She squeezes her eyes shut and nods against my hand. A single tear dribbles its way down her face. I catch it with my thumb, then drop my head and capture her lips. They're soft and wet and warm. Blood surges to my dick, but I keep the kiss sweet and gentle.

Several seconds later, she pulls back, her mouth glistening with moisture from mine. "I love you," she whispers, "against my better judgment."

I could do without that last bit, but I'll take it. "I love you too. And I promise we will figure this out, okay?"

I don't know how, but I'll find a way, even if it kills me.

34

"Feel Me Now" - If Not For Me

Walker

Heath's in the shower, and—much as I want to join him—I would be smart to use this time to get more research done. Once he's out, all bets are off.

We spent most of yesterday in bed. I should be satiated, but my hunger only grows every time that lazy smile trips across his face. It's dangerous, this game we're playing, but I'd like to be an ostrich and bury my head in the sand.

It can't last, whatever this is. But I'm stupid or crazy enough to think that maybe there is a way through, one where we end up together and happy and ridiculously in love instead of bitter and angry and separated by pain and hurt and resentment so deep it'll suck us down if we pause for breath.

I fasten one more button on his shirt, which I snagged from the floor. I don't have anything on underneath it, but I won't be wearing it for long. I should be able to take half a page of notes while I wait for him to finish his shower.

If we can stay out of bed long enough, I may be able to convince him to go out tonight. We subsisted solely on takeaway and the puny

233

contents of my fridge yesterday. I'm ready for civilization again.

I open my laptop and fire it up. Outside, the rain from yesterday has switched to thunderstorms. A loud crack shakes the house. On second thought, maybe staying inside is a good idea.

The welcome screen lights up, and I type in my password. Besides me, Heath's phone pings with an incoming text message. I glance at the screen out of habit and see Maeve's name.

I swipe to unlock the phone. We really need to have a conversation about his lack of security. The guy is way too trusting.

Maeve's text is at the bottom of the screen. *Is it done yet???*

I wrinkle my brow, trying to figure out what she means. Maybe she's asked him to fix something for her?

As I set Heath's phone aside and open the notes file on my laptop, it goes off twice more. *Damn it, Maeve.* At this rate, I won't get anything done before he's out of the shower. I unlock the phone again to put it on silent, but Lux's name on the display takes me by surprise.

I click on it, and the screen fills with a group chat. There are new messages from both Maeve and Lux at the bottom.

Maeve: *Celebration tonight if Heath comes through! X*

Lux: *Yesss! I'm beyond ready to get absolutely hammered!!! xx*

What are they expecting Heath to come through on? And why didn't my own phone buzz with the notification? I grab it from the nightstand and enter my passcode. There's a text from my mum, but nothing else. I open our group thread. No new messages today.

They must have a thread I'm not part of. I double-check Heath's phone, and sure enough, everyone is in the chat except for me. It stings a little, but I *was* gone for two years. It's perfectly natural for it to be awkward to go back to what we had before.

The others don't know why I left. They have no idea Heath cheated on me, and I prefer to keep it that way. It's easier to wash your hands of a situation than to try to convince people to take sides. If they'd known, they might have been willing to get back at Heath with me, but my desire for revenge dried up the minute I left Wesbourne soil.

That's how I knew I made the right decision.

I'm still in the message thread on Heath's phone when it pings again. This time it's a text from Rhett.

Has she forgiven you yet mate?

My blood chills in my veins. There's no question that the "she" he's referring to is me, unless Heath is out there making plenty of girls angry. What's confusing is that they know I was mad at him. Maybe he told them what happened at the Archives, although using a thread that excludes me seems a little eighth grade.

It's stupid, but my thumb disregards that fact and starts scrolling backward anyway. I want to know what he told them, and then I'll put it away. The last messages are from a few days ago. I scroll until I find the most recent one Heath sent.

I know. I just don't have a plan yet.

I scroll back further. A new conversation started on Tuesday, the day we got kicked out of the Archives. I read the whole thing.

My heart skids to a stop at Maeve's words.

I need to get this paper sent in before she leaves. x

The phone drops from my hand onto the vintage rug under my feet. I reach behind me for the chair before my legs give out. The room spins as I lower myself to the seat.

Life should come with a warning label: *Prepare to be fucked over every time you venture to trust.*

Thunder claps outside, and I jump. My blood is pounding so loud, I'm surprised I can hear anything over the mad dash through my veins.

I am the mark.

I am the target.

They are all in on this together, plotting to take me down like one of the many victims we've preyed on over the years. They've lumped me in with the likes of Jenny Bailiff, who once sold a picture of Rhett doing a line of coke to the tabloids. Or that douchebag Maeve dated, who filmed her drunk-dancing while naked, then sent the video to all of his friends—one of whom was Pierce.

And Heath—Heath, who assured me less than twenty-four hours ago that he would never hurt me again. Never betray my trust. Never again give me cause to doubt myself.

He was the inside man.

Fuck him.

Fuck them all.

I reach down and pick up his phone, then hurl it across the room as he appears in the doorway. He jerks backward as it hits the side of the door with a sharp crack. A splinter of wood follows it to the floor.

Heath gives me a wary look before bending over to retrieve the phone, which doesn't look any worse for wear. He's wearing nothing but a white cotton towel. Normally it would take everything in me to keep from ripping it off him, but right now the only thing I'm aware of is the bleeding heart in my chest.

"Hey," he says. "Everything okay?"

I gape at him. "How can you possibly ask me that?"

His brows furrow, deep lines forming on his forehead. Another ping sounds from his phone, and whatever he sees there turns his face ashen. "Walker." He lifts his gaze. "I can explain."

A high-pitched laugh bursts from my mouth. "Explain? You think I give a damn about your explanations?"

He reaches out for me, even though we're separated by the entire room. "Please. Just hear me out."

"I'd prefer you never speak to me again."

"I wasn't going to do it." He tosses the phone onto the bed and starts moving toward me.

I hold up both hands. "Don't come any closer."

To his credit, he stops, but the look on his face is enough to make me want to scream and throw things at his head. How dare he look hurt and miserable? *I* wasn't plotting *his* takedown!

"I'll admit," he says, "at first they convinced me to go along with it. But when it came down to it, I couldn't let Maeve go through with it. Not when I feel this way about you."

"You gave her my notes."

"That was over a week ago. You have to believe me, Walker."

I give another sharp laugh. "I don't have to do anything. And trust me, the last thing I'll ever do again is believe you."

"I wouldn't have let them send it. Believe that, at least."

I cross my arms over my chest, as if trying to keep my heart from crashing right through my rib cage and bouncing across the floor like a rubber ball set loose. "Get out." It's nothing more than a whisper.

Heath's face pinches with pain. "I still love you." Desperation saturates every word.

"When you love someone, you don't stick a knife in their back every time they turn around."

"That's not what I—"

"That is exactly what you did," I scream, running across the room and smacking my hands against his chest. "You gained my trust, just so you could use it against me!"

His fingers clamp around my wrists like they're nothing more than twigs. I immediately regret my decision to touch him. "No, Walker, listen."

"Have they hated me this whole time?" I ask before he can get out whatever it is he wants to say. "Were they plotting revenge on me the whole time I was gone?" I can't help the keening tone that creeps into my voice. I sound weak and insecure, because I am.

"No." He shakes his head. "Maybe." A deep inhale inflates his chest, and he sighs heavily. His breath brushes across my face. "I don't know."

"What were they going to do with my notes?" I brace myself for the answer.

"Maeve was going to submit an AI-generated dissertation on your behalf."

Breath lunges from my lungs. God, she's an evil genius.

"Walker, I'm sorry."

"You knew why I left, didn't you? You knew it was because of what you did." The image of that skank on top of him fills my mind. Her tits slapping together on her bare chest, the sound of their grunts as she rode him harder and harder. I squeeze my eyes shut. Vomit lingers at the back of my throat.

"I was suspicious, yeah."

I tear my hands away from him and retreat to the safety of the other side of the room. Away from his heat, his scent, his solid body. "And yet you let them believe I was the guilty one."

His face contorts with anguish. He skirts his tongue back and forth along his bottom lip. "Yeah."

"Your father was right after all, wasn't he? You're not a man," I spit out. "You're a coward."

I try to relish the devastation that crosses his face, the satisfaction of my words finding their mark, but instead I feel empty inside, like a pumpkin that's been hollowed out for Halloween.

He runs his hand through his wet hair, pushing it off his forehead. With the other, he pinches the bridge of his nose. I can't be sure because of the distance, but his eyes look damp.

"Please go." My voice cracks like a porcelain vase that's been set down too hard, an ugly, jagged line racing up the side. "I need you to go."

This time he doesn't protest. He picks up his shorts from the bed, and since I'm still wearing his stupid shirt, he walks out without it. I don't want it any more than I want a root canal, but I'm not about to take it off in front of him.

The front door closes, and I trip over my feet trying to get to the window. I arrive in time to see him open his car door and climb inside, shirtless in the rain that's still beating down. The downpour is a solid sheet between us. I can't tell if he looks up at me. His taillights glow red as he pulls out of the driveway.

I sink to the floor, my feet boycotting standing any longer. My eyes alight on the potted plant I bought at the same time as my candles. Brown leaves curl around its central stem. I couldn't even keep it alive for four weeks.

Was everything a lie, then? Every laugh, every story, every joke, every smile? I've spent a considerable amount of time with all five of them over the past month, and not once did it occur to me that they may be faking their forgiveness.

Maybe our friendship was meant to die two years ago, when I walked onto that tarmac and didn't look back.

I rise to my feet and stagger across the room. The plant isn't heavy, and something about the weight of it feels good in my arms. I trek downstairs, clutching it to my chest like a prize trophy. When I reach the kitchen, I open the back door to where the rubbish bin is. I dump the plant inside it, pot and all, and it lands with a satisfying clunk atop all of the takeaway containers Heath and I threw out. By the time I slip back inside the warm kitchen, I'm drenched. Puddles form on the floor beneath me, but I don't care.

I was wrong when I said people can't change, that the choices you make define you for the rest of your life. People can change. They can learn and grow and become something different entirely. That's the beauty of the human race.

That's also the ugliness of it.

Because while some of us work to improve—to become better, truer versions of ourselves—others simply continue rotting, until they're only faint shadows of who they used to be.

35

"I Think I'm Okay" - Machine Gun Kelly

Heath

I've never been one to sit around and wallow in pain. It's not my style. Why dwell on it when you know it will only make you feel like shit? I prefer drowning the pain, and I'm not picky about the method.

Or the flavor.

I toss back my fourth shot of whiskey. It burns going down and has a particular pungent taste that tells me this was a bad batch. Good thing I'm too wasted emotionally to give a damn.

"Maybe you should slow down, mate." Pierce claps me on the shoulder.

I shrug him off and motion to the bartender for another. "I'm fine."

"If he wants to get pissed tonight, let him," Rhett says from my other side. "He deserves it."

I hold my refilled glass up in agreement and clink it against his before throwing it back.

"You want to tell us what happened?" Pierce says. "With Walker?"

I slam the glass back onto the bar. The only thing they know is that she and I had a falling out. It's easy to read between the lines, but I have no desire or intention of clearing up any misconceptions tonight.

"No," I say.

Never before has my heart shattered the way it did when she threw me out. I deserved it. The evidence on my phone is proof of that. If anybody else did that to her, I'd rip their fucking throat right out of their body.

But knowing I had it coming and wanting it to happen are two different things. She deserves so much better than me, but I can't stand the thought of her being with anyone else.

She *belongs* with me. Anyone with eyes in their head can see that.

It takes a fucker like me to fuck up something that good.

I wave at the bartender, but he gives me a wary look that suggests he thinks I may have reached my limit. Little does he know, my limit tonight is passed out on the floor. I still have a long ways to go before that happens.

"Let's blow this joint." I climb off the barstool, and the room sways.

"Careful, mate." Pierce grabs my arm before I can take a nosedive to the floor.

I stagger to the door. The fresh air helps clear my head, and while that means I can once again make out the cracks in the pavement *and* step over them, it also means I'm reminded of how shitty I feel. From the way he's steering me toward his car, I can tell Pierce plans to take me home and tuck me into bed like I'm a fucking child who needs to be coddled. But I'm not cutting the night short.

Loud music spills out of another club halfway down the block. I lurch toward it, forcing Pierce and Rhett to follow. The doorman gives me a pointed look when we approach. I shove a large bill into his hand and tell him to keep the change.

The music is louder here than in the bar Pierce chose. This is one of the clubs I visit more frequently. I find that a booming bass leads to more drinks, which lead to more willing women. Win, win, win.

Within seconds, my head is throbbing. I lean against the bar and order a round of whiskeys. When I turn back, Pierce has the disapproving look of a parent. It's a look I'm all too familiar with. I flip him off and turn back for the shots. Instead of handing him his, I down it right after my own. Rhett has disappeared, so I throw his back too.

I stumble toward the dance floor. Time for part two of my plan for tonight. A group of three girls are dancing together in the center, wearing tight dresses that reveal all but the top four inches of their thighs. They smile and flutter their fake eyelashes as I approach.

Score.

I join their threesome, and one of them immediately puts her hands in my hair.

"Oh my god, I love it," she says. I strain to hear her over the music. "Long hair on guys is so hot." She drags out the vowels in her words. "I'm Emma. This is Tiffany and Maddie."

"What's your name?" the one I think is Tiffany says.

I tell her, and she giggles like it's hilarious.

"Are you a surfer?" another one asks, her high-pitched voice straddling the line between hiccup and giggle. It's either Emma or Maddie—I can't be sure anymore. "You look like a surfer."

"I am." I grin at them. They could pull my pants down right here in the middle of the club, and I'd be too blitzed to give a fuck.

"Oh my god, I love surfers," one of them says. I've given up on keeping track of which one is which. There's too much long hair, bare skin, and deep cleavage.

We continue dancing, and I try to remember that I am the envy of the room. I've got three beautiful women with their hands all over me. I could suggest the four of us get a room, and they'd probably be down with it.

Eventually another guy comes over, and one of the girls leaves us to dance with him. I'm now alone with the one who touched my hair.

We're near the edge of the dance floor.

"Do you want to go somewhere?" she says into my ear.

I expect my cock to surge at the suggestion, but it remains limp in my pants. I give her a half smile. "Lead the way." If she realizes I'm too smashed to find my own way to the door, she doesn't seem to mind.

She leads me by the hand down a dark corridor. "Wait here." She darts into a restroom, reappearing several seconds later. "Okay, let's go." Pulling me into the bathroom after her, she locks the door.

When she said *somewhere*, I pictured a suite at the Carlton, or maybe her dorm room. Even the back of her car would have been preferable to the brightness of the restroom.

I squint at the lights. She laughs and tugs me toward her. The kiss is sloppy and wet. Even in my state, I can tell that it's terrible. She pulls back with a giggle and wipes her mouth. "Maybe we should try something else."

She grabs the waistband of my shorts. I'm still wearing the same pair I had on earlier. I never even bothered to change, despite the fact that they were drenched from the rain. They're dry now, and she works to undo the button of my fly.

When she finally has my cock free, she looks at it hanging limply and bites her lip. I expect that action alone to cause blood to rush down, but nothing happens.

She strokes it with her fingers, and bile rises in my throat. "I'm going to be sick." I make it to the rubbish bin right before a stream of mostly alcohol hits the inside of the can.

"Are you okay?" the girl asks. I'll give her points for sticking around. Most girls would have fled the scene as soon as they saw the greenish tint to my skin. She'll make someone a nice housewife someday.

I answer her by retching into the bin again. I momentarily register the sound of the door closing, but my insides are still clenching up.

Once the vomiting stops, I rest my head on my arms on top of the bin. What the fuck was that? I've thrown up from drinking before, but only after making it home. Of course, I've never had this many shots this close together before.

The fly of my shorts is still open, revealing my limp dick. I yank up the zipper. The last thing I need is another reminder of my own incompetence. I can't even cheat on my heart when I want to.

Fucking pathetic wanker.

The bathroom door opens, and Pierce enters. Behind him is the worried face of the girl I came in with. She gives me a tiny wave and an apologetic smile before disappearing back down the corridor.

"What are you doing, man?" Pierce crouches beside me on the floor.

"What does it look like?" I slur.

"Come on." He slips an arm under my shoulders. "Let's go."

He manages to track down Rhett, and the two of them help me outside. I spread out as best as I can in the backseat of a car that is approximately the size of a Lego model I once built.

Groaning, I hold my head as Pierce peels out of the parking space and into traffic.

"You don't have to do this, you know," he says.

I keep my eyes closed as I reply, "Where's the fun in that?"

Neither of them responds. I run my fingers through my hair and picture Walker. She's probably asleep, sprawled out across the bed like it'll run away if she doesn't hold it down. The linens all bunched up from her tossing, her tiny pajamas a crumpled mess, her head no longer on the pillow but hanging off the bed.

A searing pain starts in my chest and travels down to my stomach. I'd equate it to someone taking a hot poker and dragging it down my body, slicing open the skin and the organs with its searing tip, blood gushing out and pooling on the floor of Pierce's Aston Martin.

If Walker had never seen my phone, I could be in the bed with her. She would be splayed across me instead of the sheets. I'd wake her in an hour, and we'd have sex again, and I wouldn't have any trouble getting it up then.

If I'd never agreed to that stupid revenge plot, none of this would have happened.

Guess it's a good thing she learned the truth before I could find an even better way to disappoint her.

36

"Lightning" - Zoe Wees

Walker

The worst part isn't the rain, but that I can't enjoy the rain. Dreary days have always been my favorite. Nothing says "read a good book" like weather too bad to venture into.

After Heath left—I'm forcing myself to think his name, like therapy for heartbreak—I didn't eat anything for the rest of the day out of fear of vomiting. I went to bed early, only to wake up at five this morning. Apparently even a broken heart can't be convinced to sleep more than twelve hours.

I've spent the last few hours packing. Leaving this beautiful house will be hard, but staying will only remind me of what I had for a few brief moments. It's time to get back to St. Anne's and my real life, the one without revenge plots and backstabbing friends and cheating boyfriends.

Not a single one of them has texted me to see how I'm doing. Not that I necessarily expect them to, since that would require Heath confessing what he did two years ago. I wish I could witness the shock on their faces when they realize that he's been the villain all along. We've taken people down for much less.

If only I hadn't told him how I feel. I can imagine the extra glee it gave him—*Heath*, damn it—to know that I fell for him again, right before he obliterated what was left of my heart for the second time.

Maybe I never stopped loving him at all. Maybe my heart has been irrevocably branded by him, unable to ever fully belong to someone else.

I remember a sleepover I attended during primary school. My friend's mum sat everyone in a circle and handed us each a paper heart. Then she told us to tear off a small piece. That one was for Adam, she said. Next we tore off a piece for Baxter, then Clive and Daniel. By the time we got to the second half of the alphabet, there wasn't enough left of our hearts to tear from. The whole thing was meant to remind us to save our hearts for the special person we'd someday marry.

But maybe some boys take giant Sharpies and scribble on our hearts until no one else could possibly want a piece of them.

If that's the case, I'll happily live out my days as a spinster. Better to be a grouchy old Oxford professor than a miserable woman chasing after any man who gives her the time of day.

My phone rings beside my open trunk on the bed. Speaking of miserable women . . .

"Hi, Mum."

"What's wrong?" Have I cried so much that she can hear the tears in my voice?

"Nothing. Just a stupid boy."

"Come over. You can tell me all about it, and we'll watch *Gilmore Girls* afterwards."

"I don't think so. I need to finish packing."

"You are not leaving without saying goodbye this time, cariño."

I sigh and fold another top before adding it to the suitcase. "I won't."

"Then you may as well come now."

"Fine." At least then I'll be able to check that off my list.

"I'll warm up the brie."

***

When I get there, Mum not only has the brie heated and on a plate with biscuits, but Rory Gilmore's face is on the TV, and two steaming mugs of tea await us on the coffee table.

"You didn't need to do all of this," I tell her, even though this is her way of showing she cares.

"Nonsense." She hands me a cup, and I use it to warm my cold fingers. The rain hasn't let up yet, and it's turned cold.

We catch up on her gardening projects and her book club friends, all of whom have made equally poor choices in men.

"Think I could join?" I blow on the surface of my tea before taking a sip.

"If it will convince you to stay, absolutely."

"Mum, you know I have to go back."

She raises an eyebrow and stares at me over the rim of her cup. "Do I?"

I give her a pointed look and reach for a biscuit. She's added prosciutto and cranberry-fig preserves to the platter this time.

"They have online classes, don't they?" she presses.

"That's beside the point. I don't belong here." I pop the whole biscuit into my mouth.

"I think it's time you tell me what happened."

I make a face and reach for more food.

She grabs the tray and holds it out of reach. "Not until you talk."

I close my eyes and take a deep breath. The whole story rushes out in two run-on sentences.

When I'm done, she looks at me with sympathy in her eyes. "Oh niñita—"

"Stop it, Mum." I reach for the cheese. "I don't need your pity."

"Listen to me." She sets the tray back down. "You cannot run from this. You must face it, or it will chase you for the rest of your life."

"I can't."

"Why not?"

I lift my eyes to her dark, probing ones. "Because I'm not strong enough to face it. Definitely not the five of them."

"I raised you to be a strong woman."

"You did, Mum. But sometimes life sucks too much out of us."

She *tsks* and sips her tea. "Maybe I was wrong about Heath. I didn't think he could do such a thing to you twice."

"That makes two of us." I spread preserves on top of my brie-laden biscuit.

"Just because he broke your heart—"

"Don't forget Dad."

"—and your father, doesn't mean you should lock yourself off from the possibility of love."

"It will be a long time before I ever think about falling in love again."

She sighs and rests her hand on my knee. "I don't want to see you become bitter."

"I won't. I'm choosing to learn from these experiences."

"That's the attitude." She gives me a pat, then reaches for the biscuits. "I'm sorry you had to see me fall apart more than a daughter should ever have to."

"Mum—"

"Let me talk." She loads her biscuit with brie and a slice of prosciutto. "I'm trying to do better. I go into relationships with my eyes open now. That doesn't mean I never get hurt, but when I do—and my taste in men is still abhorrently terrific—I like to think I handle it better than I used to."

My mind trips back to the few times I've seen her since returning to Wesbourne. She didn't fall apart the way I expected after my dad cheated on her for what must be the hundredth time. She was sad, sure, but the composure she carried would have been a pipe dream when I was younger.

"I can tell," I say. "I'm proud of you."

"And I'm proud of you, no matter what you decide to do." She brushes off her fingers. "Now, are you ready for some mother-daughter fun?"

We settle into the sofa, and she hits play on the remote. My mind drifts as Lorelei and Rory get up to their old tricks. I've watched these scenes so many times, I have the dialogue memorized.

Even though it would make my mum happy, I can't stay. Not after everything that's gone down. There's simply too much for me in England and nothing left for me here.

Oxford is calling, but there's one thing I need to do first.

When I left last time, I did so quickly, throwing my stuff in a bag with the assurance that my mum could ship everything else to me later. Tears blurred my vision and dribbled onto the clothes as I shoved them into my trunk. I was a snotty, sobbing mess.

This time, I've grown. I've matured. I'm not the same girl who ran back to Oxford with her tail tucked between her legs, crying over a broken heart. This girl is different. She's stronger and more grounded. She knows what she wants and what she deserves.

I'm not anyone's toy to discard when they're done playing. And I deserve better than what I was dished out at the hands of the people I thought were my friends. If they think they can drive me back to England, they're in for a little surprise.

There is a language they're all fluent in, and I'm not referring to English. Words aren't necessary, because actions bear the weight of communication. One move from me, and every single one of them will understand my message.

There's nothing like a little revenge to get everyone on the same page.

Maeve taught me well. Step one: discover the weakness. That must be why they invited me to poker night. They needed to discover the best place to strike me.

Lucky for me, I already know their weaknesses.

And even better, they all share the same one.

37

"I'm a Mess" - Bebe Rexha

Heath

I haven't been on the water for two days, thanks to the big storm that rolled through and stirred the ocean like a witch's cauldron. Unfortunately, hitting the surf today has done little to eliminate the dull ache that's taken up residence in my chest like a stray dog making himself at home under a porch.

Rather than jeopardize my status as the world's biggest asshole, I've only solidified it by not confessing to everyone what actually went down between Walker and me. They all still think she left for some inane reason, leaving the rest of us behind without a single word of explanation. If they knew I cheated on her, it would change everything.

But Walker was right. I'm a fucking bloody coward.

I slap the water with my open palm. The sting distracts me from the pain in my chest for one second, but then it's right back, tripping me up and keeping me from fully inflating my lungs.

I carry my board back to the shop, where Seeley has already closed up for the day. I shouldn't have stayed out so late, but I kept hoping that the next wave would be the one to dispel this stupid ache. If

253

anything, it's only increased in intensity.

I can't keep my brain from imagining what Walker is doing. Has she already returned to Oxford? Maybe she took a red-eye so she could get away as quickly as possible.

Seeley tosses me a towel as I walk through the back door. I always forget to bring one. Her gaze lingers on me as I prop my board up and dry off. Only once I've finished and thrown the towel into the laundry hamper do I meet her eyes.

"You going to tell me what's wrong?" She hovers her hand over the till, ready to cash out for the day.

"Don't know what you're talking about."

"So I'm supposed to stand here while you thrash your way through my shop?" She gives the hamper a pointed look. I follow her gaze. My towel is draped over the side, hardly in the basket at all.

I close my eyes so she won't see me roll them and toss it in. "Happy?"

"I'd be happier if you'd tell me what's up with you." She begins to set out stacks of bills on the counter in front of her.

"I'm fine." It comes out harsher than usual.

She slaps a wad of money onto the counter. "Don't play this game with me." Her cheeks flush even through her tan.

"Seeley, I swear to god—"

"I thought we were friends."

I flick the wet strands of hair out of my face. "Of course we are."

"Then quit bullshitting me. Something's wrong. You haven't been yourself all day."

I haven't been myself for much longer than that. "Just a shitty weekend, is all."

She walks around the counter. She's wearing a purple sports bra and denim shorts. The painful throb in my heart grows stronger as she approaches. When she's standing right in front of me, she stops and places a warm hand on my bare chest. "Mine wasn't so great either." Her voice is low-pitched, and my dick pulses with piqued interest.

Attaboy.

It's been roughly seven months since we last hooked up. Being with Seeley is easy, because she has no expectations. She doesn't expect me to call, and she doesn't get upset when I'm too busy for more than a wave as I head through the shop. I know what she likes. Bonus points for the fact that she isn't hard to please.

She rises onto her tiptoes, palm still pressed against me, and seals her mouth over mine. She tastes like those lemon drops she keeps on the counter for customers, which she has a personal weakness for. Her body burns hot beneath my hands, which have found their way to her waist on instinct.

I tug her closer, eager for the feel of her breasts against me. She lets out a raspy breath as I trace the curve of her spine with my thumb. Blood rushes south at the sound. My dick is ready for this. After my embarrassing fail on Saturday night, it's comforting to know that he still knows how to perform.

I pull back, but only so I can pepper her jaw with kisses. She tilts her head to give me better access, and I nibble on her earlobe in response. Her scent is different. Not a clean coconut, but a tropical mixture, the kind you'd get from a bottle of sunscreen. It smells nice, but it's not what I'm expecting.

Her neck is too tempting, and I place a soft bite in the space behind her ear. She doesn't gasp, doesn't even give a sharp inhale. I do it again. Still nothing. That's weird, but whatever. Maybe she's not into it this time.

I move to slide my fingers into her hair, but it's stuck in a tight ponytail. When has she ever worn—

Fuck.

She's not Walker, you fucking moron.

I pull back abruptly. I don't need a mirror to tell me that my face is flaming, but the one behind the counter mocks me anyway.

Seeley's brows have risen until they're nearly to her hairline. "What's going on, Heath?"

I shake my head and look at the floor. I can't meet her eyes. "I'm sorry."

"You're sorry for what? For kissing me? For stopping?"

"For—" I shove my hand into my hair. "For all of it?"

"Look, I know something's wrong. I just thought I could help you forget for a little bit."

I thought so too, but it seems Walker plans to haunt me everywhere I go. "And I appreciate it. But I can't. I'm sorry." I exhale loudly. "It wouldn't be fair."

"Fair to me?"

"Yes." *And her.*

"I'm not looking for anything serious. I thought that's what we both wanted—a casual fling that we can pick up and lay down whenever we want."

I nod, eyes still on the floor. "Yeah, I thought so too."

"Then you don't need to worry about hurting me. I'm pretty indestructible."

Hundreds of images flash through my mind: girls leaving my hotel room in tears, angry text messages when I didn't call after three days, even the handful of slaps I've sustained and deserved.

"I think it's better if we stay platonic friends." I venture a look at Seeley's face. It's blank, without a hint of disappointment.

"If that's what you want." She retreats behind the counter. Several seconds later, she thumps a bottle of tequila onto the wooden surface. "As a platonic friend, maybe you wanna talk about it?"

She pours us each a shot, and we throw them back in sync. When she holds the bottle up in question, I nod. I can do one more.

"So, who is she?" she says.

I halt with the glass halfway to my mouth. My eyes catch on Seeley's for two seconds, then I throw back the shot. I slam down the glass and wince.

She ducks under the counter again, and I really hope she's not going to produce a different alcohol. I need to be able to drive home. She slaps my keys down, and the sound jolts me.

"It's her, isn't it?"

Fuck. I'm going to need an Uber after all.

"I'd like another please." I scoot my glass across the counter.

"I knew it!" She says it like she's just beaten the Cortana level in *Halo 3*. "She's the one on your keychain."

I wiggle my empty shot glass in front of her, and she dutifully refills it.

"You are not driving home," she says.

"No shit." The tequila burns down my throat.

"I saw the way you looked at her that day, like a kid catching his first wave." She points the mouth of the bottle toward my chest. "You can't fake that kind of look."

"You'd be surprised."

She shakes her head, sending her ponytail whipping around her shoulders. "You can't fool me, Heath. There's a reason you carry her picture around with you. And there's a reason you're drinking all of my tequila." She frowns at the nearly empty bottle.

"Save me the speech, Seeley."

Her shoulders lift like she couldn't care less about what I want. "She's a lucky girl."

"She doesn't think so."

Seeley scratches at a mark on the counter with her blunt thumbnail. "You sure about that?"

Considering Walker threw me out of her house and is probably on her way back to England, yeah, I'm pretty sure. "She made her feelings clear."

"Do you believe everything people tell you?"

"Do you always ask this many questions?" I swipe the bottle from her hand and tilt it toward my lips.

"As my platonic friend and employee, I care about you." She grabs the tequila while I'm midgurgle. "And that's why I'm cutting you off." She caps it and sticks it back under the counter.

A dull haze is starting to creep over my senses. I need to stop using alcohol to numb the pain. It only makes me feel stupid. "Just leave it alone, See. She said she doesn't want anything more to do with me. Seems pretty final to me."

"Did you tell her how you feel?"

An abrupt laugh tears out of my chest. "You mean that I love her and that I'm a fucking mess when she's not around? Yeah, sure did."

I hate the look of pity that comes into her eyes.

"I always knew this would happen, okay?" I say. "I'm a huge fuckup, and I knew someday I'd disappoint her so much that she'd be done, once and for all. It was nice while it lasted, but now it's over."

"You can't seriously believe that."

I spread my arms wide. "I have no reason to believe anything else."

"You are not a fuckup." She comes around the counter toward me, and I put a hand out to steady myself. Her fingers curl around my cheeks. "You are good and funny and loyal."

I drop her gaze. Something pinches in my chest. "Too bad she doesn't agree."

"A person's depth is harder to hide than you think, Heath."

38

"Who's Afraid of Little Old Me?" - Taylor Swift

They say revenge is a dish best served cold. I prefer to strike while the iron is hot. If there's one thing I've learned since being back in Wesbourne, it's that cheaters need to learn their lesson. Otherwise, they'll continue flaunting their betrayal like a badge.

I'm not under the impression that consequences ensure a person stops their bad behavior. But they certainly shouldn't be rewarded for it. If God has chosen to use me as his instrument for doling out punishments, who am I to refuse?

My plan has several steps. The first, and arguably most crucial, is one final chai latte from Cafe de Olla. I have yet to find a cafe in Oxfordshire that makes them the same, and I intend to savor this cup like it's my last day on earth.

Who knows, by the time everything's done, it might be.

That familiar scent of freshly baked muffins and rich espresso tickles my nose before I even open the door. As I head to the line forming behind the till, my eyes skim past a familiar form.

My feet receive the message before the rest of my body, so I lurch forward when they stall. I catch myself on the rubbish bin next to me.

The man turns then, and it's not Dr. Riordan after all. He has the same shaggy black hair, the same brown skin, and is around the same height. He's even wearing a beige tweed jacket similar to one I've seen Riordan wear to class. But it's not him.

I sag in relief against the bin. For a few suspended seconds, I was back in that room, and he was putting his hands on me and threatening my degree if I didn't have sex with him.

What the fuck kind of world is this anyway, where university professors hit on students half their age, while their wives keep dinner hot for them at home?

The man turns with his steaming coffee for the sugar station next to me. He gives me a quizzical glance, and I realize I'm still leaning against the bin. Brushing a few pastry crumbs from my sleeve, I approach the counter.

I place my order, but my heart races around my chest like a dog chasing a rabbit. How am I going to handle walking the halls of St. Anne's knowing that Riordan could be waiting for me around the next corner?

Since learning about Heath's betrayal and the way my supposed friends were planning to screw me over, my brain has been circling the same subject, concocting the perfect plan to get back at all of them.

But in the bedlam, I've forgotten an important character, one who also deserves my attention.

The barista calls out my order, and I retrieve my latte. An empty sofa beckons from the back wall. I wasn't planning to stay, but now that I need to add a few more steps to my plan, I want to get started.

Fortunately, I can do everything from my phone. The first order of business is simple: call St. Anne's.

The receptionist redirects me to the dean of students. After I tell him I'd like to drop my two courses with Dr. Riordan, the line goes quiet.

"I'm sorry. Did you hear what I said?" Maybe the connection between the two countries is unstable.

"I did, Ms. Halifax." He clears his throat and riffles some papers. "May I ask why you'd like to drop those particular courses?"

"I—" I stop and consider. "I am shifting direction." I squeeze my eyes shut. I'm such a coward.

"I see." He waits several beats. Is he reading over my file, searching for answers to the blanks I'm giving him? "So you no longer wish to study English literature?"

I bite my lip. This is not going the way I anticipated. "I do. It's just—" Why can't I tell him what Riordan did? Just blurt the words out and maybe stop him from doing it to another student?

"Ms. Halifax?"

"He approached me. Dr. Riordan." I say it in a rush, the words hardly audible in my mad dash to get them out of my mouth. "He suggested that we go somewhere alone, and when I resisted, he assaulted me. Not sexually, but I think that was his intention if someone hadn't come along."

The silence on the other end of the line grows. This—*this*—is why I didn't want to say anything.

"I'm terribly sorry that happened to you," the dean finally says. "We take these kinds of accusations very seriously."

"Good." My heart rate slows to a normal speed. "Are you going to fire him? I don't know what the protocol is in situations like these."

"I'm afraid we can't go around firing professors after one accusation."

"But I told you what he did." A young couple at the table next to me looks my way. I lower my voice. "I told you he assaulted me. Who knows how many others he's done the same thing to."

"And while we will certainly conduct an investigation, you must understand. Dr. Riordan is a tenured professor. Lots of students come to St. Anne's specifically to study under him."

I clench my jaw. I knew it would do no good to say anything. "In that case, may I please have Mrs. Riordan's phone number?"

The man's soft chuckle comes over the line. "I'm sorry, Ms. Halifax. I can't give out phone numbers, even if I had access to them, which I do not."

"I appreciate your attempt at *helping*. Feel free to move me to whichever course would be a good substitute for Riordan's. I won't be returning to his classroom."

"If there's anything else I can—"

I hang up before he can finish his inane sentence. If St. Anne's has no intention of punishing Riordan, I'll have to do it myself.

I picture his office from the handful of times I've met with him there. I shudder to think of how closely I brushed against danger. The room is disheveled, decorated in the way favored by men who would rather read a book than clean. There are photos on the wall behind his desk, and one in particular stands out in my memory.

In it, Riordan's wife is wearing a nurse's uniform. She's average-looking, with nutmeg-colored hair and a slightly lopsided smile. Their two small boys are standing in front of her. The picture is older, so the boys are likely in secondary school by now.

What kind of sick monster hits on students only a few years older than his own children?

I try to remember the name of the hospital Mrs. Riordan works at, but I'm not sure the professor ever mentioned it. He probably pats himself on the back for separating work and home like that.

It doesn't matter. I'll start with the four main ones in Oxfordshire and work until I find her.

* * *

My latte has grown cold by the time someone gives me a glimmer of hope.

"Riordan? Yes, I believe we have a nurse here by that name," the receptionist at John Radcliffe says.

"Great. Can you connect me to her?"

"Sure, love. Who should I say is calling?"

I scramble for an appropriate answer. "Her sister-in-law." I do remember that Dr. Riordan has a sister who lives in London.

Soft music floats through the phone. I walk to the counter to order another drink. As I'm returning to my seat, fresh latte in hand, a click sounds on the other end of the line.

"Hello?" The voice is soft, like a bird alighting on a branch. "Renita?"

I want to scratch Riordan's eyes out for hurting this poor woman, who probably never suspected her husband could ever do something as banal as cheat on her. "It's not Renita," I say. "You don't know me, but I'm one of your husband's students."

"Oh." Mrs. Riordan's confusion is evident. "Is everything okay with Sunil?"

His name is Sunil. For some reason, this angers me. I don't want him to have a first name, to be a person. I want him to burn in hell for what he tried to do. "He's fine. That is, I'm calling to warn you that you may want to get tested for HIV."

She lets out an audible gasp. I picture her clutching her throat in her scrubs, as if it will stop the words from moving past her ears and into her soul. "Why—why would you suggest that?"

She knows what I'm telling her, and we both know that she knows. But I understand her hesitation to accept the truth. Although I saw it with my own eyes, I still wrestled the entire way home with whether it had actually been *my* boyfriend in that bed.

I imagine what will happen next. Will she rage at him? Throw an iron at his head? Toss his clothes into the front yard? Pick up the boys from school and leave without telling him? The options are endless, none of them boding well for *Sunil*.

I only wish I could be there to witness the whole thing myself.

"I'm sorry to be the one to tell you, Mrs. Riordan," I say, "but I have it on good authority that your husband has been sleeping with his students."

39

"Gives You Hell" - The All-American Rejects

Heath

It feels weird to not be going to the Archives with Walker. I've spent the majority of the past few weeks next to her in that room. Going to work today feels like coming home after a long vacation.

Not that I have much experience with vacations myself. My dad doesn't believe in relaxing when you could be making money.

I grab a knife and stick it into the jar of mayonnaise before spreading some on my bread. Tonight is poker at Pierce's place. It will be the first one without Walker since she returned to Wesbourne. How mad will Maeve be if I skip out?

I have no desire to sit there while the four of them discuss Walker as if they didn't just pretend to be her friend for an entire month while plotting to sabotage her behind her back. If their plan had worked and Maeve had sent that paper in, Walker would have been expelled.

Besides, sitting there and imagining her in the empty chair across from me sounds like a brand of torture even I wouldn't choose. Before I can change my mind, I text Pierce.

Me: *Hey, don't think I'll make it tonight*

He responds a few minutes later.

Pierce: *What's up, mate?*

Me: *I caught a bug over the weekend*

Seems like a rock-solid excuse, one not even Maeve can argue against. But I'm wrong again, because a few minutes later, my phone buzzes with a text from her.

Maeve: *You can't skip poker just because the Walker scheme is over.*

God, does Pierce keep anything from her?

Me: *This has nothing to do with her. I'm sick*

Maeve: *Come on, Heath. I've known you for ten years. During that time, you've been sick once.*

Maeve: *I know you two were hooking up.*

How the fuck could she possibly know that?

Me: *Is that what Walker said?*

Maeve: *Nobody needed to say anything. It was blatantly apparent every time you two were in the same room.*

Me: *Is now when you lecture me about sleeping with the enemy?*

Maeve: *Nope, but I'll see you at 8. x*

Fuck. I can't go to poker night and not set the record straight. I thought I could buy myself more time. Maybe with another week to think, I could come up with an explanation that doesn't make me want to hurl myself from a building every time I think about it.

Given the way Walker responded to my latest betrayal, I have no idea how the rest of them will react. Losing her was hell itself, but I never believed for a second I deserved her. My friends are all I have left. If I lose them too—

My dad walks into the kitchen. He takes one look at my half-fixed sandwich and smirks. "Packing a brown-bag lunch?"

"Yeah, Dad." I grab the mustard and squirt it onto the bread. "Want me to make you one?"

He laughs and drapes his suit jacket over one of the barstools. After rooting around in the fridge for a few seconds, he retreats with a premixed protein shake. "Sure, son. I'd like a slab of dedication between two pieces of ambition. Think you could fix something like that for me?" He closes the fridge door and leans against it.

"Sorry. We're completely out of asshole sandwiches." I tear open a package of salami and plop the entire stack onto the bread.

The veins in Dad's throat bulge as he drinks his shake. His eyes have that crazy, maniacal look they get right before he punches someone. For some reason, I don't care if he hits me this time. I kind of hope he does.

I have a hankering to take an old man down.

The nonchalance comes easily to me. It's the one thing I know gets under his skin with alarming speed. He equates it to not giving a fuck, and there is nothing worse in my dad's book than a fucker who doesn't give a fuck.

I reach for the cheese. "Hey, Dad. Do you know where the closest bus stop is? I was thinking about riding it to work today. Trying to save fuel and the economy, you know."

I don't get to see the sour expression on his face, because I'm dutifully focused on my sandwich. But there is no mistaking the cold tension radiating from him.

Scratch what I said earlier. There is nothing worse than a fucker who doesn't give a fuck about anything but the environment.

He slams his empty shake bottle onto the counter. "You care about dolphins but not this family?"

"I'm not the one who goes around smacking everyone that gets in my way."

The slap spins my head and causes bright starbursts to flare across my vision. I blink to clear it.

"I don't know what you think you'll ever amount to, working in that stupid shack and turning your back on everything I've built for us."

Dad steps closer, wheezing slightly. "But if you think you're getting a dime from me when I'm gone, you can forget it."

A smirk desperately wants to take up residence on my face, but I keep it neutral. "You don't know me if you think I have any interest in your fraud money."

Several blood vessels in his eyes have burst, giving him a serial killer look. He could murder me if he wanted, especially since I refuse to hit back, which only infuriates him more. "Your little girlfriend might think differently." He sneers, and my mind reels.

How could he possibly know that Walker's back? And if so, has he talked to her? Threatened her? Shit. The possibilities are endless, and if she's not talking to me, I have no way of finding out what he's done.

"That little surf shack of hers can't be a huge moneymaker, especially if she has you on payroll. We both know that bike of yours is above your pay grade."

I hope the relief that floods my body isn't visible. He's referring to Seeley, who knows how to take care of herself.

"Haven't you heard?" I take a big bite of my sandwich and chew while I talk. "Your fraud money is already supporting her. She's going to have my bastard children, so it's only right that I give her something. That's what you always taught me, right, Dad?"

This time I dodge the blow. The man is as predictable as the tide. Crafting the exact phrases that will bring him to the edge of his sanity is like child's play.

"If you think I'm going to let my son shack up with a woman like that—" He lurches for me, but I skirt around the kitchen island. He grabs at nothing but air.

"A woman like what? Is she really that different from all of your mistresses?" I bounce lightly on my feet so I can be ready to dodge whatever he does next.

"Don't you dare talk to me like that!" He runs at me, but he forgets that I'm thirty years younger and in the best shape of my life. By the time we make it around the island twice more, he's panting. He bends over and rests his hands on his knees. "You're nothing but an ungrateful twat. I ought to throw you out on the street and see how you survive without my cash keeping you afloat."

"You could, but then what would all of your friends say?" I take another huge bite of my sandwich.

"You pathetic little cunt. You're a disgrace to the Lawrence name."

I gesture toward him with my sandwich, mouth still full because I know how much it bugs him. "This may surprise you, but you don't get to determine my worth."

He gives me one more seething look, nostrils flaring, before turning and leaving the kitchen. My body relaxes in his absence. Whoever thought that douchebag deserved to walk the planet was clearly high at the time.

The idea comes to me so quickly and vividly, I can't believe I haven't thought of it before. All these years, I've helped carry out a multitude of revenge plots against strangers and randos from the street, when right in front of me was the perfect scheme to take down my own dad, once and for all.

I perform a quick Google search to find the phone number for HMRC. Within seconds, an automated answering machine is asking which option I'd like to choose. I opt to speak to a representative. I've never trusted those creepy robots.

After a few minutes on hold, a brisk female voice answers. "Welcome to Her Majesty's Revenues and Customs. How may I assist you today?"

"Hello," I say. "Who do I need to speak to about reporting tax fraud?"

40

"Look What You Made Me Do" - Taylor Swift

Walker

Everything is going according to plan.

While the quality of the photos I've rounded up isn't professional grade, the items are hot enough that I'm hoping the committee will be willing to overlook any slightly pixelated backgrounds or less-than-aesthetically-pleasing styling.

Rhett's was easy. He sent it himself a few weeks ago. I have to erase the whiskey bottle in Canva and do what I can to clean it up, but the whole thing only takes half an hour.

The guitar glitters in multiple shades of green, all bleeding together like a watercolor of a forest. It's propped against a leather armchair, but it's easy enough to determine the focal point.

Pierce's is a little harder. I'm able to access professional photos off various websites, but all of them are watermarked by the museum or gallery in question. I finally locate one where someone was stupid enough to put the watermark only on the solid white background. That's an easy fix. Thank you, Canva.

I personally find the painting abhorrent, but based on a quick

Google search, I seem to be in the minority on this. It looks like the type of thing a toddler would create on their mum's kitchen walls in a fit of rage, all bright colors and nonsensical patterns.

Give me a Monet any day.

As suspected, Lux has a photo on her Instagram. That was never in question. The trouble is that the picture (downloaded through a backdoor site) loses quality from the original. With what are becoming mad Canva skills, I'm able to polish it up enough for the committee.

She's displayed the bags on shelves I assume were custom-built for that purpose. Each one is backlit so that it looks like a Chanel store is masquerading as her closet. The whole thing is pretty impressive.

Maeve's is the most difficult. She has sent me photos in the past, but they're all on my old phone, which is unfortunately still in England. After multiple password resets, I'm able to gain access to my cloud storage and find an appropriate picture there. A little cropping work later, and we're golden.

The photo was taken at a gala three years ago. The three of us are wearing exquisite gowns and elaborate updos. Maeve's necklace was the star of the show for obvious reasons, emphasizing her slender neck and prominent collarbones.

Whitney Rivendale's phone number was listed on the gala's website, right below her name and *This Year's Host*. I left her a voicemail before starting on the photo touch-ups. My phone rings beside me now, and her number pops onto the screen.

Here we go.

"Ms. Newhoff? It's Whitney Rivendale, returning your call," she says when I answer. Her nasally voice reminds me of those actresses who play older, adoring mothers of delinquent teenage sons whose actions they refuse to acknowledge as problematic.

"Thank you for calling me back." I inject my voice with the brisk polish an assistant would use. "I'm calling on behalf of my employer,

Pierce St. James. Is it too late to submit a few items for the auction?"

She sighs on the other end, and I picture my plan sliding through the cracks like sand on a dock. "The auction list goes to the printer this afternoon, along with the invitations. I'm not sure—"

"I think you're going to want these items, ma'am."

There's another sigh. "Maybe if you tell me what they are . . ."

I quirk my mouth. Just the opening I need. "For starters, I have a two-hundred-piece vintage Hermes bag collection."

I wait for the inevitable pin drop.

"I'm sorry, did you say *two hundred* pieces?"

"That's right, ma'am. I also have Simone Caldwell's *Emancipation*, which I imagine should be pretty popular."

Ms. Rivendale titters through the phone, probably waving a freshly manicured hand in front of her flawless face. "Those items are— Well, you're right. They will cause quite a rage."

I grin to myself. *More than one kind of rage.*

We make arrangements for me to email her the rest of the details and photos. "I'll have everything to you within the hour," I assure her.

"Any later than that and we won't be able to include them, much as we might wish to," she says, her voice rising in pitch.

"You don't need to worry," I say. "I do have one more request. Could I pick up Mr. St. James's invitation, along with those of his three fellow donors?"

* * *

I peruse the list one final time, ensuring there are no typos or missing words. A smile creeps onto my face unbidden.

From Mr. Pierce St. James, Simone Caldwell's Emancipation,

From Ms. Lux Colombia-Clarke, a collection of two hundred vintage Hermes handbags,

From Mr. Rhett Cole, a custom Fender Stratocaster owned by musician Rodney Giles,

From Ms. Maeve Wilson, the Amarilla Pearl *necklace*

I attach the four photos I doctored in Canva and hit send. Whitney assured me the invitations would be ready for pickup tomorrow afternoon, in plenty of time to have them delivered to Pierce's flat during poker night.

Heath's going to wonder why he wasn't included. While the rest of them open their envelopes and see what I've done, he'll be sitting there, imagining something worse waiting for him at home.

It won't come.

I spent hours thinking this through. Bestowing the same punishment on him as the others doesn't seem right. After all, they were going to sabotage me by going after something important to me. It's only fair I do the same to them.

But he destroyed what was left of my heart after mangling it the first time. He drew me in, taught it to beat again, then reared back to deal it one final blow.

That deserves something much more than a basic revenge plot.

Heath deserves a broken heart of his own.

Maybe he'll live in fear of something happening weeks from now. Maybe he'll feel ignored and left out of the scheme. Or maybe he'll understand the subtle message I'm sending him: *Just because you haven't grown, doesn't mean I haven't.*

The air swelters tonight, and I regret my long-sleeve button-down the minute I step outside. Gone are the balmy days of summer, replaced by the oppressive heat of hell's personal sauna.

I check again to make sure all four invitations are in the car. The envelopes look like the midnight sky, a stormy-blue linen embossed with tiny gold foil stars, names scrawled in thick calligraphy on the front. They weighed heavy in my hand when I picked them up from the calligrapher's, each containing a "small" gift as a token for considering the invitation.

The Atlantis looms above the other buildings downtown, its eighty-plus stories reaching for the darkening sky. I can't tell which flat is Pierce's from down here, but I can picture them all sitting around the table in the game room, antes already submitted, cards in hand.

I park in the underground garage and take the lift to the lobby. I recognize the elderly doorman. He's been a fixture at the Atlantis for as long as I've been coming here, since back when Pierce bought his flat four years ago.

He smiles at me the way a grandfather might, not the exuberant ones who toss you into the air, but the ones who watch from the sidelines of every piano recital and gymnastics competition, chest puffed out proudly and telling everyone within hearing distance, "That's my granddaughter." I didn't have one of those, unfortunately, but I've seen enough of them to know what I missed out on.

"Miss Halifax." His eyes twinkle with suppressed mirth.

"Hello, Leonard." I stretch my arms out to give him a hug. His burgundy uniform is scratchy against my cheek.

"How are you, my dear?" he says. "It's been ages since I've seen you."

"I've moved to England to study at Oxford full-time."

His eyes widen, and he pats his chest like he's looking for something. "Well, of course you are." He fishes a pair of glasses from the inner pocket of his suit jacket. "Let me get a better look at you."

I smile as he studies me head to toe.

"You're just as pretty as you've always been. You here to see Mr. St. James?" He continues without waiting for an answer. "The others are here already, I believe."

"Actually, I can't join them tonight." I pull the envelopes from my bag, pleased to see they haven't been crushed. "I was hoping you could make a delivery for me, though."

Leonard takes the stack from my hand and flips through them. "Surprising them, are we?" His voice sounds conspiratorial, and he winks.

"Something like that." I smile at him one last time before heading back to the door. "You'll get them up there tonight?"

He gives me a mock salute. "You can count on me, Miss Halifax."

"Thank you, Leonard. You're the best." I blow him a kiss and return to the car park.

Showtime.

41

"My Kink Is Karma" - Chappell Roan

Heath

I can't afford to win tonight. The asshole I accused of jumping ahead of me in line doesn't exist. He's nothing more than a figment of my imagination, created for the sole purpose of keeping my friends happy.

Someone should warn you about the dangers of breaking someone's heart. No one tells you that when you lean forward to drive the sword home, you impale yourself on its double-ended blade.

Pierce is the dealer tonight. His cocktail is blueberry-and-cherry flavored, but I've long since forgotten the actual name of it, let alone how many I've had.

Maeve thumbs the pearls at her neck. She's nervous about something, but it's hard to say what. Her words have an extra bite to them tonight.

Lux twists her glass around and around on the napkin, slowly shredding the paper into wet, ribbony strips. Rhett is unusually quiet, furiously texting every once in a while.

We're really good at pretending. That's one of the first skills we learn, alongside how to address the staff and determine a good mutual fund from a bad one. Nothing screams money like a face locked into a smile that conveys nothing.

No one has said her name yet. It's like we've collectively agreed it's better to pretend the whole thing never happened. Maeve gave up on sending in the paper when I told her to fuck off. I suspect they think I've gone off the deep end.

Lux raises the bet, offering her maid on the altar for breaking an antique candy bowl. The game continues in a monotonous fashion. How long before we all grow tired of this childish routine?

Maeve is interrupted from placing her bet by a knock on the door. Everyone looks at Pierce, the same thought visible on all of our faces.

Is it her?

Not so good at hiding emotions, then.

My heart slams against my ribcage as we wait for Pierce to return. He does, less than a minute later, alone. I can't decide if it's relief or disappointment flooding my chest.

He tosses a stack of black envelopes onto the table. They slide off each other like sand in the wake of a wave. Maeve snatches them up.

"What is it?" Rhett lays his phone face down on the table.

"Just invitations or something." Pierce sits back down and steeples his hands, ready to get back to business.

"They interrupted our game for that?" Rhett mutters, as if any of us care about the outcome.

Maeve passes out the envelopes. "They're for the PCC gala." She hands one to Lux before tearing the last one open herself. I don't know if she's hidden mine as a punishment or if she's waiting for me to beg for it.

I couldn't give two fucks about some stupid invitation. The only thing I want is to get out of here.

Rhett and Pierce both toss theirs aside, apparently not caring any more than I do about some fucking gala.

"Can we get back to the game?" Pierce says.

Lux and Maeve both have their heads bent over their invites as if they're from God himself. Neither respond.

"Fuck me now." Rhett picks up his phone again.

Pierce stands up and asks if anyone needs a refill. I hand him my empty glass. The ice hasn't even had time to melt. When he reaches the door, Lux says, "Um, guys? You may want to open your envelopes."

He snags his envelope from the table and slices it open with the penknife he just happens to keep in his pocket, because of course he does. Since the gods have smiled upon me and decided not to grace me with an invitation, I have to determine the contents of these bloody things by watching everyone else's face.

Lux is chewing on her bottom lip and twirling her hair around her fingers. Maeve looks ready to murder someone—not me, for once. Pierce's glower is deep enough that his eyebrows meet in the middle of his forehead. Rhett is still playing on his phone.

"Is this legitimate?" Pierce throws his invitation onto the table. Another sheet of paper is tucked inside, along with a gold bracelet.

Maeve lowers her own page and looks at him. "I want to say no, but . . ." She picks up her envelope and studies her name on the front. "This is Emily Gershin's work."

"Who the fuck is that?" Pierce says. He's clamping the back of his chair so hard, it's in danger of snapping.

"A calligrapher on Twenty-Third. She's the best of the best." Maeve takes a long swig of her drink.

"How does that make this whole thing legit?" Pierce says. "Anyone could have hired her."

Maeve shakes her head and drains the rest of her glass. "She only does big events. Society weddings, galas, balls. There's no way she would have taken on a job of four invitations."

He lifts the single page from the table and shakes it. "You're telling me *everyone* is reading one of these right now?"

"Not everyone . . ." Lux's eyes flit from me to Rhett.

"Dude." Pierce slaps Rhett's shoulder. "You're going to want to see this." He tosses the unopened envelope at him.

Rhett catches it and tears it open with the enthusiasm of a sulky teenager on family vacation. He scans the invite and shrugs. "Another boring-as-fuck event. So what?"

Pierce fishes the loose page out of Rhett's invite and thrusts it into his face. "This." He points halfway down the page.

I toss my cocktail back. "Anyone care to fill me in on what the fuck is going on?"

Pierce tosses his own sheet to me. I read over the list of donations. How can something so inane be causing this much drama?

Then I read it.

Holy motherfucker.

I finish the list, expecting to find my own name, then reread the whole thing twice. It's not there.

"What the *fuck*?" Rhett's voice is loud enough for the neighbors to hear. He stands up and knocks his chair over backward. "What kind of sick joke is this?"

"I don't know, mate," Pierce says.

"I'm not donating my guitar to some stupid charity thing." His voice cracks. He sounds like a twelve-year-old in the throes of puberty.

"You think I'm going to allow my family's heirloom pearl necklace to be auctioned off?" Maeve says.

"I spent five years collecting those bags," Lux wails. "Some of them are one-of-a-kind."

"Let's stay rational." Pierce releases his grip on the chair and starts pacing the room. He turns to Maeve. "Don't you have to have photos for these things?"

She already has the website pulled up on her phone and turns it so we can all see it. There are photos of Rhett's guitar, Maeve's pearls, Lux's bags, and Pierce's painting on the list of donated items.

"What's the host's number?" Rhett rights his chair and scoots up to the table. "I'm going to set the record straight tonight."

"You may not want to do that," Lux says. She has stopped twirling her hair and is once again aggressively rotating her glass on what's left of her napkin.

"If the invites have already gone out, it'll make you look like a dick to withdraw your donation now," Pierce says.

"I don't care! That guitar is priceless." A red flush is tinting Rhett's cheeks.

"The real question is, who would have the audacity to do something like this?" Maeve says.

The room quiets as they all ponder this.

"Do you really need to ask that question?" My voice sounds too loud, like someone talking during a funeral.

They all look at me as if they forgot I was even in the room.

"You've got to be kidding me." Maeve's mouth is the only thing that moves as she talks. A red smear across a black-and-white background.

I drop my shoulders. "It's the only thing that makes sense."

"Does she know about—" Lux cuts off and blinks, then stares down at her hands wrapped around her glass.

"She knows," I say. *She knows, and we're all screwed.*

"Fuck," Pierce mutters. He falls into his chair and puts his head in his hands.

"If she knows, then why isn't your name on here?" Maeve asks, brows pinched together. "You were the one supposed to be collecting intel."

"No idea," I say. The only thing I've come up with is that she's sending me a different message. Not "screw you for screwing me," but something much worse. The weight of her dismissal, as if I'm not even worthy of her thoughts, let alone her revenge, is much heavier than the weight of her disapproval could ever be.

"It's actually pretty brilliant," Lux says quietly.

It's fucking genius, is what it is. She knew exactly where to strike each of us. A prized possession, a public humiliation, a brutal sacrifice.

"We can't get out of this without ruining our image," Maeve says in a stunned hush. She's still clutching the page in her hands, the once-smooth surface becoming full of wrinkles and creases.

"This means war," Rhett announces, and throws his envelope and invitation into the middle of the table, scattering poker chips everywhere.

"What do you propose to do?" Pierce says. "She screwed us over because of what we did to her."

"Technically, we never *did* anything." Maeve's lips press together. I'm going to guess that being bested tastes as pleasant to her as rotting prawns.

"And what we were *going* to do was in retaliation for what she did two years ago," Lux adds.

Shit. Now is when I pipe up and tell everyone what actually happened that summer, why Walker had every right to exact the revenge she did.

"The bitch leaves the country without a single word, then expects us to welcome her back with open arms and *not* get revenge?" Maeve says before I find the courage to open my mouth and confess everything.

"For the record, I don't think she wanted us to know she was here." Lux frowns at her glass and shudders. "Based purely on the atrocious hat and hair she was sporting at WNX."

"Who cares why she did it? I want my guitar back." Gone is Rhett's cool rockstar persona. In its place is a raging toddler who didn't get the toy they wanted for Christmas.

"You're shit out of luck, mate," Pierce says. "Just get someone to bid on it for you."

Rhett mumbles something into his glass as he takes a drink.

Now is as good a time as any. It's not like waiting will make this any easier.

I take a deep breath. "There's something I need to tell you."

They all stare at me. It's obvious from their expressions that they're expecting something along the lines of "I'm heading out" or "I finally got my own place."

They see me as a disappointment, but none of them expect this. They don't think I'm stupid enough to ruin something that good. All these years, they thought she was the villain.

I'm about to ruin the second-best thing in my life.

"Oh my god. You were in on it too?" Lux blurts out.

I shake my head slightly, then clear my throat and trace a line of moisture on my glass with my thumb. "I cheated on Walker two years ago. That's why she left."

You could fill a stadium with the silence in the room. I keep my focus on my glass. Condensation runs down the side. I'm thankful to have a place to plant my eyes that doesn't stare back at me with judgment or condemnation or horror.

Cheating is a fatal mistake. When Maeve caught her boyfriend with another woman, we planted porn on his work computer and reported it to his boss.

I can handle physical pain. I have my dad to thank for that. When you're used to being a human punching bag, there isn't much that can faze you. But even I can't take this deadly quiet.

My eyes dart to Pierce's face. His brows are deeply furrowed, but he's not looking at me. "What the fuck, mate," he says quietly.

I expected more relief than this. It feels good to finally own up to my mistake, but I'm afraid I've lost everything.

"Get out." The hiss comes from Maeve, sitting on my right. When I don't move, she says it again. "Get. Out."

I open my mouth to share my defense, but I don't have one. There is no excuse for what I did, no explanation that makes it okay. I stand before she can repeat herself.

No one tries to stop me as I head toward the door. I don't expect them to, but it still hurts. I'm glad they know everything, know that Walker has done nothing to deserve their wrath. That she should have had their support through the worst time of her life, but because of my cowardice, she had no one.

But I'm sad for myself, because this was the last thing I had. I might not have appreciated it the way I should've, but that doesn't mean I want to let it go.

There's only one thought that comforts me as I walk to the lift.

At least I'm no longer a bloody coward.

42

"Empty Room" - Jamie Miller

Heath

It isn't until the morning sunshine blasts my face that the full impact of what I've done hits me. I fessed up to a two-year-old wrong, cleared Walker's name, and stopped being afraid of everyone else's opinion of me.

A restless energy burns through my veins, stronger than usual. My friends may not be planning to forgive me, but I'm confident I can win them back. Everyone screws up. The key is making sure you become a different person, someone who'd never do it again.

I pull on a pair of board shorts and yank a T-shirt over my head, not stopping to see if either of them are clean. I reach for the keys to my bike but hesitate when my eyes land on the keys to Grenadier. Walker's smiling face beams back at me. I lift the keychain off my dresser and stare at the photo. Several scuff marks mar the surface of the plastic, but they can't hide her radiant joy.

I'm the bastard who stole that from her. I gave her a reason to believe that people can never change, that your mistakes define who you are for eternity. She never wanted to believe that she could fall for a man like her father. I made her think she had.

But I'm not like her father.

I never was and I never will be.

I swipe my keys and bolt downstairs, barely taking the time to slip into a pair of flip-flops on my way to my bike.

It takes me forty minutes to get to the other side of town. The queen is doing a walkabout downtown, making traffic a fucking nightmare.

Fortunately, I entered the address of the Airbnb Walker rented into my GPS when I took her home, otherwise it would take me forever to find the place again. It's still creepy as fuck, but it's also understandable why she was drawn to it. It has a mysterious charm, kind of like the candy house in Hansel and Gretel.

I can't see any lights on inside, but it's also the middle of the morning. Plenty of sunshine is pouring through all of those huge windows. I hope I'm not too late.

I press the doorbell with my thumb. Its harsh buzzing resounds through the house. I wait a minute before pressing it again. I don't have a clue what I'm going to say, just that I will talk until she slams the door in my face. Seeing her again will be worth everything.

There's one of those old brass knockers on the door, so I try that. I'm guessing if she didn't hear the buzzer, she's not going to hear the knocker, but it can't hurt to try. I tap it against the plate for a minute straight. There's no sound from inside the house.

Damn.

I circle to the back of the house and hit the call button on my phone. Maybe she's playing music and can't hear anything from downstairs. Or she's outside and too far from the front door.

The back garden is deserted, and Walker's phone rings straight to voicemail. I give the kitchen door a few raps for good measure, but my hope is pretty much nonexistent at this point.

She must have been here last night, because someone had those invitations hand delivered. I shove my hands into my hair and rap my knuckles against the door one last time. All is quiet inside.

I turn to head back down the steps when my eyes catch on the rubbish bin next to the house. Sticking out of the top is a potted plant, the kind Cami would be quick to adopt and talk to in that baby voice that makes me embarrassed to be related to her. Its leaves are withered and brown.

Beside it is my shirt, the one Walker was wearing when she threw me out. It's undamaged and mostly clean. I dig it out and toss it over my shoulder. A faint hint of coconut hits my nose. I turn back to the driveway.

Her car is gone, something I should have noticed right away. I sit down on the broken concrete steps at the front of the house, careful to avoid any large cracks. I pull my phone out of my pocket and check flights to England.

There are several leaving WNX this afternoon and tonight. I have no idea if she'll be on one of them or if she already left Wesbourne first thing this morning, but I do know I'm not losing her a second time.

I've never been much of a planner, and I don't see a reason to start now. I tentatively decide to get on the first flight back to England, hoping I can catch Walker while she's still at the airport in London. Aside from that, I'm winging this thing.

My bike spits gravel as I tear out onto the street. The traffic hasn't lightened since I left. If anything, it's worse. A long line of cars snakes across the bridge. The light turns green three times before I finally make it through the intersection and onto the steel structure.

I tap my thumbs on the handlebars as I wait at another light. The next flight to Heathrow leaves at 12:15. Buying a ticket and getting through security will take some time, which means I should already be at WNX, not stuck in the world's slowest traffic forty-five minutes away.

The light turns again, and we crawl forward, only to stop again after just six vehicles make it through.

"This is fucking ridiculous." I tug my phone out of my shorts pocket. It's 10:50. If I miss this flight, the next one won't leave until 7:35 tonight. By then Walker will be long gone, tucked into the Oxford bookcases, where my chances of finding her are slim.

I don't know how I'll find her in an airport crowded with thousands of people, but there's no way I'm stopping until I try. I should've told her everything the first time we were together instead of letting that stupid fear get in my head. Now she's probably already halfway across the Atlantic and out of my life again.

When I reach the next intersection after the bridge, I turn right onto a smaller street. Hopefully this one will be less crowded than Twenty-Fifth. Several blocks down, though, I come to a barricade. One of the policemen manning it points to the next street over.

"You'll have to go that way, sir."

I stifle my curse and turn the bike around. Why in the bloody hell did Queen Celia think today was a good day to parade around downtown? Any other day of the year would have been preferable to this one.

After being deterred by several more barricades, elderly women trying to preserve their ancient sedans, and traffic lights that refuse to turn green, I give up on side streets being a shortcut. I merge back onto Twenty-Fifth. My teeth clamp down hard.

I check the time again—11:15. The plane leaves in an hour. I'm at least fifteen minutes away. There aren't many options.

They always take the pavement in the movies. Or dodge between the lanes. In reality, it's a lot harder than it looks.

Still, the sidewalk is clear for several blocks. None of those bloody displays they like to put outside in nice weather. As long as no fucking pedestrians pop out of a shop in front of my bike, I should be fine. The last thing I need is to hit somebody.

I rev the engine a few times. I'll need to cross lanes to get over there, so I flip on my turn signal. The guy next to me doesn't even look. I edge my bike across the line, and he nearly clips me with the front of his Volkswagen.

"Bloody bugger!" I yell at him, but he pretends not to notice, just creeps his hatchback forward.

I don't wait any longer. As soon as I'm even with his back bumper, I nose into the lane. There's little the car behind him can do, because traffic has slowed to another stop. I don't even wait for it to start up again, just hit the gas and hop the curb. The bike lurches onto the pavement, and a clear streak of cement stretches before me. I jam down the pedal.

The lights still prove problematic, since I have to stop for cross traffic. But at least I can move as soon as they change, instead of waiting for fifty drivers ahead of me to put down their phones and tap the gas.

A siren blares across the sea of car roofs. A police officer stuck in the middle lane shouts obscenities at me. I laugh and flip him the bird before gunning it through the intersection.

The airport looms ahead of me. I haven't checked the clock recently and have no clue if I still have time to make the flight. Or worse—if they'll even have room for me on the plane. I brush that last thought aside. There's always room left in first class.

I park the bike in the departures lane, not giving two fucks if someone tows it.

The only thing that matters is getting to Walker before she leaves.

43

"The Bolter" - Taylor Swift

Walker

I would pay a lot of money to have seen the reactions of everyone last night as they opened their envelopes. Lux would have worn a look of complete shock and confusion. Pierce would have been dark and brooding, not much different than usual. Maeve would have seethed, her brows and lips pulling together in the center of her face. Rhett would have thrown a tantrum, complete with drinks sloshed onto the wall and knocked-over chairs.

And Heath—he would have sat through the whole thing, wondering what the fuck was going on. Why he'd been skipped over. Why he didn't receive the biggest punishment of all. Then when it hit him that he *had* been dealt the worst hand, he would have crumbled like a crème brûlée at a subpar restaurant.

I could have left after delivering the invitations, but instead I got a good night's rest and said goodbye to the manor. My hair is now freshly washed, my laundry is all cleaned and tucked into my trunk, and I even stopped by my mum's this morning to say goodbye and drop off my car.

Everything is done, so why is there a giant, gaping hole in the center of my chest where my heart used to reside?

My friends deserve everything they got. They were going to completely destroy any chance I had of graduating Oxford, or at least of doing so with a spotless record. Heath deserves to live a lonely, miserable life for betraying me twice. He knew I was falling for him again, but that didn't stop him from working to bring me down.

Cheer up, I tell my heart. *You got everything you wanted.*

I step up to the desk and hand the attendant my passport and ticket. There was no way to turn off the email reminders about remote check-in, so there are currently a handful of them sitting in my inbox. As if I would trust a computer to get me properly checked in.

This world is so screwed.

The attendant welcomes me with a smile and directs me to the first-class lounge. "Someone will come to the lounge to take care of your bag."

I thank her and head in the direction she points. Thank god for WNX's concierge service. The airport is crowded today, and I'm glad I gave myself plenty of time. Traffic was a mess downtown, too. Something about the queen paying visits.

I drag my huge trunk onto the autowalk and have a flashback to last time I was here, when the little girl threw up all over her mum. If it hadn't been for her, none of the past month would have happened. I wouldn't have run into Lux in the bathroom, she wouldn't have told everyone I was back in town, they wouldn't have hatched a plot to get into my good graces, just so they could bring me down . . .

I wouldn't have given Heath my heart a second time, in spite of knowing that he's bad news, that he's just like my father.

Maybe it's this comparison, or the *click, click, click* of my trunk wheels against the seams in the tile floor, but I have a sudden flashback to my dad walking toward his car, dragging his suitcase behind him. That tiny breath of hope when the pavement stopped him, only to release him again immediately.

He has always run away from his problems. He's too much of a coward to face the messes he's made, the pain he's caused, or the people he's left behind. It wasn't even the cheating that hurt so much. It was the fact that he ran, without apology, without a backward glance, without a goodbye. I woke up more than once as a child to find him gone when I came down for breakfast. Every time my mother broke the news, we both knew we'd never see him again unless she decided to give him another chance.

Only a coward runs from his mistakes. A strong person can admit when they're wrong, apologize, and do what they can to make things right. Only a coward runs in the face of conflict, afraid to be caught looking less than desirable in the light. A strong person stands up, ready to fight for what he wants, what he deserves.

Up ahead, a little girl throws her arms around her father's neck. He picks her up and swings her around, her little feet flying out behind her. My heart clenches. Hopefully she will never have to experience the pain of waking to find her daddy gone, escaped in the night because she wasn't important enough for him to say goodbye.

I move past them, ignoring the lump that has decided my throat is a good place to hang out. I'm doing the right thing, I remind myself. But then why does it feel like I'm leaving everything behind?

Why does it feel like I'm doing what he did?

I'm running from my mum and her relationship issues instead of telling her I hate being a witness to her drama. I'm running from my friends because they hurt me, instead of telling them the truth and allowing them to be there for me.

And Heath—I'm running from him because I can't face the fact that I'm turning into my own mother, that I'm as in love with him now as I ever have been, in spite of the fact that he betrayed me twice. Because deep down I do believe him, I do think he was telling the truth when he said he did it because he was scared.

I understand that fear. It's what is propelling me across the concourse. I halt in my tracks, and my trunk bumps into me from behind. People swerve to avoid running into me, and I refrain from calling out apologies.

My mind whirls as quickly as the foot traffic around me. It was never because Oxford offered more than Wesbourne. It was always because it felt like an escape from reality, a safe house protecting me from the ugliness of the world outside, from the people I left behind. People I love desperately and still need in my life. Without them, everything feels drained of color.

I've been living half a life in Oxford, content to close in on myself in order to avoid facing the pain of the past. But in doing so, I hurt the people I'm closest to. I made them think they didn't matter to me, that our relationship wasn't worth salvaging. I was so terrified of becoming my mother that I never stopped to realize I had become my father.

It takes some effort to turn my trunk around. The thing weighs almost as much as I do. People keep pushing past me, intent on reaching their flights, and I have to fight my way to the other side of the concourse to join the crowd moving the other way.

I take the autowalk again, grateful for the chance to stop pulling an entire month's worth of belongings behind me. I don't have a plan from here, and that thought terrifies me more than any of the others.

My mum will be thrilled to have me stay with her. I'll have to decide if putting up with her string of boyfriends is something I can deal with over my breakfast oatmeal. Oxford isn't a problem either. If I'm honest, my decision to become a professor had a lot less to do with my ambition and a lot more to do with feeling stuck.

The knot in my stomach has nothing to do with logistics and everything to do with facing my friends. What I did was pretty bad, and none of them are quick to forgive. They may never speak to me again. Am I willing to live with that?

I'll have to be if I am to have any hope of becoming everything my father isn't: strong, confident, and unafraid of conflict. They may not speak to me, but that doesn't mean I can't try to patch things up between us. After all, they're as much victims of this entire thing as anyone. If I hadn't left, and if Heath had told the truth . . .

It doesn't matter now. All that matters is facing the mess and cleaning it up.

As I step off the autowalk, a woman bumps into my hip, causing me to lurch into the man beside me. I'm about to shout something nasty at her when my eyes are pulled to the flow of traffic on the other side of the concourse.

Pulled to *him* as he runs toward the departure gates.

44

"Sorry" - Buckcherry

Heath

Are airports always this crowded? God, this is a fucking nightmare. How in the world am I supposed to find her in this mess?

I scan every face I can, but there must be tens of thousands of people here. I couldn't look at each one if I had all day. Which I don't. My flight leaves in three minutes. I dodge other travelers as I run toward the terminal. At least I don't have luggage slowing me down.

The gate looms ahead of me. I can already see that the door is closed, the seats in the waiting area all empty. But I still slap my palms on the attendant's counter and beg her to let me on the plane.

"I'm sorry, sir." She keeps her eyes focused on her computer screen. "They are already preparing for takeoff."

"But I have a ticket." I reach into my pocket and pull out the now crumpled piece of paper. "First class."

She doesn't even bother glancing at it. "I'm really sorry. There's nothing I can do. They can get you on a different flight at the ticket counter. Now, if you'll excuse me." She sidesteps me and walks away.

Fuck. Fuck, fuck, fuck.

I slump into the nearest chair. It's stupid to feel like I've missed her by a matter of minutes when she was probably already in England this morning. Now I'll have to wait until tonight to fly out. By the time I reach Oxford, she'll be cloistered away and able to avoid me for the rest of her life.

I try calling her once more, but she's either blocked me again or turned her phone off. I lean forward and dangle my cell between my knees. It feels pointless to sit here, but I don't have the energy to get up, let alone walk back across the giant concourse to the ticket counter.

After a few minutes of sulking, I force myself to rise. Nothing's going to change if I stay sitting here. I better get my shit in order if I am to stand a chance of getting Walker back.

I head toward the front of the airport. My stomach growls, reminding me that I haven't eaten anything today. I'll get my ticket changed and then grab some food.

I keep my eyes focused on where I'm headed, not bothering to meet the eyes of the people around me. It's only hearing my name called that snaps me from my trance.

"Heath!" she says again. I recognize the voice. I also recognize that this is nothing but a hallucination.

I turn in the direction of the sound. I blink rapidly to clear the mirage, but she's still there, still running toward me, a humongous suitcase at her heels. Is anyone else seeing this, or have I officially gone mad?

"Heath!" There's a note of desperation in Walker's voice, like she's been trying to get to me and had to put up a fight. She's closer now, only a lounge of massage chairs between us.

People are starting to look. They look at her, then back at me, as if trying to decide if this beautiful girl is actually headed toward me. I'm still trying to figure it out myself when she launches herself into my arms. Her trunk clatters to the floor behind her, but she pays no mind. She wraps her arms around my neck and her legs around my waist.

I stagger backward with the unexpected momentum. I've never felt anything better in my life. A thousand of the best waves couldn't rival this moment. I bury my face in her neck, in that divine coconut scent, and inhale deeply, filling my lungs with it, with her.

I don't know how long we stand like this, just that it isn't long enough. I could hold her like this for eternity, and it still wouldn't be enough. I let my hands roam her back, wanting to convince myself that this is, in fact, happening and not a figment of my imagination.

She feels like a million dreams in one, both everything I ever hoped for and all the things I was too scared to. "I'm so sorry," I whisper into her neck.

Walker's hold on me tightens.

"I'm sorry for hurting you." I increase the pressure of my arms so she can feel how sorry I am. "I'm sorry for not being the man you deserve. That I tried so hard to push you away. That I disappointed you."

She gives an answering half sob. Her face rubs against the skin of my neck, and strands of her hair catch in the stubble on my jaw, which I didn't take the time to shave off this morning. I want to bury myself in her and never come up for air.

People are starting to notice us. A tiny woman with white hair nudges the man beside her and smiles at us. A teenager snaps a picture with her phone. A businessman on a call steps around us and shoots me an annoyed look.

I scan for a place where we can have some privacy, but we're smack-dab in the middle of the huge concourse, people streaming around us on both sides. "Walker," I say quietly. "We're making a scene."

"I don't care," she mumbles.

"Now I know I must be hallucinating, because you never want to make a scene."

"I'm sorry for leaving," she says. "Again."

I rub brisk circles on her back. "You don't need to apologize for that. I drove you away both times."

My neck is growing damp from her tears. "Hey." I shift her in my arms so I can get a glimpse of her face. She keeps it buried in my shoulder. "As much as I love holding you right now, I'd like to kiss you even more."

She sniffs loudly, then moves to slide down. As she brushes against my cock, it springs up to remind me that it also has an opinion on this situation. Her face is blotchy from crying, and I take it with both hands.

"Hey." I wipe her cheeks with my thumbs. "Don't cry."

A hiccup escapes between her lips. "I'm sorry for ever letting you think you're not enough." Her arms slip around my neck, and she drags her body against me. "You've always been more than enough for me."

I capture her mouth then, staking my claim on her here and now. She opens beneath me, letting me in to explore, to conquer, to ravish. A tiny groan slips out of her as I flick my tongue over the roof of her mouth. I hope she can tell how sorry I am and how hard I intend to work to earn her trust in the future.

She responds by tilting her head, proving that she trusts me, that she's willing to put the past behind us. Her hands are on my chest, buried in the fabric of my T-shirt. I move my lips to the side of her neck, nipping and biting the sensitive skin there.

"Heath," she whimpers. "I need you inside me."

"Soon, baby." I pull her earlobe between my teeth and suck.

"Now. Like right now."

I let out a surprised laugh. "Babe, we're in the middle of the airport."

"There's always the bathroom," she says before kissing me again.

My cock surges in response. *Bathroom indeed.* I pull back and immediately miss her mouth. "You sure?"

"Please," she whispers against my lips. "I need you so badly." She flicks her tongue across mine, and I'm a dead man.

"Okay." I drop one more kiss on her lips before backing away. "But we'll have to be strategic about it."

I pull up a map of the airport on my phone. There's a public restroom down the hall, away from all the foot traffic. I grab her trunk in one hand and her palm in the other. "Come on."

45

"Everytime We Touch" - Cascada

Walker

Heath goes into the bathroom first. I'm supposed to stay outside with my trunk for a full minute before following him inside. I'm not sure I even make it thirty seconds before I barge through the door and lean my suitcase against the wall.

He shakes his head with incredulity, but his mouth lifts in a smile.

"Is it empty?" I whisper. It's a small bathroom, but it still has a handful of cubicles.

"For now." He yanks me inside one of them and closes the door behind us.

Now that we're here, I suddenly feel nervous. "What if we get caught?"

"We won't if you're quiet." He grabs me and clamps his mouth down over mine. I groan and reach for his hair. He pushes me against the cubicle wall. The coolness of the metal seeps through my clothes.

Heath's hands stray downward until they reach the bottom of my skirt. I couldn't have chosen a better outfit for this if I tried. The skirt is short and pleated, and there are—

"No fucking tights this time." He bites my lip gently as his hands move to the sensitive skin of my upper thighs. I gasp as his warm palm grazes my panties. I frantically try to remember which pair I put on this morning but decide it doesn't matter, because he's even seen me in the hospital-appointed pair I wore after I had my appendix removed.

His fingers toy with the seam of my underwear like they're hesitating at the door. "Heath," I moan, and press against him.

He grins and drags both fingers against me. "Your panties are soaked."

"No shit." I lean my head back against the wall as he torments me with his hand. My eyes fall closed, and I shudder as he skirts his fingers back and forth between my mound and panties.

The distinctive sound of the door opening cuts through everything. Heath clamps his free hand over my mouth before I can make an audible sound. My eyes grow wide as it becomes obvious that someone has entered the cubicle next to ours.

Heath squeezes his eyes shut and doesn't remove his hand from my mouth. His mouth quirks in silent laughter. Inside my panties, his hand has stopped moving, but he opens his eyes and starts sliding his fingers back and forth again.

I try to shake my head, but he's holding it fast against the wall. He ignores my frantic eyes, taking special pleasure in my discomfort. He slips one finger between my folds, then grins when my eyes roll back in my head.

The person beside us takes a long time finishing up. Meanwhile, Heath takes an equally long time working me over. He has yet to remove his hand from my mouth, not trusting that I am even less willing to give us away than he is.

His fingers both drive into me with enough force that I would cry out if I could. Now I have to stifle the noise, because even with his hand over me, I don't trust the sound not to escape.

The toilet next door flushes, and I mentally encourage the person to quickly wash their hands. The tap runs in the sink, followed by the obnoxious hand dryer. I roll my eyes as the seconds tick by. Heath smiles widely, pulls his hand away, and kisses me. I meet his mouth with a vengeance, now that I can do something with the burning inside of me.

As soon as the door whooshes shut behind our intruder, my legs weaken. *Finally.* Heath pulls back his mouth and hand, and I whimper at the loss of contact. Squatting, he drags my panties down my legs and helps me step out of them. Rather than leave them on the floor, he tucks them into the pocket of his shorts. My groin grows hot.

He yanks me away from the wall and spins me around. "Put your hands on the back of the tank."

I have to straddle the toilet to do so, but I comply. The porcelain is cold beneath my hands, a sharp contrast to the heat blazing a trail from my thighs to my head. The unmistakable sound of a zipper greets my ears, followed by the rip of foil. I peer over my shoulder as he rolls on the condom. Moisture forms in my crotch, and my hips buck backward of their own volition.

"Easy." He steadies me. In one quick motion, he flips my skirt up and over my back. He takes the same two fingers as before and slides them through my drenched folds, over and over. I bite down on my lip, not wanting to cry out but needing to so badly.

A sharp gasp flies from my mouth as he thrusts them inside me, propelling me forward. I hold on to the toilet tank as he does it again. And again. And again.

"You like being fucked in different ways, don't you?" His voice is sand in my swimsuit, stinging wind on my cheek, biting cold against my skin. I arch my neck, longing for his touch. He drives his fingers in even further, curling them and making me tighten around him.

"Heath." It's no more than a whimper, because that's all I'm capable of right now.

As slow as molasses, he draws his fingers out of me, only to replace them with his cock. Stars flash at the edges of my vision as he inserts his tip inside me. I grind against him, eager for him to fill me, but he doesn't capitulate.

He grips my hips with both hands, and I mimic the gesture with the lid of the toilet tank. My legs are splayed wide to accommodate both the commode and Heath. I lean my cheek against the cold porcelain to relieve some of the heat camping out in my face.

He uses my hips as leverage and pushes inside. I jerk my head backward, and a cry escapes as he fills me to the breaking point. He pulls back fractionally, then drives home again. I tilt my hips higher and push them backward. He hisses through his teeth as he finds a new angle.

His right hand slides from my hip bone to my pussy, now a quivering mess. Using his fingers, he renews his torture of my clit, pressing it, stroking it, pinching it. I cry out as my insides coil around him, so tightly I'm not sure they ever intend to let go.

I don't care if anyone comes in. I don't care if they arrest us for public indecency. The only thing I care about is getting more of Heath.

With one final thrust, he sinks deeper into me, causing both of our orgasms to break at the same time.

46

"Dancing in the Flames" - The Weeknd

Walker

"Put this on." He hands me a helmet.

"What will you wear?"

He sticks it on my head and fastens the chin strap. "It's difficult to get hurt when you're only going five miles an hour. Traffic is a nightmare." He swings his leg over the bike and fires it up.

I straddle the seat behind him and wrap my arms around his waist. I've never ridden on a motorbike before, but my normal fear has vanished, maybe in the face of postcoital bliss or because I trust Heath.

It doesn't make sense, choosing to trust him, but there is something different about him now. My mum's words kept running through my head. *One mistake shouldn't define a person.*

Heath isn't a cheater. He's never looked at other women, I've never caught him texting someone else, and when we're together, his focus is solely on me. Those aren't the actions of a cheater.

I should know. I had one for a father.

Heath made a mistake. A stupid, awful, heart-breaking mistake. But I also understand why he did it. Sometimes when you're scared, it's hard to see past anything but an instinctive reaction. For me, it was running. For him, it's always been self-sabotaging. We both have some growing to do, but at least we'll do it together.

We cruise down one street after another. He's doing his best to avoid the traffic pileups, which have gotten better since this morning. Every time we stop at a red light, he rests both hands on my thighs. My whole body tingles from that single touch.

An hour later, I'm already burning for him again. Our close proximity on the bike only amplifies the need I have for him. I shift against him, and he looks over his shoulder at me, a devilish grin on his face.

"You gonna make it another ten minutes, or should I pull over now?"

Considering we're currently making our way across the bridge, I pinch his side through his T-shirt. "Just hurry."

He revs the engine and zips around cars like he's in a video game and not real life.

"I prefer to arrive alive," I say over the noise of the wind and traffic.

When we pull up to the driveway of the manor, I wonder who is throwing a party. Four cars are lined up outside, the tail end of a cherry-red Maserati blocking anyone else from entering the premises. I pull the helmet off.

Heath slips the bike through an opening between the gate and the vehicle. As we roar along the narrow strip of gravel, I recognize the rest of the cars. Red Maserati, black Aston Martin, dark green Bentley convertible, white vintage Ferrari Spyder.

Arrayed on the porch in a variety of positions are their respective owners: Rhett in a pink tank and denim cutoffs, Pierce in a white shirt and gray slacks, Maeve in a houndstooth dress and black boots, and Lux in a white tennis skirt and polo.

Oh, fuck.

Lux lurches from where she is propped against the porch railing when she sees us. She darts across the lawn, and Heath has to stop the bike so he doesn't run over her. "Oh my god, Walker." She practically pulls me off the bike and into her arms. "I am so sorry."

She crushes me against her rose-scented body. When it becomes clear she doesn't intend to let go any time soon, I drop the helmet in the grass and bring my hands to her back. She wiggles us back and forth until I'm sure that I died on that motorbike and this is some form of purgatory.

"Okay, my turn." Maeve's voice cuts through our little reunion. She frees me from the human Velcro, only to attach herself to me instead. She smells luxurious and expensive, like a bottle of cognac and velvet. "I had no idea."

She releases me as quickly as she grabbed me, and I stagger backward a step. Heath is still on the bike, but he has cut the engine. His eyes are glued to the handlebars, and he seems unwilling to look anyone in the eye, even me.

"Are you twats coming up? I'd rather not have to move," Rhett calls from the porch, where he's straddling the railing and leaning his back against the post.

Lux and Maeve tug me toward the house. I look back at Heath. "Are you coming?"

He meets my eyes for a second before dropping them again. "I'll be there in a second."

So much for getting it on in that giant bed of mine. Or taking a bath together in the clawfoot tub. I allow myself to be led to the steps of the place I called home for a month. Fortunately my lease isn't up until the end of the week, or the cleaning crew would be in for a surprise when they showed up.

Pierce wraps stiff arms around me when I reach the porch. "We're terribly sorry for everything, Walker. I feel like absolute shit over what happened."

I nod against his chest because I don't know what else to do or say.

Do I say it's okay? It's not. Do I say all is forgiven? I'm not sure if it is yet. Even Heath and I have a mountain of issues to work through.

After Pierce releases me, Rhett beckons me over to his precarious perch on the banister. I approach him, shaking my head. Leave it to Rhett to make even an apology selfish.

He slings an arm around my shoulders when I'm close enough. "Just so you know, I wasn't in favor of the plan, but they outvoted me."

Maeve tosses a cushion from one of the rocking chairs and hits him square in the chest. "Liar."

His mouth drops open. "I never lie."

She rolls her eyes and hurls another pillow at him. This one causes him to sway slightly.

He throws up his hands. "Okay, fine. I lied."

With one final cushion, Maeve manages to hit him before he can place his hands back on the banister, and he falls off and into the bushes below.

"Oww!" he bellows.

She throws her head back and cackles. "Serves you right, douchebag." She replaces the cushion and sinks into a rocker.

Lux saunters over and leans against one of the huge white pillars. "For the record, I was here to apologize first." She crosses her ankles in front of her.

"She's right, but I was here just a few seconds behind her," Maeve says.

"It doesn't matter who was here first." Pierce crosses his arms over his chest. "What matters is that Walker knows we didn't understand the full situation."

"Or any of it," Rhett mutters as he reenters the porch, dusting off his backside. He shoots Maeve a glare before climbing back onto the handrail.

"Do you forgive us?" Lux reaches for my hand.

"I—" I study the four of them. The last thing I expected was for them to make an effort like this. How could I not forgive them? "Of course," I say.

"Woohoo!" Rhett throws his hands in the air, loses his balance, and promptly falls back into the bushes.

"I think you're safer on the ground," Maeve calls to him. "Maybe we should get you a walker, one of the ones with tennis balls on the bottom."

He lifts a hand from the flower bed, middle finger extended.

"I still can't believe Heath cheated on you," Lux says, gripping my hand tighter. "I honestly didn't think he had it in him. You two were always so sweet togeth—"

"Just because a couple is sweet in public doesn't mean everything is sweet behind closed doors," Maeve says. "You should know." She gives Lux a knowing look.

Lux ignores her. "I wish you had told us."

"I didn't want to cause drama within the group." I tug my hand back under the pretense of arranging my hair. I can only imagine how disastrous it looks after that helmet.

"You caused a lot more than drama by leaving without saying anything." Maeve's voice comes out sharp. She softens it. "We were worried about you."

I never stopped to consider how my leaving would affect all of them. I was primarily focused on getting away before the conflict blew up in my face.

That's what my dad was doing too. Not thinking about anyone but himself.

"I'm sorry," I say quietly.

"Water under the bridge." Pierce lays a hand on my shoulder. "Want me to beat up Heath for you?"

I raise my face to his in surprise. "What?"

He nods to the driveway, where Heath is still sitting on his bike, playing with his phone. "Just say the word."

I frown and shake my head. "It's all good."

"What does that mean?" Maeve sits forward in the rocker. "What's *all good*?"

"Heath and I. We're good. We talked, and—" My cheeks flame with heat. "It's all good."

"Tell me you are not taking that bastard back," she says.

I blink at her. "I'll keep my mouth shut, then."

"Walker, you can't be serious." She pushes herself out of the chair, which threatens to swallow her tiny frame. "He cheated on you."

The situation feels like a mirror image of countless conversations I've had with my mum. Only this time, I understand a little about what she must have felt every time I yelled at her. I lift my hand to my mouth to bite a nail. "I'm aware."

Maeve swats it away. "Don't start that again. Listen to me, Walk. Cheating is a hard no, remember?"

"It's her decision, Maeve," Pierce murmurs.

"He cheated on her!" she shrieks.

My heart trips, and I cast a look at Heath, still on his bike. His eyes lift at the same moment, evidently having heard her. His chest expands as he inhales. He sticks his phone in his pocket and turns the key. The engine roars to life.

"No," I yell, and race down the porch steps. Rhett lifts his head from the flower bed where he's still sprawled, but I ignore him, focused on one person only.

Heath lifts his head as I approach, but he doesn't kill the engine. I tug the helmet from his head and toss it aside. I grab his face in both hands. "Please don't go," I say against his mouth. "Stay. With me."

I taste his hesitation, so I kiss him harder. When his fingers thread their way into my hair, I know I've won. I break off the kiss. "Come on." I tug his hand. "They'll have to forgive you."

"I'm not sure they *have* to do anything," he says, but he follows me to the porch. Rhett has picked himself up from the ground and joined the others. They form a barricade at the top of the steps, arms crossed and chins jutting out.

"Guys." I entwine my fingers with Heath's. "You can accept us both or reject us both, but you're not splitting us up. If I can forgive Heath for what he did, then you sure as fuck can too."

They switch their attention from us to each other. Maeve mutters something to Pierce. They converse for a few minutes among themselves, long enough that I start to get nervous.

Heath tugs on my hand. "Hey." His eyes are so warm and deep, I want to climb into them and never leave. "No matter what happens, we have each other, okay?"

His fingers find my chin and lift it up, high enough that he can seal his mouth over mine again. At least if they decide to kick us out, we can head inside and finish what we started earlier. If they decide to keep us, it's hard to say how long until they all leave.

Someone clears their throat. "After a lengthy discussion, we've decided—"

"Just kidding! You can stop kissing now," Lux calls. "Of course we accept you both."

Heath pulls back enough to meet my gaze. "What do you say? Make them so uncomfortable that they leave?"

I grin and tug him back down to me. "Deal."

47

"All My Love" - Noah Kahan

Heath

We didn't go with traditional Halloween decor—jack-o'-lanterns on the steps and skeletons in the front yard. Since the house already looks like something out of a horror movie, Walker decorated the outside with the creepiest stuff: white gauze that looks a bloody lot like cobwebs, lights that flicker at odd intervals, and a fog machine aimed at the front door. From the eaves, she hung black Spanish moss, which has a tendency to stick to my hair whenever I walk underneath it.

We bought the house last month. It took some sweet-talking from Walker and an offer of double the value to convince the owners to sell. Now that it's ours, I have a hard time imagining the future anywhere but within these hundred-year-old walls, complete with the creepy-as-fuck paintings hanging on them.

I drop the bag of dry ice onto the kitchen floor, and Poe runs out from under the table. Two days after we moved in, Walker announced that the place needed a cat. We returned from the shelter that afternoon with an all-black monster who immediately decided that, while he will tolerate Walker, he fully intends to murder me in my sleep one day.

I break the ice into small chunks with a screwdriver. We found a recipe online for a spooky-ass cocktail, and for the first time, I have the privilege of relieving Pierce of his duties as host and bartender.

Walker swings into the kitchen doorway. "Pierce is here."

I follow her to the porch. He's been much happier since getting his painting back, even though he had to pay a million more than the first time he bought it. When Maeve climbs out of the passenger seat of his car, I lean toward Walker. "See? Definitely hooking up."

She elbows me in the ribs and pastes a giant smile on her face as they approach. "Definitely not."

Maeve is wearing her family's pearls, also rescued from Walker's devious plot to auction them off to the highest bidder. The girls exchange hugs, and Pierce and I slap each other on the shoulder.

"Come on back." I lead them through the garden to my favorite spot. The contractors finished up last week, just in time for our first poker night.

There's a big stone terrace with a fire pit, multiple seating arrangements, a hot tub, and a large wooden table and chairs. The fire is already blazing, the table scooted up close to it. Walker placed throw blankets on all of the chairs earlier. The temperature has already dropped ten degrees since this afternoon.

"This is terrific, mate," Pierce says, looking around.

Lux, Rhett, and Walker round the corner of the house. "Dude." Rhett drags out the word as he walks over. "This place is creepy as fuck."

"It's Walker's jam." I give him a one-armed hug. He is once again the proud owner of that vintage Stratocaster, although I suspect he will never allow Walker to live down what she did.

The girls head inside to grab the cocktails. I distribute three beers while we wait, and Pierce blurts out, "Isabella broke up with me."

"Fuck. You okay, mate?" It's a relief to be the one asking instead of the one being asked.

"I'm fine," he says. "I thought she was the one, but she didn't." He tilts his bottle back and takes a long drink.

"The right one's worth fighting for," I say.

"Oh, god." Rhett wipes his mouth with the back of his hand. "You're about to become sickeningly repulsive, aren't you? What happened to that 'disappoint early and often' shit?"

I shake my head and take a swig of beer. "That shit was bogus. When you're with the right person, they make you want to be a better version of yourself."

Walker comes outside through the French doors leading from the kitchen. She's holding a tray of bubbling drinks, courtesy of the dry ice. Her eyes meet mine, and heat grows in my groin. I will be divesting her of that skirt later.

She gave up Oxford and her ambition of becoming a professor. She says it wasn't because of me. I think she did it for herself after realizing that she already had everything she needed right here. She's been spending all of her free time decorating the house, but once she's done with that, I plan to encourage her to apply to work at the Archives. My girl has manuscript dust in her veins. She needs to be somewhere that can flourish.

"Why is your girlfriend trying to poison me?" Rhett looks at the tray of boiling green drinks like it might kill him from close proximity alone.

"Don't drink it until the dry ice is gone," Walker says. "It should only take a few minutes."

Lux tells each of us to grab a drink for a photo. We throw arms around shoulders and toast the camera she has set up on a tripod. Only Lux shows up at parties with camera equipment. "To the best friends in the world," she calls out as a series of flashes signal the pictures being taken.

She didn't win her purse collection at the auction, but she recently announced her intention to start collecting vintage Chanel, so maybe Walker did her a favor after all.

We settle at the table and start the game. Walker is the dealer tonight, and I slip my hand up her thigh as she's handing out cards. She jumps in her seat and shoots me a lethal side-eye. I pretend not to notice and toy with the hem of her skirt, which leaves little to the imagination.

She's been spending more time with her mum. We even have dinner with Eviana once a week. She's dating a new bloke, and this one doesn't seem too bad, although Walker's still not crazy about him. I'm not sure there will ever be a guy she thinks deserves her mum, but as long as Eviana is happy, Walker doesn't say much.

"Have you gone to see your dad yet, Heath?" Rhett asks after everyone has submitted their ante.

I take a sip of my drink before answering. It has a sweet melon-and-citrus flavor. "I'm not visiting that asshole. Ever."

Walker shifts beside me. It's been a frequent source of contention between us. She thinks I should go see him, because she doesn't want me to hold on to resentment. I usually combat that by asking when she last talked to her dad.

The great Robert Lawrence is serving five years in the Ridgeford Correctional Facility for decades of tax fraud, which is the official way of saying he's locked inside a fancy-ass resort-style prison for white men with too much money and way too much fucking power. When he is released, I have no doubt he will try to ruin me. Until then, I plan to forget he exists.

A casual argument breaks out between Rhett and Maeve over whether to accept his grievance or not. I glance at Pierce, but he and Lux are having a secret conversation, one which is causing both of them to look pissed.

"Dealer decides." We set that rule at the first poker game, when a similar argument broke out over whether Lux was allowed to submit Maeve's best friend for revenge or not.

Walker permits Rhett's grievance, to which he whoops.

"Lux, is it true that Jojo Banks is going to be at your Gatsby party?" Maeve asks.

Lux looks relieved to end her conversation with Pierce. "That's what her assistant told me."

I squeeze Walker's thigh. "You ready to rub shoulders with popstars again?" I murmur.

She splays her hand so that her fingers dip down between mine. "I'd rather rub something else with you," she whispers.

My cock instantly goes rigid. I'm on the verge of sending everyone home so we can explore that idea when her face grows concerned.

"What's going on?" she says to Lux. I've missed whatever is being discussed.

"Nothing." Lux waves her hand before wrapping a strand of hair around her finger. "I'm selling. I just met with the estate agent yesterday."

"Why?" Maeve says. "You love that house."

Lux shrugs, causing the blanket to slip from her shoulders. "It's time for a change."

"Okay." Pierce sounds suspicious as hell. "Where are you moving to?"

"Carter asked me to move in with him." Then, as if her life depends on getting out of here as quickly as possible, she grabs her empty glass and says, "Anyone else need a refill?"

No one says anything. We're still coming to grips with her announcement.

"What?" She sinks back into her chair. "We've been together for a year and a half."

"Carter." I twirl the maraschino cherry on the end of my toothpick. "The same wanker who nearly got my fist in his face for treating you the way he did at the beach house?"

She huffs out a sigh. "He was worked up that day. You caught him off guard."

"Doesn't he have a *condo*?" Rhett says, like that's a crime against humanity.

"*You* have a condo, mate." I dunk my cherry into my drink and swirl it around.

"Mine's at least in the fucking Dankirk Tower. His is like, down on Twenty-Eighth Street or something," he says.

"So he has a condo," Lux says. "So what? He's not *poor*."

"Practically," Rhett mutters.

Maeve ends her analysis of Lux's face to say, "Why doesn't Carter just move in with you? Your house is much bigger and nicer."

"I think he would feel emasculated moving in with his girlfriend." Lux looks at me. "Wouldn't you feel that way?"

I gesture around us at the terrace that my girlfriend found without my help. I tap the toothpick on the side of my glass before pulling the cherry off with my teeth.

"If my girlfriend had a place like yours, I'd sell my condo immediately and move in," Rhett says with a laugh.

"It doesn't matter, okay?" Lux says. "I've already made up my mind. Now can we finish the game?"

We return to the poker and pretend not to be disturbed by this toxic relationship. In fact, if Pierce and Rhett are up for it, I am down to pay Mr. Carter Fitzgerald-Smythe a little visit, maybe introducing my fist to his jaw.

A while later, Rhett folds and announces, "I need to take a shit. It might be a while."

Walker gives me a look that says *You're in charge of bathrooms tonight.* Fucking terrific.

Lux retreats to the house several minutes later. The temps are plummeting now that the sun has fully set.

"You cold?" I ask Walker.

"A little." She gives me a smile that goes directly to my groin.

"I'll grab some more blankets." I plant a kiss on the top of her head as I stand, filling my lungs with her scent.

At the terrace doors, I pause. Voices float out from the kitchen. I'm not sure why, but I stop and listen instead of going inside.

"You can't do that, okay?" Rhett says. "You can't put yourself in danger like that."

"Who says it's dangerous?" Lux says.

"The drug world is always dangerous."

* * *

To witness Heath's proposal, go to jessicajude.com/ace-of-betrayal-bonus for a sweet bonus chapter.

Exclusive Chapter

**Read on for an exclusive chapter from the next book in the
Hand of Revenge series.**

1 Year Ago

I should have ordered car service. The traffic on Twenty-Fifth is horrendous this morning. The Wesbourne Traveling Art Exhibition has brought thousands of visitors into the city.

To make matters worse, I'm terrible at parallel parking. Blame that one on my too-busy-with-his-new-wife-and-kids dad. I can never get close enough to the curb, so I have to pull back into traffic like a fool or risk getting sideswiped. It looks like that will be the least of my concerns today, though, since no one is letting me back up in the first place.

A roar grows louder behind me, and I catch a glimpse of an old motorcycle in the rearview mirror. Instead of merging into the next lane to avoid hitting me, he whips his bike into the parking space I've been trying to get into for the past five minutes.

He. Steals. My. Spot.

I blink into the mirror, thinking maybe my eyes have tricked me, but nope. The man is straddling the bike, looking quite pleased with himself, and wearing way too much leather, even if he is trying to throw off "cool biker guy" vibes. It's literally eighty-five degrees outside.

"You prick," I yell at him. My car top is down—you don't cover a car like this with a roof—so I know he can hear me. "That spot is mine!"

He tugs the helmet from his head, and a mane of thick brown hair spills out from beneath it, way too long to be decent. It reaches all the way down to his shoulders. A slow smile spreads across his face as he swings a leg over the bike. Then—eyes locked on mine in the mirror—he flips me off. Just tosses that bird into the air and saunters away, like this is all over now that he got what he wanted.

That's where he's wrong, the bastard.

My hands tighten around the steering wheel. I briefly consider backing into his bike. The vision of its crushed shape beneath my wheels holds a special appeal, but I really don't want to scratch the paint on my car.

Horns blare at me now that I am no longer trying to park on what is clearly a full street, but am instead holding up traffic by sitting in the middle of the lane. I shift back into drive and head for the parking garage several blocks away.

Pedestrians clog the sidewalks as I exit the garage. The salon is six blocks away, and I'm in five-inch Jimmy Choos. I mentally curse that biker my entire walk. I haven't managed to get a spot in front of the shop even once in the past two years, and when the opportunity finally presents itself, some asshole has to steal it from me.

I glare at the bike as I round the corner. Sitting there innocently, waiting for its owner to come back. It's older than I am and doesn't look expensive. What would it take to shove it into traffic, let some other wanker run it over? It's not like *they'd* have a Ferrari with a paint job to protect.

But as I approach the bike, an even better idea presents itself.

I snap a picture of the license plate and head into the salon. I'm led to the VIP area, where Taleah is waiting for me. She listens to my sob story and makes the appropriate sympathetic noises, then fills me in on the latest gossip while massaging her secret regenerative serum into my scalp. I have a reputation for knowing everything about everyone, thanks to Taleah collecting juicy morsels between my weekly visits.

When she's done and her assistant starts on my blowout, I open the ALPR app on my phone. It has come in handy more than once since Hans hooked me up. It's arguably the only good thing to come out of that relationship, but it's more than most guys leave me with.

You never know when you might need to run someone's plates.

I enter the number from the bike. It's registered to Jonathan E. Lawson. I don't know the name, of course. There's no way that guy has ever set foot in the Hills unless it was to make a pizza delivery. And judging from the hair, I doubt he's been inside a decent salon in a long time either.

The ALPR gives me his address, and my GPS tells me it's in the Junction. Not that I expected anything different, but it does complicate things. For starters, I've never actually been there before. I've driven past it, of course, and heard all of the horror stories. Houses that are nothing more than shacks. Children running around like diseases. Crime that even the police are too scared to fight.

A movement outside the window draws my attention. It's the prick strolling to his bike holding a brown paper bag marked "Cafe de Olla." He swings a thick, jean-clad leg over the bike. My own thighs clench in response, startling me into dropping my phone.

By the time the assistant retrieves it from the floor, Jonathan Lawson has disappeared, leaving nothing but a cloud of black smoke and the roar of his engine behind. What the heck was *that*? The man is repulsive and the furthest thing from my type.

That makes revenge a necessity. I can't afford to have that man haunting my dreams, taunting me to get back at him.

The Junction be damned.

I'm supposed to meet several girlfriends for lunch. I use both terms loosely, because while we are friendly, I would never call them during a crisis, and while it may be noon, the most food that will be consumed at our table is three blackberries and several lettuce leaves, sans dressing.

Hardly girlfriends and hardly lunch, but I text them all the same to let them know I won't be able to make it. They're nothing but ladder climbers anyway. Now they can enjoy their salads and bitch about me all they want, all while plotting how to use their connection to me to score one of Wesbourne's wealthiest bachelors or a position chairing the next society event.

I ask Taleah's assistant to snap several photos of my new hair. She does not have an eye for these things, and I have to keep asking her to change the angle or move to a new position. Finally, she produces several that will do. She asks if I took a before photo so I can post them side by side.

I shoot her a look out of the corner of my eye. "Don't be ridiculous. Before and afters aren't on brand for me." God, what a pedestrian idea.

She skedaddles soon after that, and after uploading the new pics to Instagram, I prepare for my new mission. It's time for a little reconnaissance.

I direct my car toward the seedy side of the city, following the GPS's instructions. It glitches out several times, as if it's giving me time to change my mind.

The Junction is pretty much what I imagined. The houses are no bigger than my bedroom, and they could all use an architect and a landscape artist. Rusted-out cars sit in driveways that used to be gravel but are now nothing more than weeds. The worst one has grass higher than the porch and a blue tarp where a window should be. I shudder.

There are no children running around, which I suspect is due to school being in session. I expect to see drug deals going down on every corner, maybe a prostitute or two, but aside from several people sitting on their steps, I observe no suspicious behavior.

I find the Lawson house easily enough. It's a yellow rectangular box, with a dingy white door in the center. Someone has taken the time to plant flowers in the tiny window boxes, although I'd bet my $2,000 shoes it wasn't the biker himself. The whole scene looks cheap and old, but at least it's not falling apart like some of the others I've passed. I'm not sure how I'd feel about getting revenge on someone who lives in a hovel. I could maybe convince myself they are a disgrace to humanity, living that way, and need to be taught a lesson, but it would definitely make my mission harder.

But now that I've assured myself he is fully deserving of my revenge, Mr. Lawson is going down.

* * *

Join Jessica Jude's email list to be notified when new books launch and to receive more exclusive bonus content. Visit <u>JessicaJude.com/Newsletter</u> to sign up.

Also by Jessica Jude

Acknowledgments

No one tells you that writing this section of the book is the hardest of all. Or if they did, I wasn't listening.

First thank you goes to Jesus, without whose strength this book would've never happened.

A close second goes to Curtis, for being my biggest and best cheerleader, and for forgiving me when you discovered that "writing a book" meant creating a story, not handwriting 100,000 words. And also for listening to my late-night rambles about things that are most definitely not important but which you pretend are anyway.

Melinda, for supporting me in spite of the fact that I write romance and not thrillers. Maybe some day. Love you.

Mom, for teaching me to chase my dreams and talking me off the ledge more times than either of us can count. (Purely hypothetical.)

Jenny, my incredible editor, you deserve like half the credit for this book. You're amazing and I'm never letting you go.

Haya in Designs for creating the cover of my dreams.

All of my teachers (the nice ones)—you believed in my dream when I was too scared to do anything about it. Thank you for not giving up on me, even when I turned the English assignment into an experiment in writing graphic horror (and subsequently discovered that isn't for me).

My family, for letting me take your quirks and idiosyncrasies and drop them into my books like little treasures for you to find and squeal over. (I guess you never actually gave your permission so . . . sorry?)

Jen, for embarrassing me every chance you get so I have something to laugh about later. Thanks for believing in my dream. (I'll definitely look into large print options next.)

My kids, who are the reason I do everything. You make my world go round, even though I won't let you read this book for another fifteen years. Mama is so incredibly proud of you and the books you're already writing yourself. You're going to take the world by storm some day.

All of the authors who have gone before me and made me fall in love with stories. I can't name names, because then this section would be longer than the book itself.

My amazing ARC team, who devoured this book and wouldn't stop telling me how much they loved it, breathed it, even dreamed it. You boosted my confidence when I needed it most, you shared your love of Ace with the world, and you helped launch it far and wide. I couldn't have done this without you. (Well, I could have, but it would've sucked.)

Mariana, Natalie Beer, Brittney Jones, Sarah Matson, Joana N., Dani Mathis, Julia C., Jordan, Kylie, Charlena, Courtney, Ryann Rutz, Kassidy Smith, Ashlee Pool, Liz, Lueur, Destiny Musik, Lexi White, Nikita, Jenah C., Celine P., Angelica, Isabella Iadevaia, Mackenzie, Megan Black, Shayla Sprowls, Ky & Mel from the Plot Twist Podcast, Diana Le, Kaliena D., Becs, Chelsea MacRae, Chryslynn, Emily Beauchamp, Morgan DeGruchy O'Connor, Reece Hall, Katrina Blount, Kamelah Fernandez, Demi Heinrich, Nikki Hamilton, Heidi, Cai Sanchez, Macy, Rebecca Cowell, Samantha Link-Thompson, Stace, Bianca Kouzoumis, Maddy, Grace Dringenburg, Erin Wickson, Lya Riley, Ana Ferreira, Mystique, Ashley T., Anjessica, Rachel Berosik, Sydney Baker, Megan Lyles, Sandra Christenson, Kaytie Kirk, Zhoe Morse, Gretchen, Michelle, Jessica Dennis, Georgina Nicholls, Mercedes Hogan, Madison Perlberg, Elise Ruediger, Abby, Kalei,

Sophie Masannek, Jessica Mack, Michelle Carriveau, Brandy Frank, Elena Nacci, Dessy, Jayme Kendrick, Cadence, Dakota P, Jessica Smith, Jennah Smith, @yourstruly_aw, and @ninagrl17—you're the best hype squad a girl could ask for. Thank you for your help compiling the playlist for this book and for giving it all of the love it deserves.

And finally, dear reader, if you've made it this far, it's because you truly loved every word, and for that, I cannot possibly thank you enough. You're amazing. The end.

About the Author

Jessica Jude loves nothing better than sending her characters on an emotional roller coaster of love, angst, and drama, but in reality her life is very ordinary, drama-free, and probably boring to anyone watching. (Which would be weird. And creepy.)

She married her high school sweetheart at nineteen. Being an author is a dream she's had since she was six years old and wrote her first "book," which was ten pages long, about a girl named Mary getting lost in the woods. (It was never published, but good news: Mary was eventually rescued.) When she's not writing, she's reading, reading about writing, or eating ice cream. In another life, she would live in England in a sprawling manor house with hidden passages and secret stairways, but for now, she's content with her old brick farmhouse in the Midwestern United States.

Some of the things that make her weird include:
An equal love of traveling and staying home
Hating phone calls, except with her sister
Adoring the scent of coffee but not drinking it (please don't burn me at the stake)
Quiet in public, loud at home
Borderline obsessed with Kate Middleton
Getting excited about rainy days
Loving ice cream and salads (but not together, gross)

Still a fan? Here are some ways you can ~~stalk~~ stay connected!

JessicaJude.com/newsletter

Instagram @JessicaJudeBooks

Threads @JessicaJudeBooks

TikTok @JessicaJudeBooks

Discussion Questions

1. What do you think drove Heath to make the decisions he did?
2. How do you feel about Walker's choice to forgive?
3. Do you agree that a person shouldn't be defined by one mistake? Why or why not?
4. Do you think people are capable of change?
5. What did you think about the relationships depicted in the book?
6. How did you feel about the theme of revenge in this book?
7. Contrast the friends' pettiness in their revenge plots with their loyalty to each other. How does that make you feel about them?
8. What scene in Ace of Betrayal made the biggest emotional impact on you and why?
9. What quote or moment haunts you?